D1052742

YERBA BUENA

Also by Nina LaCour

Watch Over Me

We Are Okay

You Know Me Well
WITH DAVID LEVITHAN

Everything Leads to You

The Disenchantments

Hold Still

YERBA BUENA

Nina LaCour

FLATIRON
BOOKS
NEW YORK

YERBA BUENA. Copyright © 2022 by Nina LaCour. All rights reserved. Printed in the United States of America. For information, address Flatiron Books, 120 Broadway, New York, NY 10271.

www.flatironbooks.com

Designed by Donna Sinisgalli Noetzel

Library of Congress Cataloging-in-Publication Data

Names: LaCour, Nina, author.
Title: Yerba Buena / Nina LaCour.
Description: First edition. | New York : Flatiron Books, 2022.
Identifiers: LCCN 2021034511 | ISBN 9781250810465 (hardcover) | ISBN 9781250862174 (international, sold outside the U.S., subject to rights availability) | ISBN 9781250810502 (ebook)
Subjects: LCGFT: Romance fiction.
Classification: LCC PS3612.A3528 Y47 2022 | DDC 813/.6—dc23
LC record available at https://lccn.loc.gov/2021034511

Our books may be purchased in bulk for promotional, educational, or business use. Please contact your local bookseller or the Macmillan Corporate and Premium Sales Department at 1-800-221-7945, extension 5442, or by email at MacmillanSpecialMarkets@macmillan.com.

First U.S. Edition: 2022

First International Edition: 2022

10 9 8 7 6 5 4 3 2 1

For my wife, Kristyn, who stepped into a
room and took my breath away.
Look at this life we've made together.

And for my father, Jacques, who
generously allows me to use the details
of his Los Angeles youth in my fiction.

YERBA BUENA

AN AFTERNOON IN SPRING

They rode together up the hill. Blur of trees and sky outside, groan of brakes, a current between them. With each curve of the road, the press of one bare shoulder against another, until the bus slowed and stopped.

The doors folded open, they stepped out to the street. Armstrong Drive dead-ended there—a parking lot, a ranger's station, the entrance to the woods. Sara unzipped her backpack and pulled out a thermos, unscrewed the lid and sipped. Their fingers touched as Annie took it, and Sara watched Annie press her mouth against its metal rim and drink.

It struck Sara every time—the way the air changed as she entered the forest. Cool, wet, fresh dirt, even bright days like this one dimming and softening. "Should we get a map?" Annie asked, but Sara shook her head. She knew the woods well, had no trouble getting lost or finding her way back.

She took Annie's hand and led her past the station. A group of tourists brushed by them, their faces upturned. It felt good to feel small. That's why her mother had taken her here when she was a little girl, why Sara kept coming after her mother died.

They cut onto Sara's favorite trail—the steepest, the quietest—and hiked until they were breathless, eye level with the ancient redwoods' branches, as close as they could be to the sky.

"Over there?" Annie asked.

Sara followed her gaze to a grove off the trail. She nodded, her heart quickened. They stepped as carefully as they could across the forest floor to a ring of young redwoods with a hollowed trunk at its center. There, they unzipped their backpacks, pulled out a blanket and a couple sweaters, and laid them over the pine needles.

The forest was quiet. Everyone else was far away.

"Can I kiss you now?" Sara asked.

"Not yet," Annie said. She pulled her T-shirt up over her head. She unfastened her bra.

"Now?"

Annie shook her head. "Your turn." So Sara took off her shirt, too, and Annie rushed to kiss her before Sara could ask again.

The relief of it, after the hours of waiting.

The thrill of it: two fourteen-year-olds, secretly in love.

Sara sank to the blanket, Annie atop her. They kissed the curves of necks and collarbones. Cupped breasts with their palms. Smiled, blushed, kissed deeper.

After a time, they rested together, Annie's head in the crook of Sara's neck.

"Look," Annie whispered, and Sara saw a banana slug, bright yellow, emerging from a fern. It made its way to Sara and she flinched at the strange, cold slickness of it, tried not to laugh. The slug made its way across her pale stomach, and then to Annie's. It took an eternity. They were three creatures in the forest. The girls held very still. The slug left a glittering trail of slime on their skin.

In its wake, a wave of grief: the tiny diamonds of a hospital gown. The flamingo-pink polish Sara had applied to her mother's nails in careful strokes. Yellowed eyes, cracked white lips. The nurses' concerned expressions and Sara's little brother's tantrums and how their father had stood in corners when he visited, his hands clasped behind his back. Throughout the weeks in the hospital—the sensation that Sara was hovering over an abyss. And then her mother was gone and she plunged into it.

"Hey," Annie murmured, and Sara was back in the redwood grove, her heart pounding. "What are you thinking about?"

"Nothing really."

A breeze stirred the branches above them.

"Tell me something I don't know yet," Annie said. "About you."

Her voice was close to Sara's ear, her body soft, pressed against Sara's skin. What could Sara say that would please her? Not anything from the last two years, not the months before either. Nothing from school because though it felt sometimes like they'd just met, they'd sat in classrooms together since they were small. She'd need to go further back . . . and then she found it.

"My family used to play a game together. A drawing game. We'd sit around the table and one of us would start, usually my dad. He'd draw a street or a train or a mountain. And then the next person would add something else to it. People or cars or the sky. Whoever was last would complete it, and by then the whole page would be full. I loved it so much. Waiting to see what they'd draw, thinking of something to surprise them. We'd do it for hours sometimes."

She hoped it was enough, felt Annie pull her closer.

The sun was low in the sky by then, and they were due back—Annie to her twin and their parents, Sara to her little brother to make sure he was fed. He was probably mounting his bicycle, leaving his friend's place now, heading home. Maybe their father would be there tonight. Maybe not. Either way, Sara would need to catch the bus back to town before the sun set over the ramshackle cabins and the rustic vacation homes and the wide, muddy river. Over the Appaloosa Bar and Wishes & Secrets Hair Salon and Lily's father's white steepled church.

But just another few minutes here, first, she thought.

Another kiss.

Another bird high above.

Another breeze cooling her skin.

How easy it was to forget the rest when they were small and safe in the woods.

At the other end of California, Emilie pressed a new green plant into the dirt of her Catholic school's garden. Its leaves were familiar. She looked around and yes—there was more of it, spilling over the retaining wall.

"Same plant, right?" she asked, and Mrs. Santos nodded.

"If you see a bare place in a garden, look at what's already growing. Good chance you can take a little from what's there."

School had cleared out a few hours ago. Now it was just the three of them—Emilie, her friend Pablo, and Pablo's mother—tending to the small plot that separated the school from the street. Mrs. Santos had volunteered to make it both beautiful and useful. Some flowers, mostly herbs.

"What's it called?" Emilie asked. She'd been learning the names of the plants but had missed this one somehow, growing in the shade.

"Yerba buena."

"Funny," Emilie said. "That's the name of my parents' favorite restaurant. Pablo, remember? That place on Sunset we went to?"

"The fancy one?"

"Yeah."

Pablo dropped the weeds he'd pulled into a bucket and joined her in front of the plant. He plucked a stem, dangled it in front of Emilie's face. "Here's a sprig of mint. Give me all your money."

They laughed, Mrs. Santos, too.

"So *is* it a kind of mint?" Emilie asked, rubbing a leaf between her fingers.

"Yes, it's good in tea," Mrs. Santos said. "Most of these plants are. A tea garden is an easy thing to keep. Tisane, technically. Small plants. Unfussy. I'll gather some for you. See what you like."

Verbena. Spearmint. Chamomile. Sage. Yerba buena.

"It's a bouquet," Emilie said when Mrs. Santos handed it to her.

"Use them fresh. Try some while you do homework tonight."

They gathered their things and started the walk to their houses, across the street from each other, six blocks from the school. "How's Colette?" Mrs. Santos asked.

"She's okay. She's teaching me guitar. Feel my fingers."

Mrs. Santos touched her calluses. "You've been practicing."

"Feel," Emilie said to Pablo as they waited at a crosswalk.

"Whoa."

The light changed and they crossed, and Emilie thought of Colette positioning her fingers, telling her when to switch chords. The two of them on Colette's bed, learning songs. More often, though, these past couple weeks, Emilie had been practicing alone in her room while her sister stayed, alone, in hers. The scene from a couple nights ago came back—Colette screaming at her, slamming her door shut.

They were almost to their houses now. "Tell me what you think of the tea," Mrs. Santos was saying. "Just hot water and a few leaves. Honey, too, if you want it."

Emilie waved as she climbed her front steps. "See you tomorrow."

"Come over and give me the algebra answers later," Pablo called after her, and Mrs. Santos play-scolded him, and Emilie found her front door unlocked and let herself in.

No one was around so she sliced some cheese to eat with an apple and took her plate outside to the deck. Just a few months ago, her father, Bas, and his two cousins had taken apart the old deck and invited Emilie and Colette out to help them build a new one.

"Family tradition," Bas had said. "We helped our fathers build houses and decks and all kinds of things."

"And back in New Orleans," said Rudy, the eldest of the cousins, the only one of them born before the families moved to Los Angeles, "*our* fathers helped their fathers."

Colette rolled her eyes. She'd just finished high school, but barely, her second semester transcripts so bleak that the college she'd planned to attend withdrew its acceptance. "My friends are waiting for me at the beach," she said. But it looked exciting to Emilie. The piles of wood, the cousins they rarely saw even though they lived in neighboring cities.

"Come on, sister," Emilie said. "It'll be fun."

Colette leaned against the house. She was almost otherworldly to Emilie with her extra three years and two inches of height. Her hair was longer than Emilie's, and her jean shorts were shorter, and she cocked her head and kept them all waiting. And then she shrugged and said, "Why not?"

Colette helped for about an hour before saying she had to go. But Emilie spent all day out there with them, listening to their stories, smiling along with their jokes even when she didn't understand, hammering the nails where they told her to. They taught her to use the electric sander and she'd donned a mask and goggles and worked the guardrails until they were smooth.

She leaned on the rail now, looking over a bare patch of garden where a rosebush had died and never been replaced. Maybe she could transplant a cluster of lavender. Or maybe start her own tea garden. She saw a movement through the sliding door—someone must be home. Her parents didn't keep regular work hours. Bas was a contractor, Lauren an entertainment lawyer. They came and they went and they let their daughters do the same.

Tea, Emilie thought. *Not lavender.* She would ask Mrs. Santos to help her get started. And then she heard a pounding from inside, boots down the stairs, heard Bas's shout for help.

"Call 911. It's your sister."

She grabbed the phone and dialed, followed him upstairs as it rang and the operator asked her to state her emergency, but Bas was blocking the bathroom door.

"Don't look, honey. Tell them to send an ambulance now. Tell them an overdose, say come *right now*. Don't look, Em, wait at the door for them."

So Emilie went back down and the ambulance approached, quietly, without sirens, and parked out front. Two paramedics rushed into her house and she pointed at the stairs, and then Lauren was home, too, and there was nothing for Emilie to do as the paramedics carried her sister, unconscious but alive, out the door and into the back of the ambulance, Bas climbing in behind them.

Lauren grabbed the car keys.

"I'm following them to the hospital," she told Emilie.

"I'll come, too."

"No, no, you stay." Lauren took Emilie's face in her hands. "My steady daughter, my good girl. You stay right here while we're gone."

Emilie watched out the window as the ambulance rolled away, her mother after it, all of them somehow unnoticed by the rest of the world. A few minutes later, across the street at the Santoses' house, the lights turned on. She could have crossed, told them everything, eaten dinner at their table. But she didn't. She stayed alone in the house as the night wore on. Stared at her homework, forgot to eat. The herbs from the school garden wilted on the countertop. She tucked herself into bed, held her body as still as she could. She would stay right here until it was over.

PARADISE

Two years later, Sara woke to the sound of her bedroom door opening.

"The phone kept ringing," Spencer said from the doorway, his hair matted on one side, his eyes tired. "It's Annie's brother."

Sara reached for the phone, pressed it against her ear. "Dave?"

"Is Annie with you?"

"No." She saw that it was one thirty in the morning, and her heart began to pound. Spencer sat next to her and pressed his cheek against hers to listen.

"You're sure she isn't with you?" Dave was asking.

"*Of course* I'm sure," Sara said.

"When was the last time you saw her?"

"When school got out. When I said goodbye to both of you. Then I went to work, and then I came home."

"My parents need the phone. I'm hanging up. I'll call you if we find out anything."

Sara nodded, unable to speak, cradling the phone in her hands until Spencer took it from her and set it by the bed.

"Wait," Spencer said. "Shouldn't he be able to figure it out? Like if he closes his eyes and concentrates?"

"What are you talking about?" Sara asked.

"I thought twins could do that," Spencer said.

"Oh." Sara took his smaller hand in hers. "I don't think it works that way."

In the morning, Sara made their usual scrambled eggs for Spencer, though she felt too sick to eat.

She took down their mother's plates, chipped at the rims now, their floral patterns fading. After a time, she'd climbed her way out of grief, but now Annie was missing, and she felt it closing in again. The terrible weightlessness, something cavernous below.

Spencer slid into the breakfast nook. When she carried his plate over, she saw a blank page and a pencil on the table. Their drawing game, just for two now.

"You start," Sara said, so Spencer began to draw.

She sat across from him, light through the gingham curtains, pan cooling in the yellowed sink, the family drawing from years ago hanging on the wall by the window.

Spencer was sketching a cloudy sky, blending the pencil marks with his fingers. He passed it to her when he finished. She drew the tops of trees. "We have to go," she said. "Can we fill in the rest later?"

"Okay," he said, and stuck it to the refrigerator with a magnet. "Or maybe Dad will."

"Maybe," she said.

Together, on the porch, they put on their shoes before heading in opposite directions to their schools.

Sara kept her backpack light in case she'd be heading straight out again. Stepping off the bus across the street from campus, she hoped to see Annie out front—her curly brown hair and jean jacket, her bad-girl posture undone by the sweetness of her face. *You scared me,* Sara would yell, and Annie would grab her around her waist, and they would try to look like just friends. Sara imagined tugging at Annie's belt loop. *Don't disappear again,* she'd say. *Promise me.*

I promise, Annie would answer.

But she saw Dave and Lily huddled by the entrance with Crystal and Jimmy. Annie wasn't there.

"What should we do?" Crystal was asking.

"*Leave,*" Dave said. "Split up and look for her. It's bullshit that my parents dropped me off here."

"I'll look in town," Crystal said. "But I'm kind of freaked out. Shouldn't we double up?"

Jimmy nodded. "I'll go with you."

"You two can look together," Sara told Dave and Lily. "I'm fine by myself."

"You sure?" Lily asked, and Sara said yes.

"I have my car. We can go to Monte Rio," Lily told Dave, and Dave agreed.

Sara felt her backpack's lightness, felt a fierce and desperate hope.

"I have to be at work at four. If anyone finds her, call the motel, okay?" Her friends nodded. "I'm going to the woods."

————

She rode the bus up Armstrong Drive alone, rushed past the ranger's station and to their trail. She trusted the woods. All those afternoons they spent in it. But still. She braced herself for the moment she'd find Annie, hurt or unconscious, bleeding or broken. Or worse. It was foggy and cold. She called Annie's name but was met with silence. She climbed higher and higher and off the trail, found their grove. No one was there. She hiked down to the main path, discovered other trails.

Sara would find her—she was certain of it. She searched for more than six hours, and to calm herself she imagined Annie appearing cross-legged, leaning against the soft wood of a tree trunk, smiling at the sight of her. She imagined their kiss, Annie's singsong voice as she asked Sara what was wrong. There Annie would be, perfectly fine, and the world would be right again, and she would not lose another person she loved.

And then her watch read three o'clock. She would have to leave the woods to make it to work on time. So she told herself that the phone would be ringing when she reached the office of the Vista Motel. It would be Dave, and he'd say they'd found her. She left the shade of the forest and waited in the sun for the bus to take her to Monte Rio.

The Vista Motel was one town over, no better or worse than the others. Its main office had a supply room off the back. All the buildings—twenty single rooms and three suites with mini kitchens—were one story. Visitors could drive right up to their room doors. And behind the rooms was a private lawn for motel guests with access to the river. They'd sit in lounge chairs under white umbrellas and sip whatever beverages they'd brought with them, and when the weather was warm enough they'd walk down the stairs to the rocky beach and swim.

"Did anyone call for me?" Sara asked Maureen when she got there.

Maureen, working a crossword, shook her head without looking up.

"You're sure?"

"Been right here since 8:00 a.m. 'Parakeet,'" she said, and filled in the letters. Then she took a clipboard and handed it to Sara. Only six room numbers were checked, the peak season over now.

"I'm waiting on a call. It's important. If it comes while I'm cleaning, will you come get me?"

Maureen nodded.

In the supply room, Sara pulled on a pair of latex gloves. She found the rolling garbage bin without a busted wheel. Grabbed a bucket of Windex and sponges and cleaner and garbage bags and balanced a roll of paper towels on top. She pushed everything out the back door and into Room 5. Off came the sheets and the blanket. She emptied the trash from the bathroom and beside the bed. She grabbed empty beer bottles from the dresser and newspaper pages from the floor. Annie had always suggested they sneak into a room one day, use it for just a few hours. "Doesn't it sound good?" she had whispered into Sara's ear. "A locked door? A *bed*."

"Believe me," Sara had told her. "There is nothing appealing about any of those beds."

"Why not?"

"They're gross."

"It's only people," Annie had said. "Only bodies. What's the big deal?"

So, just a couple of weeks ago, on the afternoon of Annie's sixteenth birthday, Sara had cleaned Room 12—one of the nicer rooms that overlooked the lawn—as thoroughly as she could. She bought six candles from the drugstore and carefully peeled off the pictures of Jesus and the Virgin Mary before setting them up: one on each of the bedside tables, three on the dresser, one on the TV stand. She brought her boom box from home with Alicia Keys's latest album because Annie always nodded and swayed when "No One" came on.

That night, Annie met her a few blocks away for ice cream, and when they were finished, Sara said, "I forgot something at work. Come with me?"

As soon as they were off the street and out of sight, Sara grabbed her hand. "Are you ready for your present?" she asked.

Annie blushed.

Maureen had already given her the room key, so Sara took Annie straight to the door and let her in. She lit the candles. She started the music. She opened the mini fridge, where the half bottle of pink wine that a couple had abandoned in their suite that morning awaited them and divided the wine between the two plastic stemmed glasses that the motel supplied to guests. Then she turned to see Annie watching her, eyes shining, and Sara was overwhelmed. *To be looked at in that way. To be loved by this beautiful girl.* She might have lost her composure had Annie not stepped forward right then, put her hands through Sara's hair, and kissed her.

The night was perfect. Well—almost. There was the moment Sara went to kiss the inside of Annie's elbow and saw a mark there. Felt light-headed for a moment, close to tears, until she told herself it was nothing. Not the stuff of her father or his friends, nothing like her mother. It was a scratch, maybe. It didn't mean anything.

Where was she? She ran the vacuum across the room. Dave must have heard something by now. She would dump the trash and then go check in with Maureen. Maybe the call had come when she was busy with a guest. Or maybe Maureen hadn't taken her seriously when she'd said it was important. She rounded the corner to the Dumpster and startled. A boy was there—just a couple years older than she was, standing knee-deep in trash.

He froze, eyed her warily. He had greasy hair that fell into his eyes. His clothes were grungy, but that was the style, after all, so it didn't tell her much about him.

"Hey," he said.

"Gross," she said.

He grinned, relaxed now. She noticed a small chip in the corner of his right front tooth. "These are perfectly good magazines," he said, showing her what he'd found.

She rolled her eyes and dumped the contents of her bin. He started toward the new trash. "Nothing good in this one," she said, and went to wheel the bin back around the corner.

"Hey, wait," he called. She turned, impatient, as he hoisted himself out of the Dumpster. "I was wondering . . . any chance I could take a shower in one of the rooms you haven't cleaned yet? I'll be quick."

At first she thought she'd say no, but she saw hope in his

face, and it sparked her own. She would let him use the shower. She would wait outside the door. And while she did this good deed, while she helped someone who needed it, Dave would call to say he found her.

But even though she did it, and the boy thanked her afterward, his hair wet and his face clean, Dave didn't call. And he still hadn't called when she checked back after an hour. When the sheets were drying and she went in again, Maureen walked around to the other side of the counter.

"Honey," she said. "I know you. You wouldn't tell me something was important if it wasn't. If anyone calls for you, I'll be out this door yelling your name before they're finished saying hello. Understand?"

"Okay," Sara said.

"Anything you want to talk about?"

"No," she said. "But thanks."

She couldn't give words to it. Not yet. She wanted to keep Maureen the way she was—her dyed black hair and her low-cut shirts, all business and kindness, the kind of boss who just two weeks ago had handed her the key to Room 12 with no questions asked. She didn't want to hear what Maureen thought or see her face grow concerned. She just wanted the waiting to be over. She wanted the fear out of her body.

So when she saw the boy again from the window of Room 20, this time brazenly on one of the lawn chairs under a white umbrella, flipping the pages of a magazine, she told herself that once she was finished making the last of the beds, if he hadn't left by then, she would go out there and sit with him.

When she approached, he lifted his hand in a wave.

"What are you doing?"

He shrugged. "Isn't this what people are supposed to do here?"

"If you're a paying guest, yeah."

"Are you here to kick me out?"

She shook her head.

"Then join me."

She sat on the chair next to his, but not before scooting it a few inches away. She was blond and pretty. Tall like her father. She was used to keeping her guard up so that boys and men didn't get the wrong idea. But there was something about this boy that told her he was okay.

"This is a nice place," he said. "I can't believe people actually live here. It's like paradise."

"Not quite."

"Are you kidding? I mean, look at it."

"No, I know," she said. "It's gorgeous. I know." She understood why people came and sat where the two of them were sitting. The river, the redwoods—they amazed her, too. "What are you even doing here?" she asked.

"I'm headed to LA, but I need new spark plugs."

"There's a garage a couple blocks away."

"Yeah. They said they could fix it in an hour, but I'm a little short on cash at the moment. Any ideas where I could get a short-term job? It's just a Civic. It's cheap to fix."

Sara shrugged. "Not really."

"Well, here," he said. He wrote something on the corner of a magazine page and then ripped it out and folded it. "If you hear about anything, call me?"

"Okay." She rolled her eyes, slipped the paper into her pocket.

She didn't know how to feel when she saw the cars out front. Whether another dinnertime with just her and Spencer would be better, or if the loud voices of her father and his friends might drown out her dread.

Even though they were in the living room when she walked in, there was a hush to the house. The TV played the local news, its volume turned down low.

Two guys, brothers whose names she couldn't keep straight, sat in the window playing cards. They glanced up when she walked in but then back to their hands. They never talked to her. But Eugene was on the sofa.

"Hey," he said. "Hey, Sara. Come sit."

He patted the cushion next to him and Sara sank into it, noticed how tired her body was from the searching and the cleaning. She leaned forward, cradled her head in her hands.

"I barely see you anymore. Growing up and getting too busy for me now?"

She'd known Eugene all her life. Her mother and his wife had been best friends, but then her mother died, and Eugene's wife left him.

"My friend is missing," Sara said, head still buried, eyes still closed.

"Missing," Eugene said. "Huh."

The room was quiet again, taut with something, but it didn't have anything to do with Sara. She was too exhausted to care. "We've looked everywhere."

She felt a shifting of weight on the sofa. When she opened her eyes he was still there, a new beer in his hand. "Well." He sipped. "She'll turn up." Another moment passed. "You know you can come to me if you ever need anything, right?"

She looked up at him. She nodded.

"Good," he said. He patted her back.

Just then the lights of a police cruiser flashed across the wall.

"Fucking Larry," one of the card players said from the window. She listened to the car door shut and Larry's footsteps come up the walk. The men tensed the way they always did when he came by. They'd grown up together, but Larry's uniform divided them.

Sara's dad opened the door, didn't invite him in. "What can I do for you?"

"Hey, Jack. We're looking for a friend of your daughter's. I have a couple questions for her."

"For Sara?"

"She here?"

Her father stepped to the side to make room for her in the doorway.

Sara answered the officer's questions—the last time she saw Annie, if she remembered what clothes Annie had on. She remembered everything, of course, still couldn't keep her eyes off her, even after more than two years of being together. If Larry had asked a question about their relationship she would have told him the truth. She didn't know why they were hiding it, exactly. A few kids were out in school and it wasn't terrible for them. But secrecy had become what she and Annie were used to. A sacred thing, between them. They wanted to keep it close.

"Are you aware of any risky activities Annie might have been involved in?"

Annie in the candlelight, the mark on her arm. Maybe she should tell him. But it might have been nothing, and Sara had no way of knowing for sure. "No," she said, and hoped that Jack would believe it.

"Any drugs?"

It had been nothing. Sara shook her head.

Larry turned to Jack. "You have a reason to know any different?"

Her father's face, impassive. His tone steady like it always was. "Now why the fuck would I know anything about that?"

"Just making sure."

Larry left and her father and Eugene and the other guys opened another round of beers. Sara checked on Spencer down the hall, sound asleep in his bed. She grabbed the spare keys from the kitchen drawer and stopped in the living room.

"I need the truck for a little while. Okay?"

Her father gave her a single nod. "Careful out there," he said.

She drove a mile through the dark to The Pink Elephant. They were too young to get in, but they met there anyway most nights under the neon glow of the sign. She would show up and wait and her friends would have news and everything would be okay again.

As she neared, she saw that Dave was sitting on the curb, his forehead on his knees. Lily's arm was around him, and Jimmy was talking and talking the way he always did when he was nervous.

"They're gonna drag the river," Dave said when Sara reached them.

First, all that registered were his swollen eyes, how sick he looked, the way a person could waste away over the course of so few hours. And then: his mouth, the same shape as Annie's and just as soft. Sara thought maybe she could close her eyes and kiss him, open her eyes and find him transformed into his sister.

And then she said, "*What?*" and he said again, "They're going to drag the river."

She pressed her hands against her eyes until it hurt too much. There they all were, still, under the pink neon light of the sign. "I don't understand," she said.

"It seems too soon, doesn't it?" Jimmy said. He stuffed his hands in his pockets. "She hasn't even been missing for that long. I don't know why they'd do it so soon. I think it's probably a mistake? I mean, why jump to the worst-case scenario? Are you sure the hospitals aren't wrong?"

"They're going to drag the river," Sara repeated.

Lily wiped her eyes and looked at Sara. She nodded, solemn.

Jimmy said again, "It has to be a mistake. How can everyone be so *sure* she isn't in a hospital somewhere?"

"Because we're fucking sure, okay, Jimmy?" Dave said. "We've called every single hospital. We've looked *everywhere*. We are 100 percent fucking *sure*."

"Sorry," Jimmy said. "Okay. Sorry."

Lily clasped her hands together and lowered her head in prayer.

———

After Sara's mother died, they returned to the house, three of them now. A little boy, hardly more than a toddler, who could not be consoled after the tiniest sadness: milk gone curdled and dumped out of the glass, a hole in his sock, a missing toy. A man who joked and laughed with his friends but howled in his bedroom at night so fiercely he woke his children. A twelve-year-old girl, every part of her tender and ragged. It hurt to eat and it hurt to be hungry. To be awake was to be in despair, but her muscles grew sore from inertia.

Then Spencer came in one night and scooted his body against hers. She was used to being close to him, to smoothing his hair when he cried, to kissing his forehead. But this night it was different. He nestled his face between her shoulder blades. She felt his belly rise and fall against her back. Felt the synchronous beating of their hearts.

He needs me. He needs me. He needs me.

I need him. I need him. I need him.

He brought her back to life.

Back home from the Pink Elephant parking lot, her father's friends gone, she went to Spencer's room and climbed into his bed.

"Hey," he mumbled.

"Can I sleep here?" she asked. *The river.* She couldn't get it out of her head.

He nodded, and she turned over. She scooted her body until she felt his stomach against her back. She waited for his breathing. She waited for his heartbeat. She hoped he might still possess the power to heal her. But her fear was a wild, dangerous thing. Her body shook with it. Spencer didn't notice. As soon as he was sleeping again, she went back to her room.

Diamond-print hospital gown. Pink polish. The slug and the redwoods. How it felt to be held, and how it felt after. Hope, turning hollow.

The panic was so powerful she thought she might double over from it, didn't know how to be still. Her room felt too big for her, full of too much air. She needed to be contained. She took some boxes out of her closet to make room, carried her blankets in. She slid the door shut and screamed into her pillow. She lay in the dark, shirts and dresses she'd outgrown dangling above her. She wanted to stay, felt safer, but she heard a knock at her bedroom door.

She found her father waiting. He looked past her into the room: her bare bed, her blankets spilling from the closet.

"You're sleeping in there?" he asked.

She was raw with fear and here was her father and she wanted to tell the truth.

"I'm scared," she said. He placed a hand on her shoulder. He hadn't touched her in a long time. She felt the tremor of memory, something long ago buried—a time before Spencer, before death, when she was a little girl who laughed with her parents in the bright sunshine on the bank of a river.

A time before she knew the river could swallow a person whole.

She said, "They're going to drag the river in the morning."

When she looked at him again, his cheeks were wet and his eyes were closed.

"Dad," she said. "Let's go look for her, okay? Let's go driving and find her."

She felt the warmth of his hand, knew he could help her. And then he squeezed her shoulder and let go. "Listen," he said. "Girls your age—they don't just disappear. She's gone and that's the end of it."

"Not Annie."

He sucked in a breath, cast his gaze down the darkened hallway. She wanted him to face her instead. Felt like she might disappear while he wasn't looking. *Stay with me,* she wanted to say. *Help me get through this.*

"I've lived in this town for a long time," he said. "I've lost friends of my own. You keep going. You'll learn."

But Annie's mouth, kissing hers. Annie's head in the crook of her neck.

"We're more than friends," she said, and his eyes darted back to her in surprise.

She tried again. "Help me find her."

He turned away and walked to the front of the house. She told herself he was finding his keys. Maybe fixing coffee to keep them awake during the ride. He was getting his shoes, and he'd come back and say, *Let's go.* She waited, imagining it—how it would feel to not be alone.

She used the bathroom, returned to her room, certain she'd find him waiting for her and ready to go. But he wasn't there. He wasn't in the living room either.

He was gone.

She went to flick off the light in the kitchen and saw something familiar on the table. Spencer's smudged clouds, Sara's redwoods. And now a river, too, with a girl—Annie—

floating facedown in the water. Sara gasped, dropped the drawing, didn't want to look. But the image stayed with her anyway. Annie's curly hair, her jean jacket, all her father's careful lines.

She returned to her closet and closed herself in.

Early the next morning they gathered on Annie's deck—Sara and Dave and Crystal and Jimmy and Lily. The boat started in Monte Rio, made its way slowly forward. None of them had slept. There was nothing to say.

They had seen this done before. Every summer tourists poured in, most of them college kids with rafts and inner tubes and too much alcohol. The tourists crowded their streets, left trash on their beaches, and every couple of years, one of them drowned. Sara had seen bodies lifted by hooks out of the muddy water, but never the body of someone she knew.

Lily sat next to Dave, holding his hand. Crystal and Jimmy huddled together, sharing a blanket. Sara stood behind the others, biting her nails until she bled. And then the boat appeared in the distance, casting down its hook, lifting it back. Dave and Annie's parents were on the boat and Sara didn't know which would be worse—straining her eyes to see or having it all too close.

They waited for the boat to pass them but it didn't. It stopped the length of several houses away, close enough for them to see the people gathered on one side of it, looking overboard at something below.

The giant hook lowered and Dave moaned, started rocking back and forth. Lily said *Shhhh, it's all right, it's all right.* Cries came off the boat, traveled the distance between them, and the hook lifted Annie out of the water.

The faces of her friends, red and wet and swollen. The panic in Dave's eyes, the blankness in Crystal's. How hard Jimmy and Lily tried to soothe the others before Jimmy rushed to the side of the deck to throw up and Lily went in to call home but forgot her own number. Sara stood still as it all swarmed around her. The sobs that carried across the river. The arc of Annie's dangling body, water pouring from her clothing and her hair.

She tasted blood, realized she was biting her finger again, shoved it in her pocket.

Inside, against her fingertips, a paper, folded in two. She took it out, unfolded it. Saw the boy's name for the first time: Grant.

Grant with his car in need of repair. The car that could take her away from here. From Lily's father's voice, here now and praying. From Dave's gasps for air, each of them a stab at her heart. From the abyss that would swallow her the way it did when she lost her mother.

She saw her father, gaze cast down the dark hallway.

The drawing he'd left for her to find—too horrible to comprehend.

She couldn't stay. Not here, in this town that stole people away.

She made it through the house to the door.

It was still the early morning. She rode the bus to the motel. She spotted a Honda Civic by the side of the road, and when she got close enough to see in, she exhaled. He was there, still asleep, his legs bent in like a paper doll's, his mouth open.

She knocked on the window. He startled, saw her, sat up.

"I was getting my beauty rest."

"I'm going with you," she said. "We need to leave today."

She waited on the sidewalk with her backpack while Grant talked to the mechanic. "They have to finish a job first, so it'll be a few hours," he said when he came out. She didn't have a few hours, felt the need to go *now,* but she'd promised him money and they had to go get it. At first, she'd thought of Maureen. She knew her boss would give her the money if she needed it, but she also knew Maureen would try to make her stay. Lily always had a little cash from working at the church, but Sara couldn't bear to see her friends again so soon, their tearstained faces, her own heartbreak, reflected. It was possible, she thought, that she'd never be able to look at them again.

So that was it, then. Only one person left.

She led Grant down the main street and onto a narrow one. It had been a long time since she'd walked to Eugene's house. She hoped he'd meant it when he said he'd help her.

When Sara was a kid her family spent weekends over there, her parents drinking beers on Eugene's deck overlooking the river, Sara holding Spencer's hand as she guided him down the wooden steps from Eugene's house to the pebbled shore. Even before Spencer was born, sometimes Sara and her mother would lie out on Eugene's dock, the sun warming their skin.

She remembered it all as she approached the house—the snack trays Eugene's ex-wife would set out for them, chips and slices of melon—and wondered where she went after Sara's mother died, why she hadn't remained a part of their lives. They were almost to the river now, and Sara didn't want to look. She was glad she could barely see it behind the trees.

The door swung open and there was Eugene, alone, just as she'd hoped.

"Sara." He narrowed his eyes.

"I need help," Sara said.

"Come in," he said. "You, too, whoever you are."

They walked in and Eugene shut the door. The redwood walls, the shag carpet, the sliding glass doors to the deck. Sara knew it would be familiar, but this was more than that. She could almost hear her mother's voice. She could have doubled over from it.

"Now tell me. What's going on?"

"I need to get away. I'm leaving today and I need money."

"Leaving for where?"

"It doesn't matter. I just need some money to get there. Whatever you can spare. I'll get a job and I'll send it back."

He leaned against the closed door and looked them over.

What happened in that moment? What particular stillness, what particular light? The dust rose from the carpet when Sara shifted her weight, glittered, dispersed. She watched as Eugene's gaze left her body and settled on Grant's. The edges of the room rose, floors tilting downward to the center. Almost imperceptible, but Sara felt it.

And then, yes, here it was.

"Money's something that's got to be earned, Sara."

He was looking at her body again, wasn't trying to hide it. She was used to men looking at her that way, but didn't expect it from Eugene. He locked eyes with her and unfastened his belt. Turned to Grant and snaked it out, loop by loop.

"What the fuck, Eugene?"

"Hey," he said. "You came to me. I should be calling your father. It's your choice what you do. I'm going to lie down for a while." He tossed his belt on the chair and headed down the hallway. "I'll leave the door open just in case."

They were alone, then, in the living room with its fucked-up slanted floors, and it was dim and dusty, but the light that shot through the bent shutters was brutal in its daytime brightness. Nowhere their eyes could rest.

She turned to Grant.

"I'm gonna do it," she said. "We need the money."

Grant swallowed and nodded. "Okay."

"'Okay,' you're doing it, too?"

"Yeah." His eyes were scared, but there was more than fear there, something she couldn't quite place.

"I don't want Eugene's . . . I don't want any part of him inside me," she told him.

"We can probably set limits? Tell him what we'll do?"

"Okay," she said.

They looked toward his hallway, his wide-open bedroom door. Somehow, the floor had become flat again, the light through the blinds only light. She walked and Grant followed. Eugene was sitting in his bed, still dressed, and it struck her that he hadn't been sure they'd do it. He didn't want to look foolish.

"I'll get you off," Sara said. "But you can't fuck me."

"Saving yourself for someone special?"

She could feel Grant trembling behind her, and his fear made her stronger. "Take it or leave it," she said.

"What about you?" he said to Grant.

"I guess . . ." Grant said. "I guess I'll do whatever."

"I'll take it, then," Eugene said. "I've got three hundred dollars in cash."

"Show it to us."

"Stay here."

He came back with the money and she counted it.

"A'right then?" he said.

"Yeah," she said. "All right."

She couldn't think about it, wouldn't allow herself to. Not her father the night before, not the horrible thing he'd left her. Not the hook or the river, not her friends after, not what happened in Eugene's house.

All that mattered was the money in her pocket and the car that ran again and Grant, driving quickly enough for her to catch Spencer on his ride from school to his friend Henry's house, where he went every afternoon. And here they were in the distance: two boys, peddling up the street.

"Pull over," she told Grant, and leaned out the window to call Spencer's name. He heard her, stopped riding. She meant to open her door and get out but found that she couldn't, her palms suddenly sweaty, a knot in her throat. She could see Spencer trying to make sense of Grant as he walked his bike to her window while Henry stayed up ahead.

"I need to talk to you," she said.

"Okay."

When she didn't move or say anything else, he opened her door and she stepped out.

"We have to go."

"Where?"

"Los Angeles."

He smiled, and relief pulsed through her, until he said, "Ha. Funny."

"I'm not joking," she said. She didn't want to say the words, but she had to tell him something. "They found Annie."

She tried to breathe. She saw that he understood. "I can't go back home."

He nodded. "But we don't have money."

"I got some. I have enough for a little while."

"Where would we even live?"

"We'll figure it out."

"What about Dad?"

"What *about* Dad?"

"Sara."

"*Spencer.* There is nothing for us here. Please."

Her hands were shaking. She tried to still them but couldn't, so she hid them behind her back.

"Spencer, please. Just get in the car."

He looked at his handlebars. He touched the bell with his thumb, gently, and it chimed so quietly she could barely hear it. He did it again and again, over and over, as a minute stretched by and then another.

What was happening? All those meals she had cooked for him. All the times she'd tucked him in and kissed his forehead and said I love you.

But he wasn't saying yes. He wasn't coming with her.

"Okay," she finally said. A sob rose in her throat, but she turned to the concrete and forced it away. "I'll call you when I get there. As soon as I have a phone number I'll give it to you. Ask Henry's mom to let you stay at their house for dinner every night, okay? And go to her if you need anything, ever."

Spencer nodded, but she could see that he didn't understand.

"Stay away from Eugene," she said. "Do you hear me?"

"Why?"

"Just promise me."

"Okay."

"*Promise* me."

"I promise."

But she could tell he didn't know what was happening, and she barely did either. Only that she couldn't stay. She didn't want him to see her cry, but how could she help it? She had known he would go with her and now he wasn't. She had known she would never leave him and now she was. She held him against her as her chest heaved and then she folded herself back into the car. Managed to shut the door. Grant started the engine, pulled onto the road, and Spencer stood watching her, eyebrows furrowed, as they passed him and went on.

"It would be hard to have a kid with you," Grant said. "Probably better this way."

Sara turned to the rear window. There was her brother where she had left him, staring at the car as it disappeared. They drove down River Road, past the shops she'd been going to all her life. Past the liquor store and Lily's dad's church, and then Grant steered the car toward the bridge.

She pressed her hands over her eyes as they crossed the river.

The road changed, smoothed out beneath them.

"Here we go," Grant said. "Goodbye, paradise."

Amazing, how little three hundred dollars was when it came down to it, nearly one hundred already spent at the mechanic. They held their breath as the tank filled at the station in Forestville.

"I can drive if you want," Sara said. Before long it would be dark and the journey was almost five hundred miles. She had never traveled so far in her life. She reached for Grant's keys. *Please say yes.* She needed to be tethered to something. She wanted the responsibility of keeping them within a lane, of following freeway signs and turning when she was supposed to.

He looked relieved, handing her the keys and slumping into the passenger's seat, and she felt their compatibility, told herself that it was a good sign. But once she buckled the seatbelt, she felt herself back in Eugene's bedroom. His teeth on her nipples, his rough face against her ribs. She'd tried to please him with her hands, tried not to see the way he watched her do it. "Get out of here," he'd finally said, so she'd left for the bathroom, where the sounds of Eugene and Grant were muffled, and then out to the deck, where she couldn't hear them at all.

But more than that—worse than that—was Spencer's confusion, his bicycle bell, how it felt to let him go. What had she done?

She felt sick as she started the ignition.

Once she was on Highway 5, nothing was familiar. She had left home and she felt she might leave her own body, too, whatever that would mean. Surely, by the time they reached Los Angeles, she would feel like someone new. Grant didn't say a word for dozens of miles. Night fell. Exhaustion crept in, and she blinked fast to stay awake. She needed Grant to drive. She thought he was sleeping but then she heard something, glanced over, and saw in the darkness how his hands covered his face, how his body shook.

He was crying, which meant he was awake.

"Grant," she said. "I need a break."

He didn't respond, so she kept going. She sat up straighter. Opened her eyes wide. She tried to find a good radio station, but it was mostly static. They were in the middle of nowhere.

When she pulled off at the next exit, Grant was crying so hard that he didn't look out the window to see the cause of the slowdown and the turn, the roll onto gravel, the driver door opening and shutting.

The motel clerk asked to see Sara's ID.

"My wallet was stolen," she told him.

She understood that this is what her life would be now, until she turned eighteen. She didn't offer up any details, just looked him in the eye and waited.

The clerk studied her.

"Can't let you stay without ID," he finally said.

"How much is the room?" she asked, as though she hadn't heard him.

"Seventy-nine dollars."

She took Eugene's money from her pocket and counted it out. She handed it to the clerk and he sighed.

"Fine," he said.

So easy.

Grant was still crying. She opened the passenger door and leaned over him to unbuckle his seatbelt. She couldn't spare any words of comfort. To do so would slice her open. But this room was for him. She could have pulled over somewhere, climbed into the backseat, and slept until she was able to drive again.

"Let's go inside," she said. "Let's take showers."

She let him go first. He took a long time. By the time he emerged from the bathroom she felt herself itching all over, felt covered by Eugene's saliva even in the places he hadn't touched. She startled at the shadow of someone passing outside their room. The faint sound of canned laughter from a television next door made her flinch.

In the shower she scrubbed and scrubbed, the water hot, her skin pink, every part of her that could be washed clean now.

She came out wrapped in a towel.

"Should we sleep here tonight?" he asked.

"We paid for it," Sara snapped. "So yeah, I guess we should." She sat on the bed.

"Okay," he said.

A thread on the blanket was loose. She pinched the end of it and pulled. "I washed my clothes in the shower. I'm not trying to be weird."

He crossed the room to unzip his duffel, found a clean shirt and handed it to her.

"Thanks." She pulled it over her head. Glanced down to see the image of Mickey Mouse, holding a bouquet of red flowers behind his back. "What's up with this shirt?"

"My cousin got it at Disneyland," he said. "It was a gift."

She widened her eyes, almost laughed. She flipped off the switch and they fell asleep.

The motel was a mistake. They didn't know it in the morning when they woke up, or as they spent four dollars on Egg McMuffins and one cup of coffee to share. But a little past noon they needed gas.

"Already?" Sara said, trying to calculate it. It was too soon for them to be on empty again.

"Yeah but we're good. It was thirty in Forestville and we've only spent five more."

"No," Sara said.

"Oh, right." They were silent as they pulled up to the pump. Grant cut the engine and turned to her. "How much was the room?"

"Eighty."

He clenched his jaw.

"I was too tired to keep going. I asked you for help but you didn't help me." But she knew they'd been wrecks—*both* of them. She had thought she was doing it for him but she'd been wrong. They both had needed it.

"Okay," he said. "Maybe if we don't turn on the air conditioning. Maybe if we drive in neutral as much as we can."

"Maybe," she said.

But it cost thirty-five to fill up the tank and over the next two hundred miles they watched the gas run out too fast. When they hit empty they were at the base of the mountain range that separated the central valley from Los Angeles, and Sara realized that Los Angeles didn't mean anything anyway. They had nowhere to go even once they got there, no money to take care of themselves.

Grant pulled off the freeway and parked on the street. "I'm so fucking hungry. I haven't had a real meal in a week. I don't know whether to get gas or food. If we don't even have enough to get us to LA anyway . . ."

Sara looked out the window: One main road. Two gas stations. A motel. A diner. A long line of semitrucks.

"Let's get food," she said. "I want a whole plate of something."

They moved the car to the diner parking lot so that Grant could leave his stuff inside while they ate. They chose a booth along the window and sat down, were handed menus, ordered coffee. The comfort of it. The normality of it. She might not know how they'd pay, or what would happen to them next, if they'd make it over the mountains or what awaited them if they did. But she could have eggs and hash browns and pancakes with butter and syrup. She could have a cup of coffee that kept getting refilled.

Annie was gone and Sara didn't understand how the world was still the world. How could she be sitting in a diner with this plate of food, how could her feet rest on this floor, how could she unroll her paper napkin to discover a clean set of silverware inside?

But she'd already lived through that particular shock once, so she knew it meant nothing when she took a bite and it tasted good. It would taste the same whether or not Annie was alive.

They stayed in the booth not talking long after they finished their meals. The waitress brought the bill and they were relieved to see they had enough to pay and even tip, though it meant there was nothing left over. They stayed so long that she came back over to them after it was dark.

"A pecan pie just got out of the oven," she said.

Grant shook his head. "But any chance you all need help with the dishes tonight?"

Sara saw her quick glance to the bill, her relief once she'd seen that they'd paid.

"We're fully staffed but I think Bruce at the Quality Inn was talking about needing some help. You kids could check there."

Sara thanked her.

The motel wasn't nearly as charming as the Vista, but it was familiar all the same. Bruce said he only needed one person, chose Sara because she had experience. He asked if she was looking for steady work or if she was just passing through and Sara told him the truth.

"Come by in the mornings at nine," he told her. "If I find someone who can stay the deal's off, though."

Sara nodded. "Any chance there's an open room? I'll clean it so well you won't even know we were there."

"Sure, there's an open room," he said, but just as she started to thank him he added, "for sixty-five dollars a night."

She ignored his smirk, told herself that a night or two in Grant's car wouldn't be so bad. "I'll see you at nine, then."

"I'll be here."

The next morning, Sara tapped on a door and listened. Nothing. She unlocked the first vacant room and stepped inside. A bed, two side tables, a chest of drawers, a bathroom with a tub. It was much smaller than the suites she was used to, wouldn't take her long to clean. She had finished three by the time she let herself into a room and shut the door behind her, set down the caddy of cleaning supplies and sighed. She had nine to go after this one but she was moving quickly.

"Good morning, dolly," she heard, and startled. She turned to see who had spoken. It was a skinny woman, sitting up in bed in a black T-shirt and a necklace with a little silver charm. Hair wild, makeup smudged beneath her eyes.

"Oh, God, I'm sorry," Sara said.

"Don't be. I was sleeping like the dead. Didn't hear you knock."

"I'll come back later."

"No, wait. I haven't seen you here before. I'm Vivian." She leaned against the headboard and looked Sara up and down. "What a waste of beauty. What are you doing here?"

Sara didn't know how to answer. She wanted to move on to the next room and away from this. But no easy lie came to her. "My friend and I are heading to Los Angeles."

"And you ran out of money?"

Sara nodded.

"What's Bruce paying you for this?"

It struck her that they hadn't settled on a price.

"Probably close to nothing," Vivian went on. "I can get you the money much faster. Is your friend as pretty as you?"

She wanted to say they weren't interested. But the garbage bin and the gloves and the cleaning supplies, the picking of strangers' hair out of sinks and showers…the familiarity of it scared her. What if she never moved on from it? She could see herself frozen in time, stuck on the wrong side of the Tehachapi Mountains, cleaning room after room from morning until night. She needed to make it to Los Angeles, whatever it would offer them. If this was the way out, then they could do it. They'd already done it once.

Sara finished her shift, got paid for the day at the office, and found Grant leaning against his car reading an oil-stained copy of *People* magazine. She told him about Vivian. "She has the whole thing planned. She does it a lot, I guess. She says nobody cares. We won't get caught. And if we stay for one week we'll have enough to get us started in LA."

"And you *want* to do this?" Grant asked.

She stared at him. "Are you serious?"

"I'm just saying—"

"I *want* to get out of here," Sara said. "I want to make it to LA."

"I don't know," Grant said. "I mean, I see what you're saying but I don't totally get it. You got paid, right?"

"Fifteen dollars."

"You worked *four* hours for fifteen dollars?"

"How much did *you* make? Or have you been too busy reading?"

"I asked everywhere on this strip this morning. The gas stations and the fast food places and that other motel. No one's hiring. But if you clean again tomorrow and we don't eat today then we'll have thirty dollars and that's enough to get us there."

"But *then* what?"

"Then we're in LA."

"And we *still* won't have any money. Look. It'll just be a week. We'll use condoms. Vivian will handle everything for us." The truck stop loomed ahead of them, rows of trucks and lonely drivers. She wouldn't set limits this time. She would do anything Vivian told her to do and so would Grant. They could be pragmatic about it, didn't have to be people who cried in the car afterward or scrubbed their skin raw. "We'll do it for a few days," she said. "And then we'll pretend it never happened."

"I'm sorry. You can do it if you want, but I just can't."

She closed her eyes. "Thirty dollars isn't enough," she said. "We need to eat. We need at least one night in a motel in LA, even if it's only to shower. Otherwise, who's going to hire us?"

"There's got to be a different way," Grant said.

But she was searching her mind, the rows of trucks, the horizon line, the wide-open sky. "Can you think of one?" she asked him.

He didn't answer.

"I'll do it for both of us, then," she said.

They spent another night in the parking lot, and the sun rose, and Sara slipped out of the car shaky with a hunger she tried to ignore, two quarters in her pocket. She took her change to the phone booth, closed herself in, and dialed home.

"It's me," she said when Spencer answered.

"Hi." She had hoped to hear something distinct in his voice—sadness or anger or relief to hear from her—but she couldn't make out a feeling. "Are you okay?" he asked.

"Yeah," she said. "Are you?"

"Yeah. Did you get there?"

"Not yet," she said, but she didn't want to worry him. "Almost." They stayed on the line, breathing together. The street was deserted. A truck pulled onto it. She caught a glimpse of the driver, remembered what lay ahead of her, and turned toward the hillside where a woman perched on a rock, pulling something from the ground and placing it into a cup. She saw that it was Vivian.

"Gotta leave for school," Spencer said.

"Okay. I'll call again soon."

The phone booth was silent now. She listened for her own breath. *There it was.* She was still a part of the world.

Sara leaned against the glass pane of the phone booth. Vivian, in the distance, lifted the cup to her lips and sipped. What would their day be like? How many men would Vivian find for her? How much money would she make? Enough, at least, to get them over the mountains. Then they could look for a shelter to sleep in for a while. She'd find a cleaning job. She'd begin a new life.

She left the phone booth and headed across the parking lot and to the edge of the hill, where the asphalt turned to grass.

"Good morning, sunshine," Vivian said from above.

"I saw you from the phone booth. What did you put in your cup?"

"Come closer, I'll show you."

Sara stepped carefully up the incline, testing the dirt underfoot to be sure it would hold her. She could feel the small rocks and sticks through the thin soles of her canvas shoes. She sat next to Vivian on a boulder.

"Here," Vivian said, picking a stem from a tangle of small green leaves. "It's the good herb. Yerba buena. It's healing. Take this and put it in a cup of hot water. Sue in the mini-mart will give you the cup and water for free."

"What does it heal?"

It erases memories, she imagined Vivian saying. *It helps you fall out of love. It tells your future, so you can bear more easily the days in between.*

"Whatever you need it to. It's all about your intentions."

"Right," Sara said. "Okay." It was only a weed that grew out of the ground. She felt an ache, low in her stomach.

"You can choose not to believe it. Up to you. But a positive outlook will get you far in life. Be open, that's my best advice to you. So, are you ready for the day? What time are you starting at the motel?"

"Nine."

"I'll come by with our first customer around eleven o'clock. You clean those rooms as fast as you can in those two hours. Take a shower in one of them so you smell nice. It should all be just fine. I'm a good judge of character and I'll choose nice ones for you. But if something feels off, get yourself outside right away. Most of them are lonely but some of them are wicked."

Sara nodded, tamped down her dread. She stood up, yerba buena sprig in hand, and made her way to the mini-mart, where, just as Vivian said she would, a woman named Sue waved her out the door without asking for payment.

Grant was still sprawled across the backseat. She opened the front passenger door and slipped in, waking him when she shut it.

"Hey," he said, sitting up and smiling, glad to see her. It made her feel, momentarily, like her new life might be starting already. If only it were not for the day to come. All night, she had tried not to think about it, what the men might be like and what they might want from her. When she had finally fallen asleep in the early hours of the morning, she'd dreamt of Annie. She had been whispering something to Sara, whispering it right into her ear, but Sara couldn't decipher what it was she was saying.

She wondered if the words might come to her now that she was awake. *Some of them are wicked,* she heard instead. She needed other words.

"Tell me why you were crying."

"When?"

"In the car after the thing with Eugene."

He shifted on the seats, rubbed his neck. "I don't really want to talk about it."

"No, it's okay. Here, I made you this. I found it growing on the hill."

He took the paper cup from her hands and she wished she could hold on to the heat as it left her. But now it was warming his hands, and that was good, too. And he would tell her something she wanted to know.

"Are you trying to kill me?"

"It's yerba buena," she said. "It's supposed to be healing."

He took a sip. "It's good," he said. "I've never had tea like this."

"Tell me."

"Jesus, Sara, I'm still waking up. Okay. I went to the Russian River because I wanted to meet a guy."

"A specific guy?"

"No, just—I heard a lot of gay guys go there."

"Oh," she said. "That's true. But summers, mostly."

"I heard it was really small and I thought it might be easier to find someone there than it would have been in San Francisco. Or less overwhelming, I guess?"

His face was pink. He wasn't meeting her eyes. She wanted to make it easier for him. "Wait a second," she said. "You went to the Russian River for a hookup and you brought a Mickey Mouse shirt?"

He smiled. "What the fuck is wrong with Mickey Mouse?"

"You're right," she said. "Everyone knows you should wear Mickey Mouse if you want to get laid."

"Maybe that's where I went wrong," he said. He winked but he looked sad in spite of it. He took another sip. She waited.

"I didn't meet anyone, though. Or I *did*, but . . . I went to a bar and a guy tried to talk to me and I left. I couldn't do it. I don't know why."

"And then I took you to Eugene's."

"Yeah. And it was weird. I mean, I wasn't looking for anything like *that*. But the whole reason I stopped there was, I didn't want to be a virgin by the time I got to LA. I didn't want some whole thing when I finally met a guy I wanted to date. I wanted to know what I was doing. But you were smart, not to let him fuck you. I did and I still don't know what I'm doing. I'm just gross now."

"You aren't gross," she said.

"How did you know him anyway?"

She took the paper cup from Grant's hands and sipped. It warmed her and she was grateful for the fragrance of it, covering the staleness of their bodies in the enclosed space for so long.

"He's my dad's friend," she said. "He's known me all my life."

"Oh, man. I'm sorry."

"It's . . . I mean, whatever," she said, trying not to think of holding Spencer's hand as they made their way to the river or sitting on the shag carpet, her mother petting her hair. "They're all assholes. I already knew that." The sun was streaming through the windows now, the morning bright, and soon she would be heading to the motel. "Anyway, I don't think anyone ever really *knows* what they're doing."

"Thanks," Grant said.

"And it's probably going to be really special next time," she said. "For you." She leaned against the inside of the car door and assessed him. His hair falling into his eyes, the way he jerked his head to the side to see better. He had high cheekbones and a nice jaw. The little chip in his tooth was surprising and sweet. The bravado he'd shown in the lawn chair with his magazine would undoubtedly return one day soon, sure to charm tons of guys. Maybe all it would take was a row of palm trees and some ocean air, and he'd have his old smile again.

"Why Los Angeles?" she asked, and as she formed the

question she realized that she might be mistaken—he might actually know people there. They might have a sofa to sleep on, a warm meal at least.

"I want to be an actor," he said.

She nodded, tried to conceal her disappointment.

"Okay," she said. "I'm going to start my shift." But she didn't move.

"You know we don't need to do it. Not this way. You can just clean the rooms. I can tell that lady for you if you want. I can call it off for you and we can just go. Maybe fifteen dollars would get us there."

She looked out the window to the mountain range—it looked like it stretched on forever.

"No," she said. "It's all right. I can do it."

She stopped by the main office for the ring of keys.

"You're back," Bruce said.

"Here I am." She loaded her supplies and dragged the bin of sheets up the stairs before doing the same with the garbage. *Tap-tap* on the first door. She waited. No answer. She let herself in and moved quickly, as Vivian had told her to. She didn't clean as well as she had at the Vista, not even as well as she had the day before. Just well enough that she wouldn't lose this job before the week was over. With each room finished came a worsening dread until her hands shook and she thought she might vomit over a toilet while scrubbing it. *It's only people,* Annie had told her once. *Only bodies.* She called on the words for comfort, but they made her think of Annie's own body—naked on the forest floor, by candlelight in the Vista bed, being lifted from the river—and knew a body must be more than that.

By 10:30 a.m. she had cleaned all but one room on the list. She was breathing hard from the exertion, from the trips up and down the stairs to shove the dirty sheets in the laundry and empty the garbage into the Dumpster. An hour and a half before, eleven o'clock had seemed far away but now she kept watching the clock, expecting the minutes to leap forward and surprise her. And she couldn't get Annie out of her head, the way she'd touched Sara, how she'd pushed her fingers inside of her, ran her tongue along the half-moons where her breasts met her ribs. How right that had felt. How wrong all of this did.

Sara tucked the laundered bedsheets tight over the bed. The motel was quiet, Vivian and her first stranger half an hour away.

She would take a long shower in the bathroom she'd just cleaned. A small comfort to combat the mounting dread.

As she undressed, she imagined Annie arriving here at the base of the mountains, in the doorway of this shitty motel room in her jean jacket, saying, *How could you even think of letting anybody but me touch you? Come on, let's go.* She'd grab Sara's arm and they'd race down the stairs and to Grant's car, and the three of them would speed away.

Sara turned on the water, stepped into the shower. She closed her eyes and felt the heat. She washed her hair and rinsed it. When she opened her eyes again and looked down, she saw red in the water.

She put her hand between her legs.

Oh.

She had tampons in her backpack. Unwrapping one was as familiar as a homecoming. Her body, reliable, despite all that had gone wrong. And here it was: the answer she'd been searching for earlier, not from the sky or the trucks or the horizon after all. She would listen closer from now on.

She dressed quickly, made sure the bathroom was clean, and returned the supplies to their places. While Vivian was probably knocking on the doors already and waiting for Sara to open one, Sara was demanding thirty dollars from Bruce instead of the fifteen he'd given her yesterday. They settled on twenty-five and, with the cash in her fist, she ran the blocks to the Civic, past the rows of trucks, past the strangers who would remain strangers forever after all. Grant had found them a box of French fries, cold but barely touched, and an unopened packet of ketchup. He had them propped on the dashboard for the moment she came back.

She knocked on the window, so much sooner than expected. He sat up straight, looked through the glass. Clutched his heart at the sight of her.

THE FLOWER SHOP & THE STUDIO

Emilie, in the Los Angeles summer heat. Cutoff shorts, skin on the fabric seat of her Tercel, pulling up to her parents' house for brunch. And there was Mrs. Santos, tending to her front garden and waving.

"I've missed you," Emilie called out, crossing to her.

Emilie had worked as a receptionist for the Santoses' real estate business until the month before. It had been a normal afternoon in the office. She'd just finished refilling the cups of ballpoint pens and paperclips on the desks when a hush fell. She turned to find Mr. and Mrs. Santos and Randy, their elder son, standing in the reception area with a cake.

"Happy five-year anniversary!" Mr. Santos said, and they'd all cheered, heading toward her.

Randy lowered the cake onto the desk, bright purple yam and white coconut, one of the Filipino dishes she'd grown up eating at their house "Ube," she said. "My favorite." But she could barely get the words out. *Five years?* It was supposed to have been a summer job, something to pay her rent between her sophomore and junior years of college. She stared into the tiny flames of the five candles and began to cry, and Mrs. Santos said, *There, there,* while Mr. Santos pretended to get a phone call and closed himself in his office.

"You know he's terrible with emotions," Randy said. "But we understand."

"I'm being rude. You made me a cake. You've been so good to me."

And they had been. Her responsibilities consisted of answering the phones and brewing the coffee and talking to Mr. Santos about recipes and bird watching (though Emilie neither cooked nor watched birds), and on the best days Pablo came by and spun in Randy's office chair and made her spin in hers and they got dizzy and gazed at the yellowed dropped ceiling of the office as though it was sky, marveling at songs they loved or films they'd seen. Sometimes Pablo pulled up pictures of his latest collages and drawings on the office computer for her to critique. Sometimes he read sections from her essays, and everyone gave her their full blessing to print them out, every draft of them, page after double-spaced page.

"Tax deductible," Mr. Santos would tell her, extending his arm toward the printer as though bestowing upon her a small kingdom of ink and paper.

It had been so easy to stay. For the years to slip by. It had been good, but its time was over, and Mrs. Santos said, "Let's eat cake while we decide what you'll do next," and Emilie had stopped crying, grateful to be understood.

Now, in her garden, Mrs. Santos said, "Colette drove up a few minutes ago. Family brunch?"

Emilie lifted the bottle of orange juice she'd been instructed to bring in confirmation.

"How's she doing?" The same question, asked so many times over the years.

Emilie shrugged. "You never know with Colette."

"Poor girl."

"Woman," Emilie reminded her. "She's twenty-eight."

"You're all still so young. But yes. She's a woman now. Your poor parents. And you, too, Emilie. It's good to rest. Finish your studies. We always have a place for you at the office if you need a few hours here and there. Randy's loving real estate . . ."

"Too much paperwork. Tell me about these flowers. They're just like California poppies but they're *pink*."

"A hybrid. Don't you love them?"

Inside her parents' house, she set the orange juice on the counter and kissed her mother and father on the cheek. They were both in striped aprons, Lauren's hair neatly swept off her face, Bas swaying to The Neville Brothers. The waffle iron steamed, the bacon crackled. Coffee dripped into the pot.

"Will that be us someday?" Colette asked, appearing from behind her, speaking low into her ear. "Attached forever to the music of our youth?"

Emilie tilted her head a little closer, felt the thrill of Colette's attention. "I'd be fine with that. As long as we don't match aprons with our spouses."

Colette threw her head back and laughed and Emilie was flooded with love, with regret. How could she forget how much fun they had when they were together?

Their neighborhoods bled into one another, but over the

years they'd settled into a halfhearted avoidance. Sometimes they'd run into each other in cafés or restaurants. "I didn't know you hung out here," one of them would say. "It's like three minutes from my place," the other would answer.

When they were with friends, the run-ins were briefer and more pleasant. When they were each alone, Emilie felt guilty for not calling more often, not checking in to see how Colette was or if she needed anything. Once, standing in line at a café, Emilie caught sight of Colette alone at a table, reading, and she turned and hurried out. It was too difficult to know the right thing to do. Sitting at a different table would have been an acknowledgment of their distance. She could have taken a spot at the second, empty chair and read alongside Colette, but that would have taken too much pretending. They weren't that kind of sisters. They didn't have comfortable, familiar silences. They talked on the phone when it was necessary, did each other favors, got together for family gatherings, but they'd never felt easy in the other's presence.

Not since they were teenagers, anyway.

"Help me set the table," Colette said.

They gathered the blue placemats and the matching napkins, the silverware and the glasses, and took them outside to the table on the deck they'd helped build a decade ago. Colette went back inside and Emilie closed her eyes and made herself very still, listening for the ocean. It was only four blocks away, but with the traffic and the people in between, it had a way of getting lost. Colette returned with sparkling water and the orange juice and the silver salt and pepper shakers, shaped like birds.

"All together!" Lauren said, apronless now, stepping out with a platter of fruit.

"Our beautiful girls," Bas said, coming after her with the waffles and bacon. "Tell us everything new."

Colette started. She was volunteer tutoring at a place her best friend worked for—a nonprofit that started in San Francisco and now had a center in LA. "You walk up and it's this funny store where everything is time travel themed."

"I'm not following," Lauren said, pouring coffee.

"It's almost like a joke shop, but the stuff is actually cool. But it doesn't even matter—the tutoring happens in back. I go a couple afternoons a week when kids get out of school and I help them with their homework."

"You've always been great with kids," Bas said.

"Yes," Lauren said. "It sounds perfect for you."

Emilie couldn't remember a single instance of seeing her sister interact with a child. But it was possible she missed something. *Likely* she missed it. Even though the farthest Emilie had moved was from Long Beach to Echo Park, she managed to fall out of touch with her family from time to time. She'd see them again after a few weeks and there would be a new story among the other three. A dinner or a museum visit, something they hadn't told her about but that they weren't exactly hiding either.

Once, after hearing about a weekend trip to Joshua Tree, Emilie had excused herself for the bathroom and sat on the toilet, scrolling through their family text chain, making sure she hadn't missed the invitation.

"I've always wanted to go to Joshua Tree," she'd said when she returned to the table.

"You should have come," Lauren said.

"No one told me about it."

"Bas, you told her, didn't you?"

"I thought you were telling her. Of course, you were invited, Em—we thought you were busy."

"Maybe next time ask me," Emilie said, staring at her plate.

But they were together now, and it was her turn to share what was new. "Well, you know I quit the real estate office."

"It was time," Lauren said. "I mean, the Santoses are a wonderful family, but you couldn't work for them forever."

"I have to figure out what to do next, but I have some ideas. And last semester I took this women's studies class that was focused on writers and we read the most incredible plays and novels. I decided that that's what I want to study. Literature. So I changed some things around and—"

"No," Lauren said. "No. Emilie."

Emilie felt her face get hot. "I know, it sounds crazy, but I'm really sure about it. I signed up for classes and they look incredible."

"I've lost count," Colette said. "First it was ethnic studies and then women's studies?"

"Design was in between," Bas said. "If I'm not mistaken."

Emilie nodded. "Yes. Design was in between."

"So this is your *fourth* major." Lauren sighed, pushed her plate away from her. "And you're entering your . . . *seventh* year of undergraduate studies?"

It was her fifth major, actually. She was relieved they'd forgotten botany. She refilled her water glass. Was grateful when the conversation moved on.

Brunch was over and she was driving again, a few blocks from her studio apartment, when she saw the woman hanging the

HELP WANTED sign in the window of the flower shop. *Fate,* she thought, pulling over.

The school conversation clung to her as much as she tried to shake it, to tell herself it didn't matter, that they were only concerned. Most people go to college for a degree, she told herself. She went for an education. And so who cared if it was taking her a long time? She would put all of it out of her mind. Here was the mid-afternoon summer sunshine, the heat of the sidewalk, the flower shop up close. Enough to numb the sting for a little while.

It was the opposite of Pablo's family's office: everything was unabashedly beautiful. The bright and deep greens of the sidewalk plants against the blue-black shop facade. Glint of metal planters, warmth of clay pots. Inside, the smell of clean dirt and candles.

The woman who had moments ago hung the sign was now behind the counter.

"Hi," Emilie said, and extended her hand.

She had her interview right then and there. She had never before worked for a florist but she'd taken a weekend class in floral design, had made many wreaths, had even done the flowers for the low-key wedding of a college friend. And, of course, there were the lessons Mrs. Santos had given her over the years. The reverence she'd imparted.

Meredith, the shop owner, asked her to assemble a few sample arrangements and Emilie got to work.

She wanted this job. She felt its rightness. She thought the beauty of it might coax out some dormant part of her and jolt it awake.

"The florist I'm replacing had our restaurant accounts,"

Meredith said. "Olive, The Grant Club, Yerba Buena, Silver-ado . . ."

"I love Yerba Buena," Emilie said. "I had my first legal cocktail there when I turned twenty-one."

"Sophisticated choice for a twenty-one-year-old."

"It's my parents' favorite restaurant. They leap at any excuse to go. Actually, I've *noticed* the floral arrangements there. A lot of branches and leaves, right? Big blossoms—proteas, leuca-dendrons. Nothing too traditional."

"Yes, but I'd want you to bring your own vision. As long as you're good and the arrangements complement the space, the owners will be happy."

My own vision, Emilie thought. Her flora phase was so long ago and yet it came back to her, the woody smell of snipped stems, thorn pricks and sore fingers.

Meredith craned her neck to see what Emilie was doing. "Take your time with those. Let me know when you're fin-ished."

Emilie could have spent hours editing and adding, but she knew Meredith would appreciate efficiency, so after only a few minutes she stepped back, made a few changes, and declared the arrangements complete. Meredith admired them, impressed.

"Can you name the flowers?" she asked, and Emilie looked at the wall lined with silver buckets. She named as many flow-ers as she could and promised she would study the rest. She wanted a job offer on the spot. She knew it would pay next to nothing, but she would make it work.

"Write down your information here," Meredith said, hand-ing her a legal pad and pencil. "I'll get back to you soon."

Emilie faked a smile and hoped it looked genuine. "Great,"

she said. When she got to the door she turned back. "I'd love to work for you. Your shop is beautiful."

Then she shut the door behind her and felt the weight of the day.

She drove to Echo Park Lake and walked its perimeter, not ready to go home yet. The swan boats were out on the water, the downtown skyline in the distance. She tried to pay attention only to what she could see and hear, to the sensation of her feet on the path and the sun on her skin.

But she kept thinking of her family. How terrible it felt to her, to be a disappointment. And she thought of Olivia, too. Her former professor turned secret girlfriend had broken up with her half a year before for the same reason—because Emilie was still an undergrad. Even though their ages weren't all that far apart, Olivia could have been fired had the administration found out about them, and Emilie had to accept it, knew she had only herself to blame.

She got halfway around the lake, paused at her favorite spot. Gazed at the reeds, the fish flashing below the water.

Maybe her family was right to give her a hard time. Maybe she was wrong to continue as she had been. But she was enrolled in the classes, it was too late now.

She longed for the life of a fish. In and out of reeds they swam. All color and movement and blankness.

She drove the rest of the way home, climbed the stairs to her studio apartment, and opened the one window that wasn't painted shut. She hoped for a breeze. She sat on her bed and looked out. Above the garbage-strewn sidewalk, the run-down motel, the row of houses and palms on the hill behind it, was a blue sky with a single white cloud.

She would need to find something for dinner.

She opened her refrigerator. A half carton of eggs, a bottle of ketchup, a jar of jam. Some juice that expired yesterday and a carton of iced coffee. She'd order a burrito from the shop a couple blocks down. She grabbed her purse and her phone and saw that a text had come in. It was Meredith.

Why postpone a good thing?

She called her friend Alice, who always picked up for her even though she had a real job as a stylist for photographers and filmmakers and ignored almost everyone else.

"I have good news," Emilie said.

"As long as it has nothing to do with Olivia." Emilie could hear the music and conversation in the background, pictured Alice at one of the parties she was always asked to go to or waiting for someone to join her for happy hour somewhere.

"Not about Olivia," Emilie said. She took the phone away from her ear to order her burrito and then, choosing a table in the covered back patio full of palms and bright colors, said, "I got a job at that flower shop on Sunset and North Vermont." They'd never spoken about the shop, but Emilie knew Alice would have noticed it. Alice moved through the world noticing beautiful things.

"That place is absurdly pretty. And you'll be doing arrangements again! You were always so good at that."

"Thank you." She tried to hold the compliment as what it was—something true and simple—and not feel bad about possibly moving backward, twenty-five with a minimum wage job, not pursuing anything, really, not moving toward a bigger life.

"I think it'll be good," she said. "For now, at least."

Emilie spent two weeks training at the florist before she was sent out in the mornings to the restaurant accounts, her car full of flowers and leaves and blossoming branches. Tuesdays she visited a sushi place downtown, everything white and spotless. On Thursday mornings she made centerpieces for each table in a blue-tiled Greek restaurant famous for its eighty-two-year-old chef. And two mornings a week, she arranged flowers for Yerba Buena.

The restaurant at Sunset and Selma was a Los Angeles institution, revitalized in the past decade by Jacob Lowell, a chef who'd earned a reputation through his decade at the French Laundry, followed by a series of pop-up restaurants after his move to LA.

The restaurant that formerly occupied the space had been known for its steak and its duck, its formal service and decadent architecture, its decades-loyal regulars and throngs of tourists. It had coved ceilings, private leather booths, multiple dining rooms, and a Michelin star—though each year rumors circulated that it was on the verge of losing it.

With the help of a few investors, Jacob Lowell had bought the place and closed it for six months. When he opened it again, many of the walls had been knocked down, fresh plaster in white and pale peach applied to those that remained. A new sign hung over the door, the letters carved into wood: YERBA BUENA.

Bright drawings replaced the old oil paintings. The coved ceilings stayed, along with the leather booths, but now there were two bars and two large dining rooms, and the menu was unrecognizable. The old regulars complained that it was too noisy. They balked at the idea of sitting next to strangers at one of the communal tables. But the new clientele praised the lighter menu, the handmade pastas and tender meats, the delicate fish and the salads plucked from local farms, and the less fussy air of it all. The waitresses in their summer dresses, as though they were the ones going out to dinner; the sommelier, who'd visit the table with the air of an old friend eager to catch you up on what everyone's been drinking; the impossibly attractive bartenders who actually smiled when they talked to you . . . They were all irresistible.

Emilie showed up by nine on the mornings she worked there, when the restaurant was uninhabited but for her and the two chefs in the kitchen, the tinny echo of their music whenever the kitchen door swung open. She'd thought she'd known the restaurant well from all the birthday and anniversary celebrations she'd spent there with her family. Their favorite booth was there, in the center of the far wall. Her parents had learned its number—48—and requested it each time they made a reservation. But she saw it in a new way now, with morning light pouring through the windows, the stillness, the quiet. She would gather the arrangements from her last visit and wrap the old flowers in newspaper. She'd wash out the vases and urns and spread the new cuttings across the community table until she saw a place to begin. A branch or a flower. A color theme, or a texture that moved her. She liked to work on several arrangements at a time. Sometimes she put on her headphones, but most of the time she enjoyed the quiet, the faraway kitchen noises, the rustling leaves, her footsteps as she circled the table, choosing the next stem.

And then there were Jacob's footsteps, too, at ten thirty, when most of the flowers were in the urns and no longer on the table.

"Good morning," he'd say.

"Good morning," she'd say.

He was generous with his compliments, so much so that she began to wonder if he had an uncommonly deep appreciation for flowers. The way he would linger, how he'd lean closer and ask questions about colors and names—all this couldn't have been about her. When he ran out of questions, he'd make his way to the kitchen or return to the dining room but sit in a far booth, in what she could tell was his usual spot, and eat his breakfast over a stack of paperwork. She felt his presence across the restaurant as she set the newly finished vases and urns in their rightful places, as she cleared the debris and her scissors from the community table and wiped it down. She never knew whether or not to say goodbye—he appeared so engrossed—but every time she got to the door and turned, he'd lift his hand and she'd wave back.

Then, one morning, after a month of these tentative questions and answers, he said his usual good morning and breezed past her to the kitchen.

It was August and the table was laden with dahlias and pe-onies. The blooms were thick and fragrant—enough to make her swoon—but he barely glanced at them.

She placed three red peonies in an urn, added branches for height. She stepped back to see if it was working. And then the kitchen door swung open, and he reappeared. He was carrying two plates toward her.

"Hungry?" he asked.

There were thick slices of bread warm from the oven, halved farm eggs with deep orange centers, berries and jam.

"Yeah," she said. "I'm starving." And it was true.

He returned with a pot of tea and two ceramic cups.

He chose a new breakfast table, the one right in front of the community table scattered with her snipped stems and sup-plies. That's where he now sat on the mornings she worked there.

Every time she finished, they'd eat together. He brought along his stacks of papers—receipts from the farms from which they sourced their meats and vegetables, copies of the schedule to approve—and Emilie would pull a book from her purse and review for the class she'd attend later that morning.

They sat as though their early mornings began with a kiss, with her telling him about last night's dream from her place in the shower while he shaved at the sink. As though they'd discussed the arc of the day as they drove together to the restaurant, and they already knew who was going to the store and who was making dinner. By the time they parked they were full with their talking and their knowingness of one another, and now they could sit quietly, together in their separate tasks.

This lasted for weeks, and it was enough for her. She wasn't one of his young waitresses who got off on the thrill of his hand on their waists as he slid past them in doorways. She didn't want to gossip to her friends about what he was like in bed. Everyone knew that he was married. He and his wife were darlings of the food world, appeared in magazines, were guests at celebrities' weddings and birthdays. She was pretty sure that he had a kid—maybe more than one. She stayed later and later, closer to noon, when her class started. She brought her laptop and wrote papers across from him. She found herself working better when she was with him. She could be deep in thought over a poem, her fingers flying across the keyboard, and then she'd finish her paragraph and lean back and he'd be smiling at her.

His staff would trickle in. The manager, Megan; Ken, the host, to look over the reservations before returning later on; the waitstaff, to taste the new wines and the ever-changing menu. One morning the bar staff came in early for a meeting, and a bartender set his bike helmet down at their breakfast table.

"That's where Jacob and Emilie sit in the mornings," Megan said. "Let's move to the back."

A thrill coursed through her, to be recognized this way, to be mentioned by name even though most of the people there wouldn't even know that the woman quietly arranging flowers was the one they were moving for.

Then a voice she didn't recognize said, "We can go straight to the bar actually. I'll go over everything there."

Emilie turned toward her, but the stranger was already leading the others out of the main dining room. Emilie walked past them all a little later on her way to throw away the first batch of clipped stems and discarded branches. The woman—tall and slender with short blond hair, so attractive that Emilie blushed—stood alone behind the bar while the others watched her mix and pour. Some of them took notes.

When they filtered back into the dining room, the woman stopped next to Emilie.

"I've never seen ferns used this way," she said. "They're so strange with the peonies. *Beautiful* strange, I mean. I never would have thought of putting them together. Do you mind if I touch them?"

"Go ahead," Emilie said.

"These grew all over the place where I'm from."

She watched the woman trace their edges, felt an overwhelming closeness, like this wasn't about ferns at all, like she was touching Emilie instead. How intimate it was: The single fact about her life. The curve of her cheekbone, up close. The blond tips of her eyelashes. Tiny freckles across the bridge of her nose like the specks of pollen Emilie discovered on her clothing after work sometimes.

She turned to Emilie. "I'm Sara."

Emilie felt her blush giving her away but managed to extend her hand. "I'm Emilie." Sara's shake was firm, her hand soft, but there was something else, too. Something in the way they fit together, palm against palm, that made Emilie not want to let go.

"*Oh,*" Sara said. "The Emilie who sits with Jacob." They dropped each other's hands.

She wanted to deny it but couldn't. Wanted to say it wasn't like that, didn't mean anything, but what *did* it actually mean?

"It's all right, I get it," Sara said.

Emilie watched Sara say goodbye to the others. Saw her laughing with Megan about something, taking an envelope from Jacob. She breezed past her but then stopped at the door. "Nice to meet you, Emilie," she said, lifting a hand to wave, and Emilie felt herself blush again, wanted Sara's hand in hers again, caught sight of a cluster of tattoos on the inside of Sara's forearm—words, she thought—and wished she knew what they said.

"Is she new here?" she asked Jacob a little later, over their usual eggs and jam and toast.

"I wish. She's just consulting. I've been trying to poach her from Odessa for months, but I finally got her to design our new cocktail menu. Actually, will you try something? You have to go to class, I know, but just a sip. Tell me what you think. I've been searching for a signature drink. *The* Yerba Buena. This is what she came up with."

She followed him to the bar where he checked a recipe on a piece of paper and carefully measured and poured. She expected him to be confident in everything, but his bartenders moved so much quicker, were nonchalant where he was focused and precise. Finally, he handed her a coupe glass. She sipped. It tasted bitter in a way that felt like being nourished, but still a little sweet.

"Is it too bitter for you?" Jacob asked.

"It's bitter, yeah. But not too much, no." She took another

sip. "I've never tasted anything like this, but it *feels* familiar somehow."

"She's a genius," he said.

It lasted this way for so long—the mornings over toast and coffee, the quiet conversations—that Emilie thought it would last like that forever. But then, a couple weeks later, he finished his paperwork and leaned back in his chair.

"I'd like to see where you live," he said.

What could she say in response to that? Fleetingly, she wondered if this was a thing he did, like a side project, observing people in their natural environments. It was something *she* loved—being in other people's houses, seeing the colors they painted their walls and the objects they kept on their bookshelves. But when she met his eyes, his desire was plain.

"Okay," she said. "I'll give you the address."

"I'll see you later, then," he said as she left.

She went to her class and rushed home. She didn't know if he meant later today, or later as a stand-in for someday. She thought she would be prepared in case today was what he meant. She sorted through her stacks of mail and recycled the catalogs and junk. She washed the dishes that had sat for too long in the sink, and she even got out the vacuum and pushed it around, the first time in a while. She didn't think of her studio as a place for people to visit; her hopes for it upon moving in had quickly faded until it became a place to study and sleep. Most of her eating and her socializing she did elsewhere. The only people who came over were friends she didn't have to try for anymore. She kept IPAs in her refrigerator for Pablo and dried lemon verbena leaves in her cupboard for Alice, and that was enough for them.

Now she stood in her doorway and wondered what her place would look like to Jacob if he did in fact appear here, whether later today or in a more distant future. It was small. Unimpressive. Its walls were primer white, and she found herself resentful of the owner, who must have been either too cheap or too indecisive to finish the job. Half of her mismatched dishes were chipped and she had no fitted sheets that matched the top ones. The kitchen windows were painted shut—simply boiling water for tea made the glass fog over. Some nights she'd climb into bed by nine o'clock because none of the lights were bright enough and to be awake any later than that made her sad.

And also—the window on the east side had no curtain. When she was naked she had to duck when she passed it. When it was dark outside everyone could see her, doing whatever she was doing, and when she'd tried to hang a curtain rod the plaster had crumbled.

She realized the apartment wasn't equipped to impress anyone. She should focus on herself.

So she showered and shaved her legs. She brushed her teeth and massaged coconut oil into her skin. She let her hair air-dry. It was long, midway down her back, and she didn't think she'd ever worn it down to the restaurant, at least not when she had been there in the morning to work. She dressed in a pair of lounge pants Alice had brought her from a trip to Morocco, emerald with tiny brass bells around the ankles. As she pulled a black tank top over her head and looked at her reflection, she found herself wondering if this was something she actually wanted.

Yes, his attention made her feel special.

Yes, she enjoyed their mornings together.

In fact, she enjoyed them too much. She ached for the idea of more with him but she didn't, she realized now, actually ache for the reality of it. She didn't even know if she wanted to have sex with men again—her last relationships had been with women.

She remembered how it started with Olivia as she fished a pair of gold earrings from her jewelry box. Emilie had sat in the front row, always. She'd admired Olivia from the start—found her thoughtful pauses charming, her effortless use of academic jargon something to aspire to. Olivia dressed in button-downs and jeans, her hair kept natural and faded. Her nose ring changed often. A diamond one day, a hoop the next. Emilie had watched her, admired her, had asked questions in class, filled her notebooks with what Olivia taught her, underlined passages from bell hooks and Angela Davis, scrutinized Foucault.

But it really started when she visited Olivia's office hours one afternoon to talk about a paper she was writing. "It's about the liminality of Creole identity," she'd said, rushing to speak as she sat down across from Olivia's desk, not wanting to take up too much of her professor's time. "How we exist in a gray area. And I'm wondering if you think there's room for intersectionality. Like if I could talk about passing as white *and* passing as straight? Or maybe it would be better to just focus on race, I don't know." Emilie had been fishing through her bag for a notebook and pen. She opened the notebook, positioned her pen, and leaned back to see what Olivia thought.

"So, you date women?" Olivia had asked.

"Yeah."

"Sure," Olivia had said, a new interest in her voice. "Sure. You could write about that."

They waited for the semester to end.

Emilie would always go to Olivia because Emilie shared a small two-bedroom apartment with a housemate back then, and Olivia had her own half of a side-by-side duplex. She'd answer her door in yoga pants, public radio faintly in the background. They would have sex or have dinner and then stay up late binge-watching shows and dissecting them. It was the most fascinating part of academia, Emilie thought, that even trashy television could be significant if you looked at it through a certain lens.

Emilie thought that how they'd met shouldn't have been an issue—Olivia was only five years older—but Olivia had worried for her job. "I'm upset, too. I don't know what you're doing," she'd said when they were breaking up. "You shouldn't still be here." Emilie had known it was her fault. What was she *doing,* still going to college?

After the breakup she'd signed the lease to her own place—the studio—which felt, at the time, like a step into adulthood. But it quickly became just another place to write her papers, and let mail stack up, and worry about her life.

And now Jacob might arrive here at any moment. She had thrived on the tension between them, but she never thought he'd walk through her door, and as the hours slipped by, she found herself hoping that he wouldn't. She tried to study but she couldn't. She felt nauseous, and then sicker by the minute. If he didn't come tonight, she would quit the flower shop, she would never go back to Yerba Buena, their mornings together would fade, dreamlike, into a might-have-been. By the time it was eight o'clock she told herself he wasn't coming and relief washed over her. She put her kettle on, dropped two verbena leaves into a mug. She listened to the water as it heated, watched as the steam began, and soon the pot was shrilling. Just as she took it off the burner, the knock came.

Here he was in her doorway, taking up more space than she imagined he would, his hazel eyes bright with nervousness, the strands of hair by his temples more gray than silver in the gloomy light of her studio. Even his voice sounded different without the echo of the restaurant. He had barely stepped inside and was already walking circles around the studio's perimeter, picking up all the things she owned and asking her questions about them. She had collections of gemstones and shells and books with green spines.

"Do you read them?"

"Of course."

He laughed. "Are green books better?"

"Not better, just prettier," she said. "I read all books. I just keep the green ones."

He eased one out from the middle of a shelf. Set it back. Found a framed family photograph—Emilie and Colette and Bas and Lauren, dressed up and smiling. "This is outside my restaurant."

"We've been going there since I was in high school."

"Fuck, I'm old. So these are your parents? Your sister?"

"Yeah."

"You guys close?"

Emilie shrugged, felt his gaze upon her. "My sister's a drug addict. She's been in and out of rehab since we were teenagers, so . . ."

"Ah. That complicates things. How old were you when it started?"

"Fifteen. She gets better but it doesn't last. It's easier for me to sort of . . . disconnect." She heard herself telling the old story—her addict sister, her complicated adolescence. Wondered if she'd ever outgrow it. How pathetic it was to let someone she rarely saw have such a hold on her life.

It had only been a few minutes, and already she was exhausted by Jacob's questions, by coming up with answers. When he took over talking she felt her shoulders fall, her stomach unclench. She relaxed into his words. She nodded in a way she was used to, to show him she was listening, to show him how interested she was.

"It seems like you really like school," he said.

"I do. I'm ready to be done with it, though. I'm on my fifth major. All my classmates are children. *Smart* children, but still, so young."

"I liked college, for a while. Before I got the job at this little tapas place and fell madly in love with cooking and realized I was just wasting my time, sitting in classrooms every day, when I could be in the kitchen." He talked and the sky darkened through the window behind him. The motel sign's VACANCY light clicked on. She wondered if she should offer him something to drink and she wished she had thought to get something for them to eat. But he wasn't here anyway. He was in Spain, where he had somehow ended up working on a farm—he'd told her how but she hadn't followed—and now his eyes teared up and he shook his head.

"When I think of that dirt in my hands . . . That soil. I've never felt anything like it since. I love all the farms we partner with at the restaurant, but they're mostly new. City kids burning out, looking for something noble, thinking they'll find it with some seeds and a couple acres outside Santa Barbara. Soil like Marta and Xavi's? That takes time."

"It sounds incredible."

"It *was* incredible."

The sky was black by then and she was starving, wondering what was going to happen.

"I want to cook you dinner," he said, suddenly back with her, on his feet and stretching his shoulders. "I saw that Mexican grocery downstairs."

She glanced at her clock. "It closes in five minutes."

"Shit, let's go."

She was glad to get out of the studio and into the night. She would open her tiny bedroom window once they were back up. She would light a couple candles for the table she usually used as a desk, and she would set out cloth napkins, which she rarely did. She headed to the spices to find chili paste while he picked through the bins of produce for the ripest avocados and brightest citrus. She paused on her way back to him, because he was such a sight, palming oranges and avocados, peeling back cornhusks, smelling the cilantro and mint, the fluorescent lights of the open sign outside clicking off and him still there, facing her but not seeing her, placing slim red peppers into a basket.

He sliced the oranges and avocados and made a quick salad

dressing. She owned a single cast iron skillet. He blistered corn and peppers in it, seared prawns. It was one of the best meals she'd ever eaten.

She thought, maybe, this was all there would be. A delving into his past, a shopping trip, candles and cloth napkins and a meal.

But, of course, it wasn't.

They had only been kissing for a couple of minutes when he took her shirt off. He was fumbling with her bra clasp and she wanted to ask him what they were doing. What this was going to be. The taste of his mouth was a new taste. And there was the matter of his wife, who suddenly seemed real to her, and his children. Two of them, she knew now. Boys.

He had taken his pants off, untied the drawstring of hers. He was telling her she was beautiful. He was saying how much he wanted this. And there was a condom in his hand, and he was unwrapping it, and she thought back several hours ago, to the fraction of a second between the kettle's shriek and the knock at the door. She wondered how long he'd been planning it, and when exactly she fell behind. *Wait,* she wanted to say. *What are we doing?* Even as she kissed him, even as she slipped her pants over her feet, she didn't know.

It was almost one by the time he left.

Emilie's mother turned sixty and her father made the usual birthday reservation at Yerba Buena for that Saturday night. In the morning, Emilie's phone dinged with a text from Colette.

Pick a sister up?

As long as you don't mind a detour to Long Beach, she wrote back.

Bas and Lauren were visiting friends near the restaurant before dinner and had asked Emilie to pick up her grandmother. Her phone dinged again:

Fine with me.

So at six, Emilie drove the mile from her Echo Park studio to the Silver Lake apartment that Colette shared with her best friend. It was nearly winter but the sun shone bright and warm. Instead of texting when she got there, she double-parked and went to the door, smiled wide from behind her sunglasses when Colette opened it.

Colette stood in the doorway, barefoot, wearing a long red dress, cinched at her slim waist.

"Hey, sister," Emilie said.

"You're early," Colette said, turning back into the apartment, but when she reappeared in the doorway with her purse, she smiled back. "I hope the ragout's on the menu."

"Oh my God," Emilie said. "Me, too."

That evening, climbing into the car, rolling down the windows, and heading to their grandmother's house in Long Beach, Emilie felt as though she were watching them through the window of a neighboring car. They looked like sisters, no matter how they felt. Their wavy dark hair and full lips. Their sunglasses, their dresses. She was used to feeling dull in comparison with Colette, but now she was carrying a secret. She felt it in her bloodstream, turning her bolder.

She glowed with it.

Claire was on her front porch when they got to Long Beach. Eighty-nine years old, wearing a suit and sheer black stockings, a rhinestone-studded purse in her hands, a look of expectation. Just the sight of her made Emilie want to cry. Both sisters jumped out to help her into the car.

"Look at your dresses," she said. "Your lip color." She touched Colette's hair, and then Emilie's. "It always warms my heart to see you together."

Emilie loved her grandmother, her New Orleans accent, her soft brown skin, the way she lingered on details, her unapologetic regard for beauty. Her gold-rimmed stemware and extensive wardrobe, the floral wallpaper in all the rooms of her house. Emilie, throughout her years of school, had interviewed Claire for a dozen term papers. It was endlessly fascinating to her—how her grandparents had been part of a Creole exodus from Louisiana after the war, a small piece of the Great Migration. How they'd done their best to re-create home in South Central Los Angeles, opening barbershops and bakeries and restaurants, holding supper clubs and dances. They were steeped in Catholicism. They danced the second line. They perfected their gumbo and their jambalaya. Their children grew up well versed in their parents' triumphs and their regrets, in a pride in their dislocated culture, but then most of the Creole businesses closed down and their history was fading.

Claire was the eldest of three sisters: Claire, Adele, Odette. They were famous for their beauty. They never showed sadness. Their waists were so small that Adele carried a measuring tape in her pocket in case she saw a woman who might rival them. All their lives, they never lived more than five miles apart. Emilie and Colette were like them in name, in their small waists and muscular legs, in their dark hair and their childhood disputes. They were like them in their frequent phone calls but not in the feelings behind them, in their proximity but not in their secrets.

Like this one.

Emilie carried her secret with her as she drove Colette and Claire to Yerba Buena. Felt it surge into her throat when they parked the car.

Colette helped her grandmother out of the passenger seat and Emilie took Claire's other arm. They flanked her, felt her fragile elbows even under blouse and blazer.

Claire tightened her grip around Emilie's wrist, and Emilie worried that she'd feel her hummingbird pulse and ask her what was wrong. *Dear,* Claire would say, *are you nervous about something?* But they made it to the door and entered, Emilie's secret undetected.

Bas was at the bar, but Lauren stood in the front, waiting for them.

"Did you do this arrangement, Emilie?" she asked when they walked in.

Emilie nodded.

"Claire, you remember that Emilie does the floral arrangements for this restaurant, don't you?"

"Oh, now isn't this lovely," Claire said. "Now what's this flower called?"

"It's a Coral Reef Poppy," Emilie said.

And then Ken was there, eyes flashing with surprise to see her. He scanned the reservations list.

"The Dubois family," he said. "Welcome."

"You remember us!" Lauren said.

"Of course," he said, glancing at Emilie. "I have a table for you right this way if you're ready."

As soon as they got to the table, Colette picked up the small sheet of paper with the day's menu.

"Ragout!" she said.

"Hooray!" Emilie said.

"I almost want to get two orders for myself."

"It's so good."

"Yeah, and the portions are small."

Emilie could feel the eyes of her family on them, felt again how sisterly they looked tonight. She played into it, buoyed by her nervousness, by Ken's surprise, by the way the manager, Megan, had just slipped behind her and touched her shoulder in a private hello. Anyone who didn't know better would think she was just squeezing past her seat, that it meant nothing.

"We could order three and share them. That way we could get other things, too," Emilie said.

"Sharing," Colette said. "That's so cute. Let's do it."

Megan appeared at their table with a bottle of Prosecco. A busser—someone who didn't work in the mornings—was next to her with glasses.

"We wanted to start you all off with something while you look at the menu," Megan said, pouring.

Lauren beamed at Bas.

"You told them it was my birthday," she said. She turned to Megan. "How sweet. Thank you."

Bas shook his head. "Actually, it must have been . . ."

He looked at Colette and Emilie felt the familiar tug of

annoyance. Of course, he would think it was Colette, even though Emilie did the flowers here. Even though Colette couldn't even get herself to the restaurant, let alone think to call ahead about a special occasion.

Colette shook her head.

"Not me," she said.

"A little bird must have told us." Megan set a glass down at Emilie's place. Gustav came with olives and house-baked bread—only given to friends of the restaurant.

"From Jacob," he said.

"From *Jacob*?" Lauren said in wonder. "How long have we been coming here, Bas? A decade?"

"Longer than that, I think."

"He bought it twelve years ago," Emilie said, and blushed, but no one noticed.

Lauren gazed into Bas's eyes. "Tonight we made it to the inner circle."

"I'll toast to that."

"You *guys,*" Colette said. "Emilie practically works here. She's why we're getting the free food."

"You're only here in the mornings, right?" Lauren asked. "You don't know these people, do you?"

Emilie felt her face get hotter.

"Just a couple of them," she said. She raised her glass. "Happy birthday, Mom."

They clinked glasses. Colette brought hers to her lips and then laughed at the alarm on their faces.

"Who wants mine?" she asked without sipping.

"Just set it by your sister's, sweetheart. Someone will take it. Do you want me to order you a tonic?"

"Sure, Dad."

He waved their waiter over.

"My daughter would like one of your house-made tonics," he said. "And let's add an extra wedge of lime."

"Are we really getting three orders of ragout?" Colette asked, and Emilie said, "We absolutely are getting three orders," and they did, and their waiter raised an eyebrow and said, "Nicely done."

After they'd ordered Emilie excused herself to go to the restroom. She was relieved to be alone for a moment, weaving her way toward the back, past the kitchen and into the hallway, when a door swung open and there was Jacob, pulling her into his office. He pushed her against the wall and kissed her, said into her ear, "It's driving me insane, having you here and pretending not to know you."

"But you *do* know me," she said, smiling. "I'm the girl who does your flowers."

"That's right," he said. He ran his thumb over her lips. Kissed her again. "The girl who does my flowers." She thought his voice sounded sad, but she didn't want sadness, not now. Not after he'd sent gifts to her table. Not after he'd given her this secret to carry, so fierce and bright it made her glow. So she pressed closer, felt him hard against her, asked, "Can you come over tonight?"

"Fuck yes," he said.

"I have to get back out there."

"Already?"

"They'll suspect something."

"You're killing me," he said. "I'm dying right now."

She reapplied her lipstick in the bathroom, a task not so easy when she couldn't stop smiling. She tried to force her face into a neutral expression as she walked back to the table.

"Was there a line?" Colette asked.

"Mmhm," she lied.

"They keep bringing us free food."

They ate amid stories from Bas about the upscale condo conversion bid he won and Lauren about the latest blunders her law partner had made and the deal they'd just closed. Bas ordered another bottle of wine and Emilie wanted a Yerba Buena but didn't order it. She refused more wine when it came, too. She didn't understand why her parents, always fixated on Colette's sobriety, never held back on drinking in her company. Emilie would have a glass or two of something, but after that she drank sparkling water, even after Colette said she didn't mind.

Bas pulled a picture of the condo plans up on his phone and Claire cared less about the renderings and more about the *how* of it. How does the image get there on the phone screen? Would they please try to explain the internet again? Emilie laughed and commiserated—who *did* understand the internet? But all the while she was replaying the moment in Jacob's office—rush of lust, then emptiness, emptiness. The despair took her by surprise; she ushered it away and replayed the first part. *Rush of lust, rush of lust.* Desserts arrived and they groaned at the decadence before finishing every bite.

"Grandmother seems stronger, right?" Colette asked after they had kissed their parents and grandmother goodbye and gotten back into Emilie's car alone.

"Yeah," Emilie said, but she wasn't sure. Claire had gone through many rounds of chemo over the years and it was difficult to know whether her frailness was due to the treatments or simply old age. "She seemed happy, at least."

Colette nodded, rolled down her window, leaned back in her seat and turned to Emilie. "So . . ." she said, smirking. "What was that all about?"

"All what?"

"The champagne. The olives and the polenta and the extra desserts."

Emilie shrugged.

"Plus, everyone who worked there. They all know you but pretended not to."

"I do the flowers. You even said that."

"Come on. They were conspiratorial."

"I have no idea what you're talking about," Emilie said, but she couldn't keep herself from grinning.

"You're obviously sleeping with someone there."

"You would jump to that conclusion."

"The only question is why it's a secret. You're twenty-five. You're allowed to sleep with people."

"It's not that simple," she said, and then immediately knew that she'd said too much.

Colette's eyebrow arched but she didn't ask anything else, and Emilie turned up the music for the rest of their drive.

That was early October. A couple weeks later, Jacob's house was featured on a design blog she visited daily. She reveled in the home tours—the stacks of dishes on exposed kitchen shelves, the wallpaper patterns, the owners' obscure collections. How fascinating they all were. The wine country farmhouses, the urban lofts, the beach shacks with surfboards propped against sun-bleached shingles.

But that afternoon, she'd clicked on the headline, "A Chef's Family's Los Angeles Craftsman," and there was his name in the first sentence, along with the name of his wife. Emilie's vision darkened . . . then the screen faded in again and she kept reading.

They'd bought it ten years ago and had been making improvements ever since. Most of the artwork on their walls—large-scale paintings, some framed sketches—were done by friends.

She clicked through the slide show. She saw their kitchen and their bookshelves and their bed. She saw their main bathroom with the penny tiles and clawfoot tub, and their front porch with its swing, and their backyard trampoline. She saw four pairs of boots lined up in the entryway. She saw a note, handwritten by his wife: *My favorite thing about my home is sharing it with the people I love.*

And, last, was a picture of the four of them with their dog. They were all smiling, they were all lovely. His arm was around her waist.

Emilie started again from the beginning, scrolling through the pictures fast and then slowly, scrutinizing the details. She wondered if the rooms really looked like this, how much they had cleared out, if they could really be so perfect. She searched the images for clues. Zoomed in on their faces for signs of tension or despair. Studied the hiking boots for evidence of wear. She forced herself up and to the kitchen, but once her tea was in hand she returned to the table and looked again.

Night fell, she didn't eat. Her head ached but she barely noticed.

She kept reading books and writing papers. She kept arranging flowers and joining Jacob for breakfast. She answered her phone each time he called, and she was home each time he wanted to stop by. From time to time, she went to the site and scrolled through the pictures. Sometimes because she was sure she'd find it—the detail that would give them away—and sometimes just for the pain of it.

And then it was November, and Los Angeles tried its best to be festive in short sleeves and sunshine. Emilie filled her floral arrangements with reds and oranges and whites. She saw less of Jacob outside the restaurant and knew it must be because of holiday parties and familial obligations, though he was too delicate with her to mention them.

If it were not for the design blog, and the fact that he always came to her, and always left before morning, she could almost pretend that their relationship was like any other. He even met Pablo and Alice one night in the early fall after Emilie mustered the courage to ask him to.

"They're both from Long Beach," she said. "I've known Pablo since I was a kid. Alice since freshman year of college. They aren't part of the food scene or anything."

She was tugging on the threads of her ripped jeans, worried she was asking too much. When she had asked Olivia to join her at a family party, it had been the beginning of the end of them. "How are you going to introduce me?" she'd asked. "As your former professor? I don't want to be that person."

Emilie knew what was at stake, but she couldn't continue to splice her life into the Jacob and the not-Jacob. She craved one life, a whole one.

When she looked up from the torn hole at her knee, she found him smiling. "I'd love to meet them. Let's cook for them here."

She only had the tiny round table and two chairs, so she went to a home store whose catalog she received each month in the mail and relished looking through slowly, page by page, imagining that she had a house somewhere to decorate. She chose two walnut chairs that folded up when not in use and then went to the kitchen and dining section to see if they had placemats and napkins she liked. They did, and also salad and dinner plates, a set of silverware for six and wineglasses with wide mouths and skinny stems. She never spent money this way, always thought she'd wait until she had a real apartment, a reason to have nice things, but it struck her, standing in the store: Maybe this was it. Reason enough. Maybe she was in the middle of it already and just hadn't realized.

She spent over seven hundred dollars that afternoon, and her table looked perfect, and she tried not to compare it to the rest of her studio, which looked the way it always did—drab and tired, a temporary resting place for the time before her life would begin.

Jacob brought over a whole trout and two bags full of produce and fresh pasta, three bottles of wine and a loaf of warm sourdough bread. By the time her friends arrived, the studio smelled of white wine and garlic on the stove, felt so warm and happy that she was afraid Pablo and Alice would intentionally embarrass her, give her away as the fraud she was. She had never hosted a party, never had matching silverware or napkins.

But they were kind. They, too, were at their best. Pablo had good news—a gallery in Culver City was going to take him on, with a show slated for February. And Alice had gone on a disastrous date, which she recounted for all of them in painfully funny detail.

By the end of the night, they were all sprawled on the bed, tea light candles flickering and stomachs full, lips stained purple from the wine. They were all exactly where they wanted to be, and that place was with her, in her crappy studio, suddenly almost beautiful because of them. They didn't even care about the flatware or the wineglasses—she knew it. They just liked that her home was a place where they could take off their shoes and stretch out on her bed and tell stories of mortification and stories of hope and get a little bit drunk. She wanted them to stay forever.

Now, as she dressed for her parents' annual Christmas Eve party alone, she feared no night would be as perfect again. They'd sworn they'd have another dinner together soon, but the weeks passed and it was difficult to schedule anything given the way Jacob came into and out of her life on a moment's notice. *Just you guys, then,* she'd texted them. And they said yes, but it had been two months and they never settled on a date. She was reaching to button the back of her dress, wondering if she had worn that same dress at last year's party, and even the party the year before that, when there was a knock on her door that she recognized.

Jacob, unannounced, a wrapped gift in his hand.

He was warm and happy, eyes sparkling, kissing her over the threshold. "Here," he said, and spun her around to button the two buttons for her. "Open."

So she untied the string and opened the box to find a scarf. "It's from the textile store that moved in down the block from the restaurant." Emilie nodded. She had gone in one day, touched the hand-spun yarn, and wished she knew how to knit. "It's dyed with *elderberries*. Can you believe that?"

She lifted it from its box. She thought of butterfly wings and lampshades and stained glass. Precious things that light shone through. She had never owned anything so beautiful.

"Elderberries!" Jacob said. She wrapped it around her neck. "How does it feel?"

She wanted him so badly. "It feels like you," she said. By which she meant it felt like something miraculous but tenuous. Something too precious to be hers forever, but something she would hold onto as long as she could.

She felt almost otherworldly, walking into her parents' house with the scarf around her neck. Only Alice and Pablo knew that she was in love, and yet she was sure she glowed with it. She thought that anyone who saw the scarf would know that someone she loved had given it to her. But the house was full of people, and everyone was dressed up and festive, and she was nervous and warm and took off the scarf and folded it, gently, before tucking it into her purse.

The scent of shrimp and sausage and spices from Bas's gumbo filled the house. Colette stood at the stove in stockings, one foot lifted and resting on the opposite calf as though she were in a yoga class, stirring apple cider and cinnamon.

"Hey, sister," Emilie said.

"Hey, sister," said Colette. "Mom and Dad have been bickering all day. Help me keep them away from each other."

"I'll do my best."

Colette smiled and Emilie saw a smudge of lipstick on her front tooth. "Here, wait," Emilie said, and rubbed it off with her finger.

"No date?" Colette asked.

"Nope. You?"

"Not dating right now," she said. "But you are, aren't you?"

"I'm going to help Dad serve the gumbo."

"Nicely done," Colette said, like the waiter had said to them that night at the restaurant, and Emilie wanted this rapport to last, to feel normal—so much so that tears rushed to her eyes, made her turn away quickly—because she knew her sister, knew that it wouldn't.

She helped Bas dish rice into bowls, held them out as he portioned the broth and seafood, ladle by fragrant ladle. If only she could breathe it in all night, stationed here with a clear purpose. But of course the task ended, and she carried the bowls on a tray to the guests, all these extended family members and old family friends, asking her the same embarrassing questions, making her life feel so small when really it wasn't, it wasn't.

Her cousin Margie and Margie's husband, George, spent the evening chasing their twin toddlers and changing diapers, and late in the party, Emilie saw Jasper, the rounder twin, waddle too close to the fireplace and reach out a hand.

"Oh, sweetie, watch out," Emilie heard herself say, and then he screamed and yowled. Margie rushed to comfort. George appeared with ice wrapped in a dish towel. Emilie backed away, recognizing the weakness in her voice. Wondering why she hadn't shouted, *Stop!*

Always quiet and polite. Incapable of urgency or panic. What was *wrong* with her?

Margie rocked her crying boy, her brow furrowed. George did his best to keep the ice on, but Jasper kept wriggling his hand free to look at the blistering skin on his fingertips.

Emilie watched them from across the room. It seemed so recent that they were drunk kids at their own wedding, and George spilled bourbon on Margie's dress and she threw her head back and laughed and the night was bleary and the moon almost full. And now here they were: so serious, so adult. They wouldn't even look at Emilie. She was the primary witness, the one who could have stopped it.

"He'll be okay," Margie said to George, his mouth a tight line. George removed the ice for a moment and Emilie got a glimpse of a burning red welt before turning away.

Later that night in her studio, she kept thinking of it. Poor little Jasper with his tiny hand outstretched. *Oh, sweetie, watch out*. She'd been worse than meek; she'd been halfhearted. As though danger didn't really exist, as though life were something just to be gotten through. As though they were actors running lines. The living room: three walls, stage lights, and a dark theater. The food: plastic. The wine: grape juice. The fire: red-orange cellophane and a fan.

She existed outside of her life and she knew it. When faced with danger, she couldn't even shout. She barely heard a word people said, too busy making her face appear eager, nodding her head, and saying, "How interesting."

Early in the new year, Emilie walked into an Echo Park sandwich shop and there was Colette. She was with a friend, Emilie noticed with disappointment. She'd thought maybe this would be their moment. But Colette's sandwich was whole, meaning they'd just arrived, and Emilie thought maybe she could join them. She'd brought a book, had been imagining a sandwich and a beer in a corner booth because it was past lunchtime and too early for dinner and she knew there would be plenty of open tables. But maybe she would take a seat at their table instead.

She put her hand on her sister's back and Colette flinched and then saw who it was.

"Oh. You." Colette's hair was greasy and her eyes were tired. She sniffled and rubbed at her nose, and Emilie knew.

"Just ordering to go," Emilie said.

"Sit with us. This is Kyle."

"Hey," Emilie said, suddenly light-headed. "I have to be somewhere."

She wanted Jacob to make her food. She wanted the hollow of his shoulder.

"Actually I shouldn't even be here. I didn't realize how late it was."

Colette rolled her eyes. "Didn't mean to scare you off."

She wondered how much effort it required for Colette to make her voice sound so light, to pretend this was nothing of consequence.

She tried to match her. Maybe she was sober, Emilie thought. Maybe she was just coming down with something.

"No, it's just me. I'm just, you know . . . scattered as usual."

Kyle said, "Hope to hang out another time."

Who the fuck are you? Emilie wanted to scream in his face.

She cast her gaze to the empty booth in the corner, where she would have had her beer and her sandwich. "Yeah," she said. "That would be cool."

Afterward, all Emilie could think of was an evening when she was nineteen, living with Alice in their first-ever apartment. She and Alice had split the water and electricity bills. They made grocery lists and cooked giant batches of chili on Sunday nights for the other college kids in the building. She'd felt capable and confident—motivated by adult responsibility— when Colette returned from her third stint in rehab.

She and Alice thought it would be fun to have her over, to drink tea and sit on their crappy sofa. To just hang out. But Emilie and Colette hadn't hung out by choice in years, and it felt off from the moment Emilie had opened the door and invited Colette into her apartment. All she could think about was how Colette was living back home, spending her days in her childhood bedroom while Emilie's bedroom next door sat empty.

Alice brought out some cookies, set them on the water-stained coffee table they'd found on the street. Emilie was aware of the apartment's imperfections, its plainness, the shabbiness of their scavenged furniture. But for the first time, now, she was glad for it. As though the nail holes in the walls, the streaky paint on the ceiling, the worn fabric on the sofa might soften the terrible feeling that she'd overtaken her older sister.

Colette looked beautiful, sitting on the sofa with her sweater wrapped around her even though it wasn't cold. She always looked beautiful to Emilie, even at her most strung out. Post rehab, though, Colette filled out her clothes better, the whites of her eyes were brighter, her skin its lovely light brown, pink in her cheeks again.

In the exuberance of homemaking, Emilie had planted herbs in a long rectangular pot she kept in the kitchen window-sill. She offered Colette lemon verbena, spearmint, or a mix of the two.

"They're really good together," Alice said. "Especially with honey."

"Sure," Colette said. "I'll try it."

Emilie felt such pride, serving Colette tea in a deep blue mug that she'd bought herself, in an apartment with her own name on its lease. But also the *guilt*—as though the mere facts of her life were acts of betrayal. She couldn't make sense of the two.

She would focus on what was ahead of them—that would feel better.

"So what are your plans?" she asked Colette. "Are you looking for jobs?"

Colette had wrapped the sweater tighter around her. "Portfolio's hiring baristas. They'll train. I filled out an application."

"That'll be great," Alice said. "We go there to study some-times. You can make our lattes."

"Well, I haven't even interviewed yet," Colette said. "But hopefully, yeah."

"Have you considered transferring your community college credits to Long Beach? It's such a good school. We both love it. Don't you love it, Em?"

Emilie nodded. She did love it. Loved the anonymity, so many students, all of them rushing to one place or another. Loved the specialness of the Japanese Garden, how quiet it was. She often sat on a shaded bench there to do her reading, took breaks to watch the koi swim under the lily pads. She loved her classes, the esoteric knowledge of her professors. Loved, especially, when they broke character, made references to their families or their fields of study. When they cast aside the textbooks and revealed their passions—she lived for those moments. Knew that one day she, too, would be passionate about something.

She'd gone to the kitchen to heat more water, returned to find Colette looking tired, rubbing the space between her eye-brows. Bringing up the future had been wrong, Emilie real-ized. She should have kept them in the moment. They should have talked about music or TV.

"Hey," Emilie said, sitting next to Colette. "You know, for-get everything we've been saying. You're back home now, so just let yourself rest. There's plenty of time to start school or get a job or whatever later."

She placed a hand on Colette's knee, but Colette jerked away.

"You're treating me like a child. Can you please stop?"

Emilie felt the breath knocked out of her. Several months passed before they saw each other again, and even then Emilie was careful not to say too much for fear of saying the wrong thing.

She was still careful, now, so many years later.

She looked out of her window, the VACANCY sign across the street flashing bright.

My entire adult life, she thought, *I've been waiting for my sister to love me again.*

She wouldn't say anything to Colette or their parents about what she had just seen. Colette's addiction was her own, her choices were her own. It had never been Emilie's place to get involved.

A few weeks later, Emilie and Alice drove together to Pablo's art show, both of them in black dresses. As soon as they entered through the glass gallery doors they saw him. He wore a new suit and a skinny black tie and impeccably clean white Nikes. He was so proud, standing with his family, Mrs. Santos blotting tears with a pink handkerchief, Mr. Santos visibly flustered by her display of emotion. And the works themselves: huge drawings, mostly graphite on thick white cotton paper, occasional blocks of color, peach or blue or green.

They barely got to talk to him but were glad to watch as people swarmed the space and the gallery director took Pablo by the arm, introducing him to collectors while the gallery girl strode across the floor, placing small red stickers beside the sold pieces. And then one particular drawing, hung at a bit of a remove from the others, caught Emilie's attention. She weaved through the guests to get closer. Stood before it, took it in.

Line-drawn figures on one side, so spare that they lacked all detail, gathered together. Through the middle of the piece, a jagged black gash, separating one part from the other. A single figure stood on the other side, reaching toward the group of people.

Out of the gash grew a plant—its leaves deep green, the only color in the piece. She looked to the small white title card hanging next to it.

YERBA BUENA.

Her breath caught.

Is *this* how he saw her?

She felt suddenly, brutally exposed. People knew about her relationship to the restaurant—how many mornings she spent working in it, how whenever she took someone for dinner there the waitstaff paid them special attention and comped the bill.

Yerba Buena was a fantasy, yes, but it was also a chasm. It had separated her from other people, people who lived their lives without secrets.

When Alice appeared behind her, Emilie was trembling.

"Did you know about this?" she asked.

Alice nodded. "I requested a catalog from the gallery last week. See that stunner over there? It's coming home with me when the show is over." She pointed across the room, but Emilie didn't look.

"You didn't warn me."

"Warn you about what?"

"It's just—I know Pablo uses his life in his work, but I don't think it's too much to ask that he stay away from mine. My *private* life." She was livid, burning tears spilling over.

"*Emilie.* What are you talking about?"

"This." She thrust her hand toward the gash. "Me." She pointed to the lone figure. "Didn't you see the title? It's called Yerba Buena."

"Oh," Alice said. "Okay, yes. I can see why you might think it's about you."

"Might?"

"Well, it *isn't*. It's about his break from Catholicism. They grew yerba buena in the school garden. Didn't you help them?"

Emilie searched the drawing.

"See, here's a cross." Alice pointed to the top corner.

The school garden, the weeding and the planting. Mrs. Santos teaching them the names, giving Emilie a bouquet of herbs. Emilie put her face in her hands.

"Oh my God. Alice. I'm a disaster." Alice looped her arm around Emilie's waist. "I'm mortified."

"No one will ever know. If anyone saw us having this conversation, we'll say you were reliving your own fall from faith."

"Promise me you'll forget I ever thought this."

"I promise."

Just a minute later Pablo appeared behind them—finally a moment free—and they all embraced.

"So what do you think?" His face was so eager, he was high off the thrill of the night. Her old friend had done all this. She imagined what it might have been like, had she come here not knowing him, and seen this drawing and its title. How she would have felt an uncanny sensation of being understood.

"It's stunning," she said. "It's like . . . the best possible thing art can do. It's about you, but I see myself in it. I imagine everyone here does."

"Em," he said, hugging her again. "That's the best compliment I've gotten all night."

And she held him tight, knowing how close she'd been to letting a misunderstanding overtake her. How close she'd been to ruining this night. Alice winked at her and Emilie let go, awash in relief before Pablo was swept away.

VENICE

Sara and Grant made it over the mountains, past the amusement park and the sprawling suburbs, and into Los Angeles.

They drove down Sunset Boulevard where the palms were taller and more exotically beautiful than they'd allowed themselves to imagine, and the stars in the sidewalk were dirty and crowded and not at all glamorous. There were plenty of street kids and they found themselves briefly among them, but they didn't fit. They weren't punk or anti-capitalist. They wanted jobs and apartments, to be the people dropping dollars in cups. They heard about a youth shelter with showers and a job placement program, and soon Sara was bussing tables at a hip restaurant in Venice, until the restaurant manager saw her potential and hired her as the hostess.

"Wow, congrats," Grant said when she told him. They were sifting through bags of donated clothing in the shelter's common room.

"I need something dressy," Sara said. "The hostesses always dress up."

"Here, this one will work." Grant held up a blue tank top that crossed in back, and Sara thanked him and took it.

Soon, Chloe, one of the waitresses, asked Sara to take over the lease to her one-bedroom apartment. It was dark and small but right off Abbot Kinney Boulevard, only three blocks to the restaurant.

"I don't know if I can afford it," Sara said, standing in the doorway of the galley kitchen.

Chloe tapped her red nails on the laminate countertop. "You just got promoted. It might be tight, but you can eat dinner at the restaurant every night you work. You'll manage."

Sara nodded, wanting to believe it.

"Look, I understand if you don't have the savings. I can spot you the deposit—you can pay me back when you can. My boyfriend already put it down at our new place so I'm not worried about that."

Sara nodded. The deposit. She hadn't even thought of that expense.

"This neighborhood's getting insane," Chloe said. "It's smart to get a place now, when you still can. Have you seen how many restaurants are coming in?"

"I'll do it," Sara said.

Chloe held out her palm and they high-fived. "Your first place," she said.

"Yeah." Sara laughed in disbelief. She'd *made* it. Away from the river and through the Central Valley, over the mountains and now, *soon,* out of the shelter.

"Let's celebrate," Chloe said. She opened the yellowed

refrigerator and took out a bottle. Opened an upper cabinet and took down two tiny glasses—decorative, delicate things. Next came a lemon from a basket and a small knife. She poured into the glasses, left the bottle on the counter. Carefully, she sliced into the lemon peel, one thin strip followed by another, which she dropped into the glasses.

Sara took one by its crystal stem.

"*Salud,*" Chloe said.

They clinked and sipped—to Chloe's relief and Sara's first apartment.

And then something else happened, too. Sara felt her vision sharpen, her mind clear. Here was the beauty of the etched glass. Slice of lemon. Gold liquid. Here was the taste of it—a little bitter, a little sweet, some citrus brightness, maybe honey. And here was *meaning.* A home, hers alone.

She turned the bottle to read the label. *Lillet.*

"Is it wine?" she asked.

"Aperitif."

"I'm sorry, what?"

Chloe laughed. "I forgot for a second that you're practically a baby. *Aperitif.* Like Aperol, Campari . . . You drink them before meals, usually. Just a little. Hence the tiny glasses."

"I love it," Sara said. "It feels so . . . *special.*"

"Right? I know. I love it, too. I always keep a bottle in the fridge." Chloe leaned against the counter and finished her drink. "How young *are* you?" she asked.

Sara's face went hot. She thought Chloe knew. "Eighteen," she said.

"You're lying."

"Almost eighteen," Sara said. "Maybe someone at the

shelter could cosign for me." She knew that wouldn't happen, but hoped it would buy her time.

"No, it's fine," Chloe said. "The property's managed by some huge company that runs all the shitty complexes around here. They won't care, as long as they're getting paid. Just put the apartment number and address on the check. I won't change the lease or anything." She lifted the bottle. "Refill?"

Sara shook her head. Half was still left in her glass, and she wanted only the one drink. One single, precious thing.

A girl who lived alone replacing another would barely register with the neighbors, would certainly not be worth calling the management company over. But a girl and a boy moving in together—their footfall up the stairs, their conversations through the walls, both of them so young—that might be enough to arouse suspicion. At the shelter that night, Sara tossed and turned with it. Could it be a simple thing, she wondered, to move forward on her own? Could it be natural and expected? After all, she and Grant had known one another for only a tiny fraction of their lives. She had helped him as much as he'd helped her.

Tucked into her bunk bed, the girl above her snoring softly, Sara made a mental tally. She'd let him dig through the Dumpsters. She'd let him shower in the motel. She'd cleaned at the rest stop motel for those two days and she'd been ready to do even more.

Still, he was the one with the car. And there was the thing with Eugene, enough to undo everything good that she'd given him. But why was she even thinking like this? Grant was her *friend.* She could picture him so clearly on that morning, the cold French fries on the dash, the brightness of the sun hitting the window, the gladness that washed over his face when he saw her there, how he'd covered his heart with his hands.

She would tell him about the apartment, and if he asked to live with her, she would say of course. It would be riskier, yes, but they would be careful.

He was gone the next day at his car wash job. She left for her restaurant shift before he returned, and he was asleep when she got back. It wasn't until the early evening of the day after that they saw each other. She was reading a novel in the living room when he walked through the door.

"Hey!" she said. "I have something to tell you."

"Hey," he said. "Cool. Let me get cleaned up, okay? And I have to take something. My head is fucking killing me."

"Yeah, okay. But hurry up because it's really good."

He hesitated before walking past her. "Just tell me."

"No, go ahead. I can wait."

"But now I'm curious."

"Okay. Well, Chloe asked me—"

"Who's Chloe?"

"One of the other waitresses at the restaurant."

Grant sighed. "Okay, Chloe asked you . . ."

"She's moving in with her boyfriend. They just got a place but the landlord wanted them to start paying rent right away, and she still had months on her lease, so she asked me if I'd take it over."

"What do you mean?"

"She offered me her apartment."

"Are you gonna go check it out?"

"I already did."

"When?"

"A couple days ago."

"A couple days ago," Grant repeated.

She saw how sunburned he was, how tired. She saw the tightness in his shoulders and the way he flinched at some sensation before stretching his neck carefully to the side. She knew he envied her job at the restaurant—the way she dressed up for it, stayed out late, and returned satisfied from the dinners the staff ate before closing up for the night.

"Want me to get you some aspirin? I can tell you about it later."

"No, go ahead," Grant said. "So you went to see the apartment. Are you taking it?"

"Yeah," she said.

"Cool. When do you move?"

"She's moving her stuff tomorrow, so—"

"Don't you need money for a deposit?"

"She's not making me pay one."

"Amazing," he said, not looking at her. "Congrats. I'm gonna take that shower now."

He was down the hall by the time she realized he was walking away. She thought about following him to tell him he could live there with her, if he wanted to. But she let him disappear around the corner instead.

"Goodbye," she said two days later, her duffel slung over her shoulder.

Grant was sitting next to a counselor, Monica, both of them

eating breakfast in the dining room. Monica rose to hug Sara. "You can still come for meals if you need them. And if anything goes wrong, we're here for you, okay? You have my cell, right?"

"I do," Sara said.

Grant stood next. Sara hadn't known if he was going to. He hugged her and sat down again.

"See you soon," he said, but she knew he didn't mean it. He studied his cereal bowl. She cast her gaze to the ceiling, its recessed lights a blur through tears.

"Okay," she said. And turned. And left.

When they did see one another again, it was five years later, on the bustling sidewalk of Abbot Kinney. All the new restaurants had opened, as had a slew of new bars and cafés. Expensive boutiques lined the streets. Sara had grown two inches in a triumphant feat of late adolescence. She'd cut her hair into a blond pixie, had worked her way from waitressing to bartending. Grant was more like the boy she'd met by the river than the one she'd left in the shelter: charming and young, walking with an easy swagger, holding hands with a tan, older man in a linen shirt.

Grant might not have recognized her if Sara hadn't startled when she saw him. And Sara would have said hello if it weren't for the flash of panic on Grant's face. What lies had he told this man, she wondered, for him to be so stricken by the sight of her? She averted her eyes—she knew he wanted her to—but she wished she could pull him to the edge of the sidewalk, put her lips to his ear. *I'd never give you away,* she would whisper. She wished he would call her by a different name, invent a different origin story, so they could embrace like the friends they once were.

The warmth of the sun, the engines of passing cars, a burst of laughter from somewhere down the block.

They passed each other, silent, shoulder-to-shoulder on the sidewalk.

Sara rounded the corner to the apartment she had, over time, made her own. Past the bank of silver mailboxes with her name taped over Chloe's. It had taken her a year to muster the courage to do it—to expose herself in that way. She unlocked the door to the shared foyer and climbed the stairs to the second floor. The man across the hall who'd been visibly sick with something terrible the whole time she had lived there was coming out of his door, his little dog under his arm.

"Hey," Sara said.

He raised a hand, nodded his greeting. She went inside.

It was late afternoon, the only time of day natural light filled her living room. Above her was the thump of toddler footsteps, the cry of a baby, the sounds so familiar they barely registered. She took a small glass from her cupboard, noticed her hands were shaking. She poured herself a shot of whiskey and crossed to the window. Stood, sipping, overlooking the street.

The first night she'd spent in this apartment, ghosts had come to haunt her. It had been months since she'd fled the Russian River and they'd left her alone all that time. But as soon as she'd shut her door, they rushed in, as though they'd been waiting patiently until they found her alone.

Spencer, getting smaller and smaller until he disappeared. Eugene, snaking off his belt. Annie, dripping wet with river water. Her father, drawing her a picture. Her mother, on the hospital bed.

She'd doubled over, catching her breath. Rose again to her blank white walls. Felt her feet, steady on the carpet. She told herself that she'd live with ghosts if she had to. No reason to be afraid.

Little by little, she stopped being haunted. And now she'd seen Grant, and it brought it all back.

She finished the whiskey, felt it travel down her throat. Set the glass down.

Okay, she told herself. *Enough.*

It took her a long time to fall asleep that night. She tossed and turned, finally gave up and went out to the living room. She read until her eyes were heavy and the words blurred together. Finally, at almost two o'clock, she fell into sleep only to wake three hours later from the sound of an alarm in the building. She stirred. Heard another, and another. Soon the building was full of alarms sounding, people moving and shouting, and she rushed from bed. She grabbed a jacket and sandals on her way out the door.

There, on the landing, was the mother with her two little ones from upstairs. "What's happening?" Sara asked. She didn't smell smoke.

"Carbon monoxide, probably," the mother said. "We need to get out *now.*"

Sara pounded on her neighbor's door in case he wasn't up yet, but once she was outside she saw him there already, holding his little dog.

Soon everyone was on the sidewalk. The old man who lived on the third floor, wearing a gray fedora as he always did. The hipster with his blond bun and tight jeans, his girlfriend with a robe draped around her. The woman in her forties with wild curls and blue glasses. An emergency truck from the utility company arrived, and its workers spread out with purpose. An ambulance and a fire truck pulled up next, but after making sure no one was left in the building, that everyone felt fine, the firefighters and paramedics climbed back into their vehicles, shut the heavy metal doors, and pulled away.

So it was just them again, the residents of Riviera Avenue, out on the sidewalk together. Waiting. All of them in pajamas and robes with sour breath and messy hair.

The hipster with the blond bun checked his phone screen, said something to his girlfriend, who rolled her eyes. He jogged down the block and came back with a tray of large coffees and extra paper cups. He lined the smaller cups on the sidewalk and began to fill them up from the larger ones. The girlfriend leaned against the wall and ignored him, so Sara offered to help.

"Spencer," he said, and stuck out his hand. She almost laughed. First Grant, and now this. He was not *her* Spencer, but the name made him familiar. They finished pouring and handed the cups to their neighbors. "Thank you," they said to her. "Not me," she told them. "Thank Spencer."

She'd missed saying his name aloud.

The baby started to cry and the toddler tugged at her little pink sock and said in his tiny voice, "You're okay! I'm here!"

The sky grew bright with morning. People driving by in their cars slowed and stared at the group of them, who didn't make any sense together, and yet were there together, drinking from matching paper cups and waiting to be let back inside their building.

"I moved in here a long time ago," the old man with the hat said. "Longer than you've been alive," he added, pointing to Sara. She thought he'd continue, tell them a story. "I moved in a very, very long time ago," he said, but that was all. Eventually he said, "Nothing like this has ever happened."

In the silence that followed she realized how badly she had wanted to have been told a story. She craved the arc of it, the beginning and middle and end. She craved a moral, a meaning, something she could mull over in the dark.

The mother had a dime-size hole in her pajama pants, tired eyes, and a pretty face. Spencer's girlfriend let her robe drape open, almost revealing her small, perfect breasts. The man from across the hall was younger than she'd thought and she felt a pang for him. What was it that had made him skeleton thin? His dog whined and then licked his face. The woman with the blue glasses had the brightest smile, and she closed her eyes when she sipped her coffee.

The Spencer who was not her Spencer checked his phone again and sighed.

"Spencer," she said.

"Yeah?"

"The coffee's good."

"It's from the donut shop."

She nodded. She'd just wanted to say his name again.

After a while, they were given the all clear and let back into their apartments. They filed up the stairs together, said goodbye from their doorways. Sara was surprised to find her apartment exactly as she'd left it, thought that something should have changed. It was almost seven. She didn't have to be at work until noon.

She took a long shower.

She dressed for the day. She made herself a pour-over coffee, the kind they made at the restaurant where she now worked—one of the newer and most expensive restaurants in Venice.

She drank her coffee by the window, and when she was finished she crossed to the metal filing cabinet she'd bought at a garage sale. All of her bills and personal documents were meticulously sorted, so it only took a moment to find the old lease, signed by Chloe, from nearly five years before, filed along with the notices of modest rent increases that arrived every year, addressed to Chloe, increases Sara added to the monthly rent checks she always mailed on time.

She dialed the number at the top of the document, and explained how long she'd been living there, and how she hoped to get a new lease with her name on it. The woman on the phone asked questions, brought up the possibility of a credit check and a price increase.

Sara had wanted a moral from the old man's story. But in its absence, she created one for herself: she belonged there, just as much as any of them did.

They all worked and paid their rent. They wore imperfect clothing and had morning breath. They knew the feeling of being surprised into wakefulness, of rushing outside onto a dark sidewalk. They imagined carbon monoxide filling their lungs, poisoning them in their sleep. An apartment complex full of people who would never wake up. But it didn't turn out that way. It turned out with them surviving.

"Fine," Sara said to the woman on the phone. "Whatever you need."

A few weeks later, at a little past ten in the morning, Sara's phone rang with an unknown number. She was at her stove, adding kumquats to a simple syrup she was making. The head bartender had asked her to create a cocktail for their summer menu and she'd been testing new recipes for days now, trying to get it right.

"Is this Sara Foster?" a woman asked.

"Yeah," Sara said, stirring.

"My name is Leah Stevenson. I'm the social worker assigned to your brother's case."

Sara turned off the stove.

"Is he okay?"

"Yes, he's fine. His father—yours, too?—was arrested yesterday. I understand from Spencer that you're over twenty-one?"

"I'm twenty-two," she said. "I have my own apartment. Just tell me where to go."

"You're willing and able to take him in?"

"Yes, I am," Sara said. She felt a sob rise, tried to tamp it down. "Yes, I am," she said again. "I am."

"When can you pick him up?"

"Where is he now?"

"He's in Guerneville."

"I need to make some phone calls and get my shifts covered."

"You figure out what you need and let me know. We have him assigned to a foster family, a great one who I've worked with for years. He's in good hands."

"I also—I should get him a bed. A few things for the apartment."

"Yes, but I do want to let you know that it might not be for very long. Your father's hearing will be in three weeks and we'll know more after that."

But Sara was already grabbing her keys and leaving the apartment, abandoning her syrup to cool on the stove. She passed a Japanese store with futons and sleeping mats in the window every day on her walk to work—it's where she had bought her own. She would get Spencer something to sleep on and some sheets and a nice blanket. It was summer so he wouldn't need more than that.

"I can get him tomorrow," she said on her way down the stairs.

"Will you be able to stay in the area?"

"In *his* area?"

"We try to keep things as consistent as we can."

She stopped on the sidewalk in front of her apartment. She couldn't speak. She felt the heaviness of it, the way she'd sworn she would never go back. Her place was clean and tidy and stocked with food. She knew that a bed would fit in the dining alcove, had already measured it once, in a particularly sharp period of longing. She wanted him here with her. She didn't want to go back to stay.

"We understand if you can't get the time off," Leah said. "He's on summer break, so it wouldn't be too disruptive."

She exhaled, headed in the direction of the futon shop. "I work in a restaurant," she said. "I can't really afford to stay gone. If that's really okay."

"Sure," Leah said. "Should be fine."

She left at 4:00 a.m. the next morning. A thermos full of coffee, a peach, two pastries from the restaurant: one for her, one for him. She had agonized over what kind to choose. *Five years.* She no longer knew him. Ended up with a chocolate croissant and a cinnamon roll. She'd let him pick, or she'd give him both.

She had never made the drive north, and once she was out of Los Angeles and through the mountains, descending to the flat highway on which she'd spend the next four hundred miles, she saw the sign for the rest stop where she and Grant had spent those days. She felt the power of her own car, her wallet full of cash, the money in her bank account—not a lot, but enough to handle a car repair or train ticket, enough to get her out of anything. She sped past the exit.

Approaching the Russian River, dread settled in her stomach. She entertained a fantasy of keeping her engine running and honking, of Spencer flying out of the foster home and down the walk to the passenger side. The two of them speeding away together.

And yet, of course she turned off the car. She walked through a front gate and knocked on the door. The foster mother welcomed her into a living room with a bookshelf full of toys for the younger kids, puzzles and paperbacks for the older.

And here was Spencer, seated in a chair. Her brother and not her brother. He rose when he saw her.

Impossible, how long his limbs were. The acne along his jaw. Even the shape of his face had changed.

"You look different," he said in his new, lower voice, and she realized it was true for both of them.

Nine to fifteen.

Sixteen to twenty-two.

In the beginning, they'd talked on the phone now and then. She'd always made sure he'd had her current number. But as the years wore on, he had called less and less. One morning she'd called the house, hoping to catch him before school, but her father had answered. She'd frozen at the sound of his voice. Said nothing. Only breathed. "*Sara?*" he'd asked, and she'd hung up the phone.

That was the last time she'd called.

"You look different, too," she told Spencer now.

He smiled. "Yeah, guess so."

The foster mother had disappeared, left them alone together, and Sara was grateful that no one was there to witness their awkward reunion. In her fantasies, they hadn't hesitated. They'd rushed toward each other, as though the years had been nothing.

She tried. She opened her arms, and Spencer went to her.

They hugged, quickly let go.

"Look at you," she said, and put her hand on his cheek. He blushed, couldn't meet her eye.

Did he remember it the way she remembered it? Did he

remember that she had begged him to come with her, and that he had said no?

The foster mother returned with Spencer's duffel bag, and Leah arrived soon after, asking Sara questions off a list and checking her ID. Sara signed papers and then the siblings were free to go.

"Are you hungry?" Sara asked as they climbed into her car. "We can stop in Sebastopol for lunch if you want. I could use a coffee."

She started the engine and Spencer looked at the clock on the dash. "It's only eleven," he said.

"We have a long drive."

"We're going *now*? You just got here."

"I have to work tomorrow."

"Wow. Okay." He turned to the window and she allowed herself a longer look. At his broader shoulders under his thin T-shirt. The bones of his jaw, clenched. He'd never done that as a child. "I at least need to get some stuff from the house first," he said.

They were a couple of miles from the river. She didn't want to cross the bridge, but she'd do it for her brother.

"Of course," she said.

Even after so long, she knew which turns to take. Barely had to think about it. The silence between them pressed against her as she drove. "Want to turn on the radio?" she asked.

"No use."

"Oh," she said. "Right." Static played on all the stations.

And then there it was—the river. She would have closed her eyes if she could. Instead, she held her breath until it was over. But even after, as she turned left on River Road and passed under the arches that welcomed them to town, she found it difficult to breathe. She tried not to look out the windows, to only see the road in front of her, the yellow line dividing it. Soon, she'd be on the other side, and they'd be leaving.

She turned off the main road and onto their street, her throat tight, her heart pounding. She slowed the car at the corner. *Just pull up in front,* she told herself. She wouldn't have to go in; she wouldn't even have to look. But in the distance, the mailbox jutting out at the edge of the property came into view. Bright red against green leaves, just as it had been all her life. She stopped the car two houses down. Cut the engine.

Spencer cocked his head.

"Sorry," she said. "I just . . ." So soft he could barely hear her.

He opened his door. "I'll be quick," he said, and she nodded.

She waited in the car, in the shade of the redwood trees, her eyes shut, her hands squeezed into fists, until he came out again.

They stopped for lunch in Sebastopol as Sara had planned, and she saw how the town was changing. She felt at home in the restaurant she chose for them, glad when they were seated at a bright table by the window.

"If you have any questions, just tell me," she said, scanning the menu. "I work at a restaurant a lot like this one."

Spencer nodded, but he set the menu down after glancing over it. "You can order for us. I have no idea what any of this stuff is."

"Want me to tell you?"

"Not really," he said, and took a cell phone out of his pocket.

"Is that your phone?" Sara asked. She tried to keep her voice steady. He had a phone, and hadn't given her its number? But he shook his head.

"Dad's," he said. "He left it for me."

"Oh. Did he get arrested at the house?"

"Yeah."

The waitress appeared at their table and Sara ordered the hummus and crudité, the charcuterie board, the frittata. She asked Spencer if he wanted something to drink.

"Coke," he said.

"We don't have Coke but we have a house-made currant soda? Or iced tea?"

"Water's fine," Spencer said.

"Water for me, too."

The waitress nodded and took their menus.

"Why did he leave you his phone?" Sara said. "He's not asking you to do anything for him, is he?"

"He wanted me to be able to call people."

Sara nodded. "Okay."

She felt her father between them at the table. Wanted to remind Spencer of all she'd done for him as they ate. Had to stop herself from asking if he remembered how she made scrambled eggs for him every morning, how she cut the green off his strawberries.

She saw her brother in flashes, in his expressions but not in his narrower face, even though his new face was familiar to her in its own way. How many hours had she spent online, just so she could see him? She'd checked each night for new pictures, watched him grow. She'd made the images as large as she could, stared at the pixilated likeness.

She never posted anything, had joined with a fake name and no photo. She didn't want to be found by anyone else. Apart from making sure Spencer always knew he could find her, she had disappeared as completely as a person could. As far as she knew, once she and Grant had crossed the bridge, no one had ever gone looking for her.

But Spencer was across from her now. She was going to take him home with her. No reason to think of that afternoon. No reason to think of Spencer's face as he straddled his bicycle, no reason to think about anything.

"Are you ready?" she asked when their meal was finished.

He nodded and they rose together and left the restaurant.

It was dark when they got to Venice, the air still warm. She parked in the apartment's lot and took Spencer's heavier bag, even though he was as tall as she was now.

"I was thinking pizza," she said as they stood at the bank of mailboxes and she unlocked the main door. "Does that sound good?"

"Sure."

"And then, if you want to, we could take a walk after. The boardwalk's pretty close. It's wild there—all these roller skaters and performers. There's always something to watch." The door shut behind them and she led him up the stairs. "Or we can stay in if you're tired. Whatever you want. Just let me know."

She opened the door to her unit and let him walk in ahead of her.

"Here," she said. "I'll show you where you'll stay."

She'd taken her dining table out of the alcove by the kitchen and placed it against a wall in the living room. Now a futon lay in its place, neatly made with new sheets and a pillow. She'd moved her own bedside table and lamp to go beside it. In lieu of a door, she'd hung a tension rod and a curtain—blue, the color that used to be his favorite.

"I think we'll be able to squeeze a chest of drawers in here," she said.

"If I stay long enough," Spencer said.

"If you stay for a *long* time," Sara said, "I'll find us a two-bedroom place."

She showed him the bathroom and her room, told him to make a list of everything he needed and she'd pick it up the next day. He unzipped his backpack and pulled something out. Held it in his hands. She wanted to know what it was but wasn't going to ask him. He wasn't a little kid, was entitled to his privacy. But he held it up to show her.

The framed drawing of a parade, taken off their kitchen wall.

Sara, Mom, Dad, Spencer

He was smiling at her. Holding it out for her to take. It was a gift.

"Thank you," she said. But it felt dangerous, taking it into her hands. She didn't want it.

"What time is it?" he asked.

"Just before nine."

He took the cell phone out of his pocket. "Dad might call. Phone hours end soon."

There he was again, looming between them. She could almost see him in his worn jacket, his brown corduroy pants.

"You stay here, then," Sara said, setting the drawing on the coffee table, heading to the door. "I'll pick up our dinner and bring it back."

"I'll give him your love if he calls," Spencer said. He was watching her, his head cocked and chin tilted upward, eyes narrowed, taking in her reaction.

She looked away, grabbed her keys, tucked her wallet in her back pocket. He was still waiting. She turned to the door.

"*Okay?*" he said.

She stepped over the threshold, looked back in at him before shutting it behind her.

"You can tell him whatever you want to," she said. "You can give him my love, if that's what you want."

THE CANYON & THE GARAGE APARTMENT

One day in the spring, a text message.

Tell me you're free tonight. Pack a bag.

Jacob never spent the night at Emilie's studio, and she never asked him to. It was on the list of things to remain unspoken. They'd fall asleep as though he were staying, but sometime later he'd slip out. On the worst nights, she'd pretend to sleep as he crept out of her bed and ran the faucet in her bathroom. The longer it ran, the deeper the pain.

He was washing her scent away.

He was putting his clothes back on.

He was easing her front door open and shutting it behind him.

Emptiness flooded in.

On the best nights, she was sound asleep by the time he got up and she stayed that way until morning. Now, as she packed a slinky dress and hiking boots, perfume and sunscreen, a toothbrush and a green-spined book of poetry, all she could think about was how they would wake up together in the morning for the very first time.

He picked her up in his car. Sliding into the passenger seat, it was easy to pretend that this was a car they owned together. It was an anniversary, maybe. Or his birthday. Maybe one of them had some good news to celebrate, and they turned to each other and said, *Let's get out of town tonight,* and now here they were, getting out of town.

She held on to the fantasy for miles, all the way through Los Angeles and to the coast, when she went to roll down her window and saw a sticker on the armrest—a glittery blue whale, something one of his children must have stuck there—and the line came back to her. *My favorite thing about my home is sharing it with the people I love.*

He wasn't hers.

"Tell me where we're going," she said.

"We're getting close. You don't want to be surprised?"

"You've *already* surprised me." She watched him drive, felt bold, reached out and ran her fingers through his hair and down his face.

"Topanga Canyon," he said, leaning into her touch. "But that's all I'm telling you."

"I've never been."

"Never? Not even for the day?"

"No. But I did bring hiking shoes."

She realized now that she shouldn't have brought the dress. He wouldn't take her anywhere public. They'd be hiding away like they always were. But still—this was something. Something he planned just for them.

It was a small, rustic house. Remote, just as she expected. She followed him through a gate at the narrow street and onto an enclosed path, through a verdant front yard to the door. It opened directly into the living room, sparsely furnished, only a coffee table and sofa facing a wood-burning stove. There was a little window over a ledge into the kitchen. He said he'd show her the rest when they got back, but they needed to set out in order to catch the light.

They changed into hiking shoes and he led her to a trailhead just a few houses down the road. He took her hand. She liked how their shoes looked, step in step together, as they made their way forward on the trail.

Red dirt and green trees. White wildflowers growing between the rocks. Sagebrush and manzanita.

"Wait for it," Jacob kept saying. "Just another couple minutes." As if it weren't all beautiful. As though she'd need a certain vantage point to comprehend it. *All* of it was beautiful to her. All of it. They might as well have been in another country; she hadn't left the city for so long, and when she did it was always to the beach, never to the trees. She'd forgotten the way light shone between leaves. She'd forgotten the smell of dirt and rain, the innumerable shades of green, the textures of bark and the obstacle course of tree roots and rocks.

"Almost there. Just around this curve."

She heard voices from wherever he was leading her and was disappointed. She wished they could weave through the forest on their private trail for hours, but she followed him around the bend and into the bright light of a lowering sun, and there, as if dropped from the sky, were half a dozen police officers talking among each other. And a woman in a suit. And two zipped body bags on stretchers.

"What happened?" Jacob asked.

"Two hikers," one of the cops said.

"They fell?"

"One of them fell. Looks like the other one tried to go down to help and got stuck. Starved, we think."

Jacob wiped his forehead.

"Oh, man," he said. He looked at Emilie. He looked at the body bags.

"No one was looking for them?" Emilie asked.

"Transients," the cop said. "Judging from the stuff in their packs. We got a tip from some bird-watchers who saw the bodies." He turned back to his colleagues.

They stood, holding perfectly still, until Jacob placed his hand in the small of Emilie's back.

"We can still look over the canyon," he said. "We came this far."

But the sun was too bright, and she knew that the drop was probably spectacular, but it was now tinged with terror. Her legs refused to bring her any closer to the edge. She imagined Jacob falling. She imagined the helplessness of watching it. Would she go after him? These bodies. They must have been in love, for one of them to follow the other like that. She thought of bone and flesh and rock. Snap of spine, gush of blood. Cold and hunger.

"I want to go back," she said.

———

When they got back to the house he built a fire before opening the door at the end of a short hallway with a soft bed and warm blankets. She was trying not to cry.

"Hey," Jacob said. "Want to talk about it?"

"No one would know where to find us," she said. "Nobody knows where we are." She surprised herself with the words. She didn't know she was thinking them.

He sat next to her on the bed. He took her hand and kissed it.

"A horrible thing happened to those people," he said.

"I think it means something."

"They aren't us," he said.

"But we were hiking, just like they were."

"Not *just* like they were."

"Pretty close."

But that wasn't it either.

Danger was everywhere, all of the time, and they were making it worse. That glittery whale, the art above his mantel, the way the faucet ran and ran right before he'd leave her. They were doing something terrible. Something was bound to catch up to them, even if it was only themselves.

"Let me pour you some wine. You could sit outside, or read . . . Just rest for a while and I'll make us dinner. Okay?"

"Okay," she said.

She watched from the window as he went to the car and popped the trunk. He stood there, looking into it, for what felt like a long time. Then he grabbed a cooler and balanced it on his hip before shutting the trunk and turning back.

She went into the bathroom to pee but found herself taking her clothes off when she was finished. The bathtub's tile was matte green, like moss, almost soft, but she chose the shower instead—all glass with two showerheads. She turned both of them as hot as they would go. The bathroom filled with steam, and she closed her eyes and tried to feel far away, in some tropical place where not even her name was the same.

She put the dress on after all. She dried her hair and pinned it back. She applied mascara and lipstick and smudged a little of it on her cheeks. When she walked back into the main room and Jacob saw her, relief flashed across his face.

He handed her a glass of wine and poured more into his own.

"Cheers," he said.

They clinked glasses. She felt unimaginably alone.

He seared trout and served it over pasta he'd made at the restaurant before picking her up. They drank the bottle of wine, then opened another. He told her about summers visiting his grandfather, and she did what she did best: she fell out of herself and into his story. She asked all the right questions to make him remember it more fully. The sun porch where they'd spent their evenings: wicker furniture, fireflies hurling themselves at the windows, sliver of moon, and John Denver on the radio.

"I can picture you," she said.

It made her happy to listen that way.

It fed her.

It enabled her to forget about the hikers through dinner and dessert and the time it took him to undress her. But after the talking and the quiet and his mouth against hers, when they were naked and he was touching her, asking, "Are you ready?" she shook her head and said, "Kiss me harder."

They were by the fire, on the floor, her back against the sofa.

His hands were in her hair. He was kissing her the way she'd asked him to, and she was trying to get to that place—where her body led her, where she didn't think so much. Instead there was the caution tape, the body bags. The heaviness in her stomach, the tightness of her throat.

"Now?" he asked.

"Okay."

She tried to imagine them in that tropical place as the night grew colder.

Quiet morning.

Black coffee, eggs, toast.

They sat side by side at a table in the kitchen, overlooking the canyon. In the afternoon they took a long walk, winding through safer trails, no mention of going back to the place he'd wanted her to see. Returned to the cabin for sandwiches and then it was time to go.

Packing was easy. He erased every trace of them. When he opened a closet and pulled out a plastic garbage bag, it dawned on her: This was his house. A vacation house, just barely big enough for his family of four, better suited for two. She wondered if he and his wife left their kids with friends and came here for romantic weekends. She wondered if they still slept together, or if that's what she was for. Or maybe they fucked all the time; maybe she was for something else.

He said he knew a great place to stop for coffee for the drive. He pulled up in front and they unbuckled their seat belts. She could make out a cozy, bright space.

"I'll be right back," he said.

"I'll come in, too."

"Might be better if I just go."

"Oh."

He looked at her. "We can skip it."

"No. Coffee sounds good."

She watched him as he walked in and then she took out her phone. She had a signal here; she hadn't in the canyon. She keyed in the address of the cabin. Sold six months ago, to Jacob Lowell and Lia Michaels, for just over a million dollars. He was talking to the barista now. He turned to a table by the counter for lids and she could see that he was smiling.

No one would know where to find us. No one knows where we are.

How foolish she'd been to say it. It was Jacob's *house.* If something went wrong, his wife would know exactly where to look. They'd probably taken that same walk together with their children. Seen only the beauty of the canyon and not the terror.

It was only Emilie whom no one would know where to find.

Only Emilie, who didn't belong.

The coffee sloshed onto her wrist during the bumpy drive to the highway and she let it even though it stung, as though trying to stop it was futile, as though she just had to tolerate it until enough spilled over and it had cooled enough to drink. He was talking but she couldn't hear him. Eventually he turned up the music.

They were on the freeway, moving fast. He rested his hand on her thigh for a few miles but eventually took it back. The last song ended and then it was quiet.

She said, "I wonder what excuse I'm going to give my professor tomorrow morning when I don't have a midterm essay to hand in."

She faced straight ahead, pretended not to notice his glance.

"Did I know about this essay?" he asked.

She shrugged. "I've been talking about it. Maybe you haven't been paying attention."

"No," he said. "I know. That book you've been reading at breakfast. *Passing.*"

She was surprised but didn't want to give him credit for remembering. The road grew barren ahead of them, nothing but gray.

"Maybe I should tell my professor that the man I've been having a months-long affair with invited me away with him for the first time ever."

"You could have reminded me. You could have worked on it at the cabin."

"*Hm.*" She tried to picture it. Typing away at her laptop as he cooked. Making sense of her notes as she sat in front of the fire. No dressing for dinner, no undressing after. "I can't see it."

He sighed. He was exasperated with her. She heard it in his voice. For the first time in months, she remembered how weary Olivia had grown of the simple facts of Emilie's life. That she had a housemate, that she was still an undergrad. He sighed again.

"What?" she asked.

"What are you doing?"

"I don't know," she said.

It had been so hard with Olivia at the end. Emilie wondered if it would be any easier this time around.

They drove the rest of the way in silence. They exited the

freeway and the barrenness gave way to an electric Los Angeles sunset. Their windows were rolled up and she thought
of how the air she breathed had, moments ago, filled his
lungs.

"I think we should say it."

"Say what?"

"Let's just be honest about what we're doing. You're going home to your wife now. *Lia*. And your two boys, whose
names I don't know, but who are nine and six."

He turned off the ignition and suddenly it was so quiet, qui-
eter than her street had ever been.

"Seven," he said. "James just turned seven."

"What's the older one's name?"

He cleared his throat. She looked at his hand, rubbing a
stitch in the steering wheel with his thumb. She looked at his
face.

"Liam," he said.

"That's a really sweet name," she said, feeling herself soften.
"They both are."

"This was a bad idea. To go away. I made a mistake."

"Yeah, I think it was. I think you should go home now.
To James and Liam. And teach them to never make terrible
choices. To never hide themselves away."

The sky was hot pink, bright with pollution, and Emilie
needed to get out of the car.

"Let me walk you up," he said.

She opened her car door and he did the same, followed
her upstairs into the studio. He set her bag on the floor, she
dropped her keys onto the table, and they stood, face-to-face.

"I feel like this is over," he said. "And I don't know what

happened." He ran his hand over his face. She saw he was crying.

She hadn't even wanted this with him, she remembered. Not at first. She was happy to sit at the long table, working together over coffee. No, not happy. *Elated.* She hadn't needed anything more than that.

Jacob and Emilie's table.

All this time, she'd only wanted to feel special. But seeing his life—with his restaurant and his bungalow and his family, his car and his vacation house and the café he surely stopped at each time he visited the canyon—showed her how much smaller she'd made her own. She'd had so little when they started. Now, somehow, she had even less.

She folded her arms across her chest and sobbed, until finally—after holding her and letting go, after saying it didn't need to be the end, after asking if he could call someone for her, after checking the time over and over, saying he really needed to go—she nodded, and he left her.

She'd thought her life was on the verge of changing, but it wasn't. Thought she was a complete person, discovered she was mistaken. The incompleteness lingered and expanded until she could barely open her eyes. Even arranging flowers for money cost her too much, even after Meredith let her swap Yerba Buena for a bistro in Echo Park. All the strength it took to snap off stems. The energy of smiling and saying hello. The strange sadness of looking at beauty that no longer moved her. The heat of another summer, day after relentless day.

She wanted to change her mind again, switch her major

from literature to something else, but to do so would be to step into her own trap, the one she kept laying. She couldn't change course again—even she knew that.

She scheduled a meeting with an academic counselor to advise her. "I've never *seen* a transcript like this," he said, staring at the computer in awe. "You're exactly three credits away from a degree in Women's Studies, Ethnic Studies, Design, or Literature. Botany's another story—you'd have quite a few science classes to take for that one. Do you know what you want your degree to be in?"

She shrugged.

"Okay," he said. "Should we just look through the course schedule for fall and you can choose the class that looks best to you?"

"Sure."

He gave her so many choices, but they all sounded terribly boring, or terribly difficult. He was reading her the descriptions of each one, asking her about timing preferences as though she had a life to plan around.

"How about American lit or something?" she finally said. That way, all she'd need to do was read and write a few papers.

"American lit? Sure." He opened a new window, scrolled down. "Tuesdays and Thursdays at three o'clock?"

"Great," she said.

So she read Frank O'Hara.

Zora Neale Hurston.

Sylvia Plath.

She read plays by Tennessee Williams and James Baldwin's essays. She reread *Gatsby* for the sixth time—that well-loved copy with its faded green cover—and in between the classes and pages she'd crawl into her bed and sleep.

She refused to take part in the pageantry of graduation but agreed to let her mother mat and frame the diploma for her. She was surprised by the accomplishment she felt upon unwrapping it.

It was finished. She quit the flower shop. And then there was nothing left for her to do.

Bas called her one night, sharing news from Claire's doctors. Too aggressive this time, nothing to be done. Claire wanted to go home—to stay at home until the end—so he was calling to see if Emilie could help.

"You'd need to move in, but the hospice nurses will be by every day to care for her," he said. "We can cover your bills since it means not getting another job. I could cover the rent on your studio, too. You could stay in the garage apartment. You'll have some privacy that way."

"I don't need to keep the studio," she said, the phone hard against her ear. She looked around her at the sad space. It had become a reminder of all her failures. How could she have ever found it special that night with Jacob and Alice and Pablo?

"We can always hire a caretaker," Bas continued. "We don't want you to do *anything* you don't want to do."

But she wanted to. No question. She craved purpose and here it was.

She moved out on a Saturday. Pablo helped her carry what little furniture she had down the stairs to the street, where they left everything except for her green armchair and her bookshelf. *Free to a good home,* Pablo wrote on the back of a page of one of Emilie's essays. He taped it to the bedside table.

"What if the person who wants this stuff lives in a *bad* home?" Emilie asked him.

"Then they're out of luck, I guess," he said.

"Maybe the furniture's cursed. What if they do have a good home but they take this stuff and everything turns bad?"

"Em," he said, and put his hand on her shoulder.

"It was just a joke."

She looked across the street to the motel. Its VACANCY sign was on the way it always was. "Goodbye, motel," she said. "Good fucking riddance." She turned around and looked up to her windows. "There are only a couple boxes left. Do you mind grabbing them?"

Pablo shook his head. "No way. You need closure."

So they trudged up the stairs together. Pablo stacked the two boxes and then picked them up.

"I'm going to leave you here," he said. "Take your time. Say your goodbyes."

With everything cleared out, the studio didn't look so bad. She could almost remember the first time she saw it, when its emptiness was full of promise and she had plans to paint the walls some vibrant color. She remembered—suddenly—that she had told the owner he could keep the walls as they were, covered in their coat of primer. Alice had just visited Morocco and Emilie had clicked through the photos of hotels and stores and houses, in awe of the colors.

She could have painted the walls bright pink. She could have filled it with unruly plants and made salads for herself every afternoon with bright-colored vegetables and tangy dressings. She could have fixed her record player and turned it up loud. She could have cut through the paint around the windows and hosted raucous dinner parties, climbed onto her fire escape to get some sun. She could have been the kind of person who doesn't mind being watched through a window at night—she could have lived that kind of life.

Where did she go wrong?

Now she was out of time, and she was supposed to have a goodbye that meant something. She knew Pablo was thinking about Jacob when he said the word "closure." There was only so much grieving allowed when it was over someone who was never really hers. They'd told her that one night, right here, when they'd come over unannounced as some kind of tough-love intervention.

"We *miss* you," Alice had said.

"Like a lot," Pablo had added.

But she didn't have anything left to say, so she set her keys on the counter and shut the door.

Emilie remembered the garage apartment from childhood. She and Colette had stayed there a few times as a novelty, their grandparents carrying dinner out to them, setting them up with videos on the portable VCR. But she hadn't been inside of it in years. Nor had anybody else, it seemed. The linoleum floor was cracked and peeling, spiderwebs were everywhere. The rooms smelled wet, but at least it was somewhere new.

"Let's leave the door open," Pablo said. "Air it out."

They carried the armchair through the backyard, tore

open boxes, and filled the bookshelf with green spines. They took the sheets off the bed and washed them. While Pablo swept away the spiderwebs, Emilie set her crystals on the dirty windowsills.

"You should dust those off first," Pablo said, but she just shrugged. She couldn't believe she'd accomplished so much in a single day. Already, she felt defeat rushing back.

"You could live in the house, right?"

"I think we both want our space," she said.

He tapped at a discolored portion of the ceiling with a broom handle.

"I'm a little worried this is going to collapse."

"I doubt it'll kill me."

"Well, *yeah,*" he said. "I doubt that, too. But still. It's winter. If it rains, won't it leak?"

"Are you guys in there?"

Alice appeared in the doorway, just off work, arriving with tacos as promised, and Emilie was grateful for the interruption. "I'll give you the tour," she said. "It will take thirty seconds. Then we can talk decorating over lunch."

Alice nodded and set the bag outside the door.

"Here's the bathroom," Emilie said, and Alice walked in.

"Is that the only towel rack?" she asked, pointing to a piece of broken plastic.

"Yes. Here's the living room."

Alice noticed the spot on the ceiling and her jaw dropped.

"What?" Emilie said.

Alice pointed.

"Terrifying, right?" Pablo said.

"We've already discussed it. Here's the kitchen. It's just a half-size fridge but I'll probably do most of my cooking in the house anyway. Not that I cook. And here's the bedroom."

Alice crossed the tiny room to its only window. She moved the stiff curtain aside: metal bars, a fence.

"Let's eat," Pablo said. "I'm starving."

They sat around a green plastic table on the patio outside the apartment. There was a partial fence separating them from Claire's more spacious yard, punch-colored bougainvillea in full bloom.

"This patio is pretty nice, right?" Emilie said. "I could get a lounge chair or something."

"Maybe you could find a different place to store the trash cans," Pablo said.

"Well, obviously. No one's stayed back here for at least fifteen years. That's the only reason they're here." She turned to Alice. "So, decorating," she said. "I was thinking lots of bright colors and plants."

"You're joking, right?" Alice said.

"No," Emilie said. "I'm not joking."

"You can't *settle in*. It's hard for me to think about you even staying here *temporarily*."

"I want to make the most of it."

"Em." Alice set down her taco. Her eyebrows furrowed in concern. "Em. I'm sorry. But you can't live here."

Emilie pushed her plate aside. She rested her face on the table, the plastic warm against her cheek.

"You guys know that feeling, where it's like . . . you're moving through fog? Except it has more mass than fog? You can barely get out of bed. Forming words is hard."

"I guess," Pablo said. "Maybe I've felt that way a few times."

"What are you talking about?" Alice asked.

"That's how I feel all the time."

"Since when?"

"I don't know. Forever? I can't remember."

"Emilie," Alice said. "Are you serious?"

"I just want bright walls, okay? I need something to snap me out of this."

So Alice and Emilie went to the hardware store for paint while Pablo drove to his place for rollers and brushes. They came back with pink for the kitchen, yellow for the bedroom, green for the living room.

"Holy *shit*," Pablo said when the first stroke of paint touched the bedroom wall. "What's this color called? Actually, wait—it doesn't matter. This color's true name is Cheer-the-Fuck-Up Yellow.'"

They painted for the rest of the day.

"We forgot to buy tape," Emilie said, and all three tilted their heads to look at the lines where the walls met the yellowed ceiling, and then across the ceiling to the cracks and dark patches. "Good thing it never rains," Alice said. They scanned the molding around the doorways, split from the walls, exposed nails doing their best.

"Oh, well," Emilie said, and climbed the ladder she found in the garage, and tried to paint clean lines around the edges.

Emilie had romanticized death. Of course, she'd imagined Claire growing weaker, sleeping longer, needing help with the toilet—that much she knew. But she'd also thought there'd be heartfelt conversations, afternoons together in the mild January sun.

Instead there was the never-ending pill sorting. The arguments over taking them. The forced cheer of her parents, breezing in and out again. The falls and cuts and bruises. The way Claire would spend a day in bed, denying Emilie's offers of water, her breathing so shallow that Emilie would brace herself for the end, would cry as she did the dishes and talked to the hospice nurse—only to find the next morning when she let herself in through the back door that Claire was dressed and out of bed already, reading that day's *Los Angeles Times* at the kitchen table.

And then there was the day Claire told her to call her sister. Emilie opened the front door when Colette rang the bell, took a moment to look at her through the metal gate before opening it, too.

Emilie's choice to not say anything a year ago after their run-in at the sandwich shop had somehow worked out. Colette had gotten clean on her own, or in secret, or *wasn't* clean but was managing to hide it. Emilie didn't know, didn't want to ask. "I love it when I can ignore my problems and they just go away," she'd joked to Alice one day on a walk along the ocean.

But she felt only uncertainty now, opening the door. Colette seemed nervous, but that could be for any number of reasons. Their grandfather's death had been sudden, not this drawn-out affair. No deathbed conversations like the one they were about to have.

The sisters hugged.

"It's been a while," Colette said.

"Yeah," Emilie said. "Where've you been?"

Colette shrugged. "Working, mostly." She swept her hair over her shoulder and the simple gesture was so graceful that Emilie wished she'd put on lipstick, wished she'd dressed in something nicer than the uniform of leggings and T-shirt she'd been wearing each day, if only to feel a little surer of herself in the presence of her sister.

"It's really nice of you to be doing this for Grandmother," Colette said. "I mean, not *nice*. It's really . . ."

And Emilie nodded. "I know what you mean," she said, and she was able to see herself as Colette did for a moment—as capable and generous and good. They hugged, and Emilie felt her heart might break, and then they let go.

"She's in her room," Emilie said. "She wants to talk to both of us. I'm not sure what it's about."

Claire was feeling strong today, which meant she was upright in bed, leaning against pillows. Colette rushed to kiss her cheek and Emilie tried to see their grandmother through Colette's eyes. Claire was frail, her skin soft and thin. Colette sat on the edge of her bed and took her hand gently. "Is this okay?" she asked. "I don't want to hurt you."

"It's fine," Claire said. "It doesn't hurt." She sighed and a tear ran down her cheek. When Colette went to wipe it away Claire shook her head.

"Girls," she said. "Listen. I want to leave everything to you. All that I have. Your father doesn't need it. I wish I could split it down the middle, but Colette—you know that I can't."

Colette was silent.

"It's because I want you to live," Claire said. "Not because I don't love you or hope for your happiness. It's not that I don't think you're deserving."

Colette tried to say something but stopped. She nodded. Emilie couldn't tell what Colette was feeling. Disappointment or regret or embarrassment or anger—it could have been any of them. Her sister was a mystery.

"Emilie, promise that you'll help Colette. You'll find ways to make things easier for her. Pay the deposit when she finds a new apartment. Help her with tuition, if she wants to go to school."

"I promise," Emilie said, even though it made her nauseous to think of it—of Colette having to turn to her for these things. Maybe she wasn't generous or good, after all. Maybe she wasn't deserving of thanks.

She excused herself to use the bathroom and didn't go back. Stood at the kitchen counter sorting pills instead. After a few minutes, Colette emerged from the bedroom. "She's tired," she said. "I helped her lie down."

"Thanks," Emilie said.

"Sure. I'm gonna head out."

"Okay." Emilie closed the lids of the medicine tray, one after another, for each day of the week. "I didn't know," she said when she was finished.

Colette cast her gaze to the ceiling. "It's fine," she said. "I mean, she has no reason to trust me."

"*Colette.*"

"I mean it. It's fine."

That night, Emilie stayed in the main house into the early hours of the morning. She sat at the dining table, sipped water from a glass. Her heart pounded fast and hard—no number of deep breaths could calm it.

She couldn't continue like this, her days with Claire so quiet and strained, full of following rules and nurses' orders. Emilie had been tiptoeing around death like it was a secret. Forcing the medicine as though Claire could get well. They all knew she was dying. That's what Emilie was there for. Claire had been frank with Emilie and Colette, so Emilie would be, too.

The next morning, Emilie brought the glass of water and dry toast and pills to Claire on her breakfast tray. When Claire took only the pills that helped ease the pain, Emilie nodded and cleared the rest away. She returned from the kitchen and sat on the edge of her grandmother's bed. "I've been doing this wrong," she said. "I'm sorry. What can I do for you? What can I give you?"

"Bless you," Claire said. Her New Orleans drawl, her dark eyes, fluttering closed in relief. "Read me letters," she said. "Keep me clean. Don't do anything to stretch this out. It's the end, let's not pretend that it isn't."

Emilie pressed her cheek into her grandmother's hand. "Okay," she said.

Claire directed her to a key in her jewelry box that unlocked the white trunk at the foot of her bed. Emilie opened its lid. So many letters, so many photographs.

"Why do you keep them locked away?"

"Not sure. Too painful, maybe. They're from a different time."

"Where should I start?"

"Anywhere," Claire said. She rested her head on her pillow and Emilie took out a cluster of letters, unfolded the one at the top.

Her grandfather's elegant cursive—she hadn't seen it in so long.

"This one is dated November 29, 1942," she said, taking a seat fully on the bed, not perched on the side as she usually did. "'My most sweet wife. This, as usual, is my Sunday to work. I am quite tired now, but am writing, or starting to write, before I go to the show.'" Emilie paused. "Where was he?"

"In Europe. For the war."

Emilie remembered her grandfather's stories. Normandy beach the day after the massacre. He and the other members of his all-Black troop were sent to search the dead bodies for identification. He'd lost most of his memories by the time he died, but that one remained, and he'd tell the story over and over. The horror of it, still.

"And you were still in New Orleans?"

"In his mother's house. We'd married just a short time before. Keep reading."

She made her way through stacks of letters. She found birth announcements and prayer cards. A newspaper clipping about her grandparents' wedding. *The altar was decorated with tall palms, ferns and clusters of white gladioli. The bride was radiant in a gown of ivory satin with lace.* They'd honeymooned in Baton Rouge.

Albums were stuffed with photographs, but Claire's eyesight was bad, so Emilie described the pictures. A picnic in New Orleans. Claire with her sisters in white dresses. There was another letter from her grandfather, loose from the stack.

How I miss your gumbo on the stovetop. How I miss every moment of you. Over three pages in his elegant cursive, he recounted the memory of their first date.

I kissed you. I was in love with you, but I was also a fool.

Emilie read aloud for hours a day. Finished all the letters and put them in order. Started over from the beginning, each one now in place. She sorted the stray photographs. Especially loved the pictures of her grandparents together, sometimes with Bas as a child, standing in front of their houses. She read aloud for weeks, walking the floor of her grandmother's room. Sitting, legs outstretched, beside her in the bed. She read through the moans and the shallow breaths. *My most sweet wife,* she read, over and over. *I am quite tired now.*

And after three weeks and five days of reading—as her grandmother's room receded and the past blossomed in its place, as Emilie read of her grandfather's homesickness and her grandmother's yearning, of cooking and cousins and romance, of dances in New Orleans and picnics in Los Angeles, of the pains and the pleasures of love—her grandmother died.

The family gathered at the house. Lauren swept Colette into her arms. Bas spoke in hushed tones to the hospice nurse and the funeral home. Wiped away tears. Emilie stood silently, hugging her arms across her chest. Eventually they all went out to the front porch. Lauren and Bas drove away, and Emilie waited for Colette to do the same, but she sat on the rusty porch swing instead.

"I'm going away," she told Emilie.

"To where?"

"A place I think will help me."

"A rehab?" Colette had seemed sober to Emilie, but how could she really tell? She was exhausted. She was numb. She'd tried so hard to give Claire a good death that she didn't have the space inside of her for other people, not even for Colette.

"No, it isn't a rehab. It's just a . . . *place.* A group of people. Near Mendocino, on the ocean. They let people stay there and live alongside them. It's something I've been curious about for a long time, but it's supposed to be really . . . *intense.*"

"So it's like a cult?"

"No. It's more therapeutic than culty. From what I've heard."

"When?" Emilie asked.

"Tomorrow."

"The memorial will be soon, though. In just a few weeks."

"I know, Em," she said. "I know. I just can't."

And then Emilie remembered the conversation with their grandmother.

"Do you need money?" she asked, hating the way it sounded. She hadn't asked for any of this.

"No," Colette said. "I'm good." She stood up, slung her purse over her shoulder. "There's no cell service there. And we aren't really supposed to have our cell phones on us anyway. Something about distracting us from real life or whatever. But I'll call you."

Emilie widened her eyes. Shook her head. "Okay," she said.

Colette hugged her, and then a car pulled up and took her away.

———

Emilie missed the restaurant. Not the days and nights of Jacob, but the *place*. The food.

Grief made her crave it even more.

She'd been preparing for Claire's estate sale, sitting at the dining table with public radio on, and there was Jacob's voice, one in a panel of chefs discussing food justice at a summit in New York. She'd listened for a little while, sorting through a box of Claire's jewelry, and at the end of the show the host announced that the entire panel would be at a prominent Manhattan restaurant for a benefit that night. She changed the station and moved on to the next box of faux diamonds and rubies.

He was across the country.

She thought of the cocktails, the salads, the warm bread.

She would give in to her cravings and treat herself to a late dinner for one at the bar.

For those final weeks of Claire's life she'd slept inside on the pull-out sofa of her grandfather's old study. But now that Claire was gone, the loss felt too close. The emptiness, the letters, the photographs. Better to return to the garage apartment with its bright yellow living room. Better to think of Pablo and Alice helping her paint than to think of Claire's final days.

She didn't usually mind the garage apartment, but that night, as she stood in the shower, she took in its flaws. The shower's plastic walls separating at the edges, the mildew on the ceiling, the shower head so low she had to angle it upward or lean down to wet her hair.

Wrapped in a towel, she crossed to her bedroom, the carpet mysteriously damp underfoot. She chose a forest green dress she'd had for years, sleeveless with a deep V-neck, and as she buttoned it she imagined white walls and clean, shiny floors, a closet that smelled of cedar and a full-length mirror with no distortion.

She drove to Yerba Buena feeling as though she were visiting an old friend who loved her. Time had passed and they hadn't called each other as much as they should have, but they still knew each other well.

The hostess was a stranger, friendly in the way all the staff of Yerba Buena were friendly, a smile for Emilie, a sincere hope that she could find a chair at the bar for her without a reservation, and then—*Aha! Success! Come with me*. Emilie followed, past the table where she'd spent so many mornings, past urns of flowers arranged by someone else, past the front bar to the main one in the back of the restaurant, where the handblown glass pendants hung in a row, glowing gold, over the honed slab of marble bar. She was struck anew by the beauty of it. And she was relieved to see so many unfamiliar faces. Apart from a knowing smile from a junior chef who happened to be out greeting a table of friends and a quick kiss on the cheek from Megan, she could have been anyone.

She hung her purse on the hook under the bar, and sat.

Then—a rush of movement. Sara turning toward her, menu and water glass in hand. Emilie saw strong, slim arms, the tattoos on the underside of one of them, words still too small to decipher. Her face: eyes deep blue, blond lashes fading lighter at the tips.

"Hey," Sara said. A dimple when she smiled, teeth white and little crooked. "I'll be right back." *Tap-tap* with one hand on the menu, as though she were knocking at a door. Swift turn away, high reach for a bottle. At the curve of her hip, a sliver of skin between shirt and belt. Emilie watched her, face ablaze.

She remembered the first time they met—the way she'd snuck a glimpse of Sara at work right here at this bar, in the restaurant that morning. How right Sara's hand had felt in hers when they shook. And how Sara had heard about the breakfast table, made the logical assumption, and put a stop to what might have begun.

Emilie wondered if Sara remembered her, too. Hoped she didn't, so she'd have a second chance at a first meeting.

She turned to the menu but Sara was in her periphery, all Emilie could see. Minutes passed while she tried not to stare. She knew she should read the menu so that Sara could take her order when she came back. But Sara coming back now seemed impossible; Emilie wanted it so much. There were two bartenders. Each of them had half the seats. This was how it had always been, and yet Emilie found herself irrationally worried that they'd trade sides.

She needed to concentrate. She would choose a drink. Better yet, she would choose two and ask for Sara's opinion so she'd stay longer in front of her. So Emilie would hear more of her voice. Maybe they'd introduce themselves, and Emilie would take Sara's hand in her own again.

But when Sara reappeared at Emilie's place, she leaned against the bar and asked, "When did you stop doing the flowers?"

Oh, Emilie thought. *Okay.*

"A while ago," she said. How long *had* it been? "Almost a year ago." She wanted to say, *I'm a different person now.* She wanted to list the ways. The thing with Jacob was over. She was through with school. She'd moved out of her shithole studio—into a place even worse, true, but still—she'd left it. She'd attended to the decline and death of a person she loved. *I am different. I am different.*

"So, what do you want?" Sara asked.

Emilie smiled, looked down in an attempt to hide it.

Sara laughed. "What?"

Emilie shook her head. "Nothing," she said. "I just . . ." She pointed to the first salad on the menu without noticing what it was. "This," she said. "And a Yerba Buena."

"You got it," Sara said.

Emilie didn't care about the food anymore; she only needed a reason to stay. But when Sara appeared again with the coupe glass, the chartreuse liquid up to the rim, the sprig of mint that hadn't been part of the drink before, Emilie sipped hungrily. It had been good when Jacob made it. Now it was extraordinary.

"How's your drink?" Sara asked, stopping by a moment later.

"Delicious," Emilie said. "I love the mint, too." She noticed Sara, considering the glass. "What are you thinking?" she asked, knowing it was an intimate question for an almost-stranger.

"It's spearmint," Sara said. "Yerba buena would be better."

Emilie smiled.

"Spearmint's stronger, tougher. Yerba buena's a little more delicate." Sara shrugged as if to banish the thought. "It's also harder to find. So, spearmint it is."

Next came a ceramic plate of goat cheese and pea greens and radishes, carried out by a runner. Emilie took one bite and then another. She had forgotten how good food could taste.

And eating it reminded her of a time before Jacob, when he was only the famous owner of her family's favorite restaurant, and she was only herself.

She finished the salad and looked at the menu again. The ragout wasn't on it, so she had to choose something different. She'd thought it was still winter, but here were artichokes, spring onions, green garlic, and apricots. Time had passed and she'd barely noticed. She chose a pasta with fava beans, black olives, and ricotta salata. Sara came back, each return a miracle, and Emilie ordered.

"Want another?" Sara asked, picking up Emilie's glass.

"Yes. But something different this time."

"I'll grab you the cocktail list."

Emilie shook her head. She waited for long enough that Sara had to look at her, and then she said, plainly, "I want whatever you'll give me."

She watched as Sara's face changed, as Emilie's invitation registered, and she let a brief smile escape. Emilie didn't look away, even when she felt herself blush, and the blush only made Sara smile wider.

"All right," Sara said, and she waited for another moment before turning away, still looking at Emilie as if to make sure that this was what she thought it was, and then she smiled again, and again said, "All right."

Instead of the workspace a few steps away, Sara returned to Emilie's seat with the bottles she'd chosen. Sara didn't look at her, but Emilie was meant to watch. There was something rich brown with a gold label. Something lighter in a smaller bottle. Sara measured the first and then the second, stirred them with a long brass spoon in an ice-filled crystal beaker.

Emilie caught another glimpse of her tattoos as she stirred, still too far away to read them. She wanted to ask Sara, but didn't trust herself to stop at only one question. She felt her insatiability; she knew she needed to corral it. And she knew Sara must be asked that all the time, by dozens of people a night on the nights she left her arms bare, and Emilie didn't want to be among dozens of people. So she forced herself to keep the question silent and relied on the hope that, later tonight, she would have the chance to see for herself.

Here came a tiny bottle of bitters—two dashes. Sara flicked open the top of a silver jar, took a pinch of what was in it. She stirred again. And then with a tiny knife perilously close to her thumb, she cut a perfect sliver of peel from an orange, dropped it in. She placed the drink in front of Emilie, met her gaze, and smiled. Emilie was aware of how close Sara's fingers were to her; she could have grazed Emilie's breast if she reached just an inch closer.

Then Sara was off to the far corner of the bar to tend to someone else, and Emilie felt alone without her. But here was the drink, a gift if she'd ever seen one, so she raised it to her lips and sipped. It was powerful. She was not disappointed. Somehow, each time she went back to it, she tasted something different. Black tea or cherry or clove. It was difficult not to consume it too quickly; she had at least a couple hours left here; she needed to pace herself. At the same time, she wondered if Sara would be drawn back to her if she emptied her glass. She watched her float from one patron to another, rarely scanning the bar, somehow intuiting who might need her. When Emilie's drink was half-consumed, the couple next to her left and a new one arrived. They must have been around her age, still in suits after their days in offices. He wore a striped tie; she wore pantyhose. Emilie took a sip. Star anise this time. Sara breezed past her to leave menus for her new neighbors. The anticipation of her return was almost too much.

"Can I make you a couple drinks?" Sara asked the people next to her. Emilie felt the current between them, knew Sara felt it, too.

Emilie's neighbors at the bar were chatty, asked Sara questions that Emilie was glad to overhear. She learned that Old Tom was Sara's favorite kind of gin, that she was from a town up north, farther north than the Bay Area, but she didn't name the town and Emilie was crushed by a need to know all of her. She kept her head down, took another sip. And then Sara's hands appeared at the edge of her glass.

"I want to make you another one, but I don't want to get you drunk." She was leaning in so close, this exchange just between the two of them. Emilie bit her lip. *Tonight,* she thought. "Although . . ." Sara said, "I do have another hour here, at least. One more?"

So it had been decided. So Sara had understood.

"Sure," Emilie said. "One more."

Megan left an hour before closing, followed by the waitstaff, one by one, as their tables cleared. And then the last dessert orders were taken and plated, and the chefs tossed their aprons onto the laundry pile, and they ate the food they'd cooked for themselves and then they left, too, and it was only the dishwashers and waitress on the closing shift, and Sara and Emilie, and a table of friends in a corner who had paid their bill but didn't want the night to end.

"I live just a few blocks from here," Sara said, and Emilie nodded and walked out with her, not caring that she was leaving her car behind.

The streets were quiet and they didn't speak. They listened to their footsteps on the sidewalk, a faraway car alarm, their breath. At the intersection of Sunset and Marmont, Sara, as though without a thought, took Emilie's hand. Their fingers laced together. The light changed.

They crossed and walked farther, up some winding blocks, through an ivy-covered archway to a courtyard with a fountain in its center.

"This way," Sara said, and Emilie followed her up a flight of stairs and into a spacious living room overlooking the courtyard. Sara flicked on the light.

It was spare and clean, with a simple wood table surrounded by chairs. Near the window was a sofa.

"Can I get you anything?" Sara asked, shrugging off her jacket. Emilie ran her fingers along the spines of the books. She touched the throw blanket that draped over the sofa's arm, would have buried her face in it if she could. She was hungry to know all of her.

"Show me around?" she asked.

Sara poured herself a glass of water from her kitchen sink. She leaned against the wall of her hallway. "There's not much to the place," she said. "But yeah, I'll show you."

Emilie followed her to the kitchen, noticed its intricate

tilework and original art deco light fixtures. She saw the inlaid wood pattern that ran through the hallway. Paused in the doorway of the darkened first room, made out a twin bed and a small desk.

"Someone lives here with you?"

"My brother," Sara said. "But only sometimes. Less often these days."

Emilie waited to hear more.

"He's eighteen and in love."

Emilie smiled.

They went down a short hallway, past the pink-tiled bathroom to the door at the end.

Sara opened it and Emilie flipped on the light. She wanted to see.

An almost-bare room. A half-made bed with crisp sheets and a white duvet on a low wooden platform. T-shirts and jeans folded on a chair in the corner. A California flag, old and tattered and push-pinned at the edges, was the only adornment. A stack of books sat by the bed and Emilie let go of Sara's hand to learn about other parts of her. There were a handful of novels, an essay collection by James Baldwin, and poetry collections by Adrienne Rich. And then she caught sight of *Passing* by Nella Larsen. She picked it up on impulse, opened it to a random page.

"I love this book," she said.

"Me, too," Sara said.

"I don't know many people who've read it."

Sara sat on the edge of her bed. "I started working in restaurants when I was sixteen," she said. "Never went to college or anything, but I wanted to learn on my own. For a few years, I'd look up the reading lists of UCLA classes each semester and work my way through them. That's how I found it."

"What class was this from?"

"Women of the Harlem Renaissance."

"That must have been a good list."

Sara nodded. "So," she said. "Is that a deal-breaker for you?"

"Is what a deal-breaker?"

"That I never went to college."

"Of course not."

"You seem like you're from a family where everybody goes to school."

"You'd be surprised."

"I didn't finish high school either," Sara said.

"Is this confession? Were you raised Catholic, too?"

"Definitely not. Just want to put it all out there. Avoid future disappointments."

"I'm not so easily scared away," Emilie said. She turned back to the book in her hands. It was an edition she hadn't seen before, the title in bold red, pencil drawings beneath. She thought of how she'd stayed up all night writing her paper after the trip to the canyon. All the meaning she'd found in its pages when her life had felt empty. She wanted to know what it meant to Sara. "What's it about, to you?"

Sara leaned back. "I guess, how they both come from the same place but end up with completely different lives. Just based on their choices. It's fascinating. You?"

"I think it's . . . like, when you're a passing person, other people believe what they want to about you. Whatever is easier or better for them. They see what they want to, *in* you. So if you don't really know what you want—or if you know what you want, but it's bad for you—you can veer off in the wrong direction." Emilie closed the book, set it back on its shelf. "But if you do know, then, I guess, you have a lot of freedom."

When she turned, she caught Sara watching her, and before Sara could look away Emilie began unbuttoning her dress.

Agony, Sara's slow swallow, her eyes locked to Emilie's fingers, undoing button after button, all the way down. Emilie's dress fell to the floor. She stepped out of her stockings, unfastened her bra. She had never felt such simple and pure desire for another person.

Sara, still in shirt and jeans, shook her head and grinned. Rose from the bed. Crossed toward her.

THE FOREST & THE BED

When Sara pushed open the doors of Yerba Buena that morning and found Emilie at the community table, arranging flowers, she hadn't been searching for anything.

Two years had passed since she'd bought Spencer a bed and turned her alcove into a room for him. He'd stayed with her there for just over a month, until the cell phone rang early one morning, waking them. Their father, calling him home.

Sara took Spencer to one last breakfast and then to the train station, where a ticket to Healdsburg was at will call. She waited with him on the platform, watched him board, waved goodbye.

Then she'd sat back down on the station bench. She waited for the rumble and tremor of approaching trains. Dreaded the quiet between them. She wanted a physical pain to match the grief. Wanted to be marked, changed forever.

She dug the fingernails of one hand into the soft underside of her forearm. Pushed so hard she could have broken the skin. And then she rose from the bench, finally knowing what to do.

She'd propped the framed drawing on a bookshelf in the living room, hadn't ever wanted it there but wasn't going to let Spencer know. She slipped it into a canvas bag and found a nearby tattoo parlor online, called and was told she could come right in.

The door was locked when she reached the storefront. She knocked, peered through the glass. A woman waved from inside before unlocking the door.

"I'm Mindy. You're Sara? Just give me a minute." Her voice was raspy and low, her full body draped in a burgundy dress, laden in beads and fringe. "Have a seat," Mindy said. "Here, look through this."

Sara took the chair that was offered, accepted the binder of tattoo designs.

"Butterflies are what I'm most known for," Mindy said as she lifted blinds and turned on overhead lights. Sara opened to the first page. So many butterflies, so much pattern and color.

"I can see why," she said. And it felt good, to genuinely mean it, to offer a kindness to someone even while she was hollowed out.

Mindy was prepping her station now, and Sara closed the binder, wondering what it would be like to have a butterfly tattooed onto her body. To choose something beautiful.

"You know what you want already?"

Sara nodded. "I brought it with me."

"Bring it over. Let's take a look."

So Sara took the frame from the bag and carried it to Mindy. "Not the whole picture. I just want—"

"Let me take a look first," Mindy said. "At the *whole* thing. And then you can tell me what we're doing." She took the frame and turned on another light. Sara studied the image along with her, remembered how they'd drawn it together at the kitchen table by the window, sunlight filtering through the redwoods outside, steam rising from the coffeepot. Their father had started while the three of them watched. He drew one line at the bottom, and then another. "A street!" Spencer said. Next came the steps and pillars of the old bank on Main Street. They leaned in, eager to see what would come next. Their father moved his pencil, faint lines that turned—as if by magic—into places and things they recognized. At the far left side of the paper, a man appeared, twirling a tiny baton and marching.

"A parade!" Sara said, and her father winked at her, handed the pencil to her mother.

Her mother drew a marching band and a float. Sara drew their family on the steps of the bank, cheering. Spencer drew a happy sun in the top right corner, hesitated, and then added a happy cloud. When it was finished, they signed their names: *Sara, Mom, Dad, Spencer*.

"So which part are we doing?" Mindy asked.

"Just the signatures," Sara said.

Mindy nodded.

"But only *Sara, Mom, Spencer*," Sara said.

"Ah," Mindy said. "I see."

And then the work began. The words would be small—no larger than they were on the paper, and the letters would be imperfect, exactly as they were written. Mindy wiped Sara's forearm with alcohol. Sara settled into the reclining chair, heart pounding, ready for the needle to bite her skin. She welcomed the sound of the pen flicking on, the buzz it made.

"Ready?" Mindy asked.

"Yes," Sara said.

It hurt the way she wanted it to. Not terribly, but enough. She closed her eyes and remembered their breakfast. She'd taken Spencer to a place she'd known he'd like, a diner. They'd chosen a booth by the window, looked out onto the morning. Palms swayed in the breeze. Pigeons pecked at scraps on the sidewalks. She'd pushed the last two pieces of bacon to the corner of her plate, a gift for her baby brother, who was fifteen years old and not a baby. Who wasn't hers after all.

She opened her eyes. Blood on her skin. Black ink. Three names.

"I'm just going to go over these letters a little bit," Mindy said. "I want them to be perfect."

"Thank you," Sara said, and she closed her eyes again, glad it wasn't over yet.

Two years later, the tattoo was as familiar to her as any other part of her body. She was lead bartender at Odessa, a new restaurant in Venice, where she mixed drinks for celebrities and filmmakers and a constant stream of glamorous people. Her recipes were written up in magazines alongside photographs of her, flashing the camera a hint of a smile from across the bar counter. She was known for her tinctures and syrups and shrubs, her fist-size cubes of ice and her extravagant yet understated garnishes. A sprig of pink peppercorns. A caramelized orange peel. Candied ginger brushed with paprika. She turned down offer after offer from restaurant owners across Los Angeles who wanted to steal her away, but none was as persistent as Jacob Lowell.

Yerba Buena.

Each time he called her and used the restaurant's name

in a sentence, she felt the past rise up around her. Felt her youth—the weightlessness of her body in river water, her mouth against Annie's, the darkness of her bedroom closet, the morning on the hill when the sun warmed her skin and Vivian plucked the sprig and placed it in her hand.

"Design us a menu. You don't need to work for me. Just make me a list of incredible drinks and teach my staff how to mix them."

"No thanks," Sara said, over and over. Until, finally, she said yes.

She began the menu design as she always did, by visiting the space. Jacob let her in on a Monday, the day the restaurant was closed. He started to tell her what he had in mind but she cut him off. "I need to spend some time in here. Sit at the tables. Explore a while. Then we can talk," she said.

Jacob raised both hands and grinned. "Fair," he said. "I'll leave you to it."

She needed to do more than just explore, but she didn't like to explain it. Even when food journalists interviewed her, she kept her comments brief. Didn't divulge that she needed to be in the space, alone, in the quiet. That she watched how the light moved and thought about color. That the degree of sweetness could be determined by the sound of her feet across the floor as she circled the space, and the art on the walls, and shape and size of the windows.

Yerba Buena was spectacular—no denying it. The plaster in various shades—soft white on one wall, peach on another. The arches and alcoves and old, black-framed windows. The smooth, tan leather of the booths. The potted palms when you entered, like a dream version of Los Angeles. And the floral arrangements—bursting with flowers she'd never seen before. Some of them perfectly symmetrical, the color of plums; others white, with petals that shot in all directions like fireworks. So many shades of pink and green. Tiny blossoms with intricate patterns, buds on the verge of bursting open. Bouquets like gardens, spilling over. She circled each of them slowly. Returned to take in their beauty again. She'd never seen flowers in combinations like these.

A small bar was to the right of the entrance, with enough seats to accommodate diners whose tables weren't ready yet, or who'd finished their meals and didn't want to leave. It was tiled a deep red in contrast with the light colors in the main dining rooms. *Cardamom,* she thought. She could taste the flavor, knew it was right. At the far end of the space, where the dining rooms converged, was a wide, curved hallway—she couldn't see what it led to. She wove through the tables, paused at the flowers again, made her way through the hall and saw it.

Another bar, this one long and straight. White marble countertop with golden blown-glass pendants hanging above, like a row of small suns. More palms, more flowers. She felt light-headed for a moment, removed from time. Felt she'd stumbled into a different life.

"Getting ideas?" Jacob asked from the hallway. She didn't know how long he'd been there, wanted him to leave her alone. But she also knew, turning to answer, that she'd accept his job offer someday. That she'd make herself at home behind this bar.

Orange blossom.

Lime.

Smoke.

Cherry.

"Yes," she said, taking another look at the flowers. "I am. I'd like to use the kitchen."

"Absolutely."

He showed her the sacks of sugar, the citrus and the spices.

"Cardamom seeds?" she asked.

"I like where you're going," he said, offering her a handful.

After that Monday at Yerba Buena, Sara made batch after batch of her simple syrups, perfecting the proportions of each ingredient. She made a cherry shrub, sampled mezcals to find the right degree of smoke. She chose an amaro, and Green Chartreuse. She made orange blossom water, designed garnishes. One afternoon before the restaurant opened, she presented the menu to Jacob and Megan and the head chef, introducing each cocktail before letting them taste. She knew it was her finest work.

So when she arrived that morning to train the bartenders, she was confident. She was fulfilled. And then she saw Emilie, her back to Sara at first—dark, wavy hair falling past her shoulder blades, standing on her tiptoes to place a tall fern into a vase—and caught her breath.

As Sara had stirred and tasted and scrawled notes on proportions, she'd often thought of the flowers. Of how captivated by them she'd been, how astonished. How the closer she had looked, the more colors and textures she'd noticed. She'd echoed that complexity with her flavors. Nothing was simple, nothing was entirely familiar. If the flowers had been different, Sara might not have designed such a menu.

And here was the person who arranged them. Here she was, lost in her work.

The bar staff were arriving, too. The head bartender brushed past Sara in the doorway without greeting her. Sara wasn't surprised by the slight—she had replaced his menu, after all. He put his bike helmet on a table near the front.

"That's where Jacob and Emilie sit in the mornings," Megan said. "Let's move to the back."

Of course, Sara thought. Jacob *would* sit with a woman each morning who wasn't his wife. She'd met Lia a few times, had served her cocktails at Odessa.

"We can go straight to the bar actually," she said. She didn't want to waste anyone's time. She was ready to mix and pour and train them. "I'll go over everything there."

She passed the woman arranging flowers, noticed her glancing up. Sara hoped she'd still be there when they finished.

And she was.

Standing at a table, once again immersed in her work, tending to ferns. Their leaves the same shape and color as they'd been so long ago, as though this woman had harvested them from the forest of Sara's childhood on her way to work.

Sara craved them. Wanted to touch them, asked if she could, was granted permission.

The ferns—their brightness, their curly edges—it had been so long.

She turned to the woman. They exchanged names, and Emilie held out her hand.

They shook and Sara wanted more of her. She noticed Emilie's blush—undeniable—and knew that more could be hers. But then she remembered what Megan had said when they'd arrived.

"*Oh,*" Sara said. "The Emilie who sits with Jacob."

Had she misinterpreted the blush, the way Emilie had watched her? Maybe not, but it didn't matter. Emilie's lips were pink and soft, Sara imagined cupping her cheek in her palm, pulling her face toward hers to kiss. But she'd let it go. Emilie seemed uncomfortable now, self-conscious, and Sara didn't mean to make her feel that way.

"It's all right, I get it," she said.

Sara took a woman home that night, something she rarely did, though the offers tumbled forth with every night she worked the bar. She was practiced in the art of being just friendly enough, of the gentle rejection, of the absolute no when it was required. But that fantasy—cupping Emilie's cheek and drawing her closer—wouldn't let Sara rest. So when a woman stayed late, past the time her friends left, past everyone else, Sara gave in. They had sex on the sofa in Sara's small living room. The woman came quickly, and Sara felt a burst of tenderness for her—Christa or maybe Christine? It had been loud in the bar when she'd told her—but soon, emptiness came rushing in. That inevitable feeling. The reason no relationship lasted very long.

Sara lay on her back, eyes closed, accepting the stranger's touch. Her body responded, but her jaw clenched.

When it was over, the familiar swell of loss.

When she finally accepted Jacob's offer to become Yerba Buena's head bartender, at the start of her first official day of work, she snipped a hearty sprig of mint from the kitchen. In the quiet of the morning, under the row of golden pendants, sunlight shining across the marble bar, she mixed a Yerba Buena. Green Chartreuse and Old Tom gin, lime and simple syrup, cherry bitters. She added the sprig as garnish.

She sipped. Understood that the drink had been needing it all this time. Hadn't been complete without it. She never drank mint tea, never used mint as an ingredient. But now that she'd be serving the drink each night, mixing it herself, she needed it to be right.

She sipped again—the leafy brightness, the herbal and the bitter and the sweet.

Fine, she thought, pouring the rest of her drink down the drain, returning to the kitchen for a bucket of mint to keep behind the bar. Fine, for something so healing to have a tinge of heartbreak, too.

She walked through the empty restaurant and looked at the flowers. They were different now. Simpler. No longer Emilie's work.

"I don't really know what happened," Megan said when Sara asked her about it. "One morning she was here, and then she never came back. I guess things with Jacob . . . you know."

Sara nodded, and Megan moved on to her next task. She was always focused, always discreet. Sara respected her for that.

Sara was disappointed, but maybe it would be easier, she reasoned, to *not* be attracted to the woman her boss had slept with.

But here was Emilie, now, in her bed.

Her dark hair in waves across the white pillow.

Here she was. A stranger and not a stranger. Undressed, asleep, with the blankets cast away from her body. Sara watched the rise and fall of Emilie breathing. She couldn't sleep but she didn't mind being awake like this, with Emilie next to her. Sara had finally kissed Emilie's mouth, after waiting for more than a year. She'd backed her slowly to the bedroom wall, pinned her against it, lowered to her knees.

Going down on Emilie brought her back to the forest floor. She was fourteen again, everything was new. The feeling disarmed her—like falling into a memory. She could feel the dirt and leaves under her knees. And yet she wanted more of it, wanted more of Emilie. Her hands found Emilie's hips, pulled her closer. And when Emilie drew Sara back to standing, kissed her deep, and led her to the bed—when she pulled Sara's shirt over her head, slid off Sara's jeans, and touched her—Sara's mind was quiet.

She felt sun on her skin, even in the darkened room. The breeze through branches as the bedframe knocked against the wall. White sheets and moss. A pillow. Ferns.

She was in bed with Emilie. She was in the woods with Annie. She should have been dreaming—only in a dream would this make sense—but she wasn't.

Her eyes stayed open for all of it, her jaw unclenched, the pleasure felt pleasurable for the first time in ages. The first time since she was a teenager, since before she ran away.

And yet it frightened her when it was over. No emptiness this time. It frightened her, how open her heart was.

Emilie slept soundly, and Sara stared at her for a very long time. She was trying to figure out what had just happened. She was trying to trust it.

She got up and pulled on her shirt, opened her dresser drawer for a pair of soft shorts and stepped into them. She headed for the bathroom and a glass of water.

She was too awake, too unnerved, to go back to bed.

Her phone battery had died earlier in the night. She plugged it in, in the dark kitchen. It took a couple minutes to come to life, and when it did, there were four voice mails, one from Spencer's cell phone, the others from an unfamiliar Los Angeles number.

She played the first voice mail, heard Spencer's voice. *Sara, I think I'm in trouble. I . . . um . . . got in a fight? I think I, uh . . . I think I hurt someone pretty bad.*

Heart pounding, she played the next message: a stranger, calling from the police station. Spencer was there.

She dropped her water glass, barely registered the shatter. She was searching for her keys, playing the messages on speaker, pulling on her shoes, feeling in the dark for her wallet.

And then a call from down the hallway. "Sara, are you okay?"

Emilie appearing, wrapped in a sheet. Rushing forward and then gasping in pain.

Sara, only now, thought to flick on the light. The next message playing, Spencer again, *Sara, where are you? I really fucking need you right now.* Emilie, naked, a shard of Sara's water glass protruding from the arch of her foot.

Sara watched as Emilie pulled it out. Blood gushed.

Not this.

"Oh God," Emilie said. "I think I need a doctor."

Another message from the station. Sara stopped it from

playing, didn't want Emilie to hear it. Broken glass on the floor. Emilie in the kitchen now, at the sink, asking for a towel. Blood on the floor, blood on her foot.

Sara stepped over the glass and took a clean dish towel from a drawer. She knelt on the floor, wrapped the towel tightly. Tried to ignore the blood seeping through. Tried not to think of Annie or the forest. Not even of Emilie herself, the hour before.

Her brother needed her, and she wasn't there.

"I'm pretty sure I need a doctor," Emilie said again. "Will you take me?"

Sara had been right to be afraid. Right to distrust something that felt so good. As punishment: her old life, the old heartbreaks, following her into this one, here to drag her back.

"I'll get you a car," Sara said. She went to her room to gather Emilie's dress and underwear and brought them back to the kitchen. Searched her phone to find the nearest hospital.

"UCLA?" She averted her eyes, couldn't watch Emilie's reaction.

Quiet.

"Okay," Emilie whispered.

Sara confirmed their location. Was so sorry, but couldn't speak it. "Red Impala in three minutes," she said. Emilie buttoned her dress, stepped into one sandal, flinched as she pulled on the other.

Emilie's face was pale; she was shaking.

"It's just a cut," Sara said.

LONG BEACH

An hour in the spring, sitting in the front pew of Saint Antho-ny's. Emilie between her parents, Colette conspicuously ab-sent. The low monotone of the priest's voice.

They knelt. They stood. They sang.

The Lord be with you.
And also with you.

Roses at the cemetery, tombstone carved with her grandpar-ents' names for their side-by-side graves. She ached, dropping the blossoms into the dirt—not only her heart but her lungs and her shoulders, too. A deeper ache than she'd been pre-pared for.

And then, the reception, the evening upon them, the sun low in the sky. All the usual guests assembled at her parents' house—the Santoses, the innumerable cousins, the lifetime friends. Alice and Pablo, bringing Emilie glasses of water and wine. After a few hours, the first guests began leaving. Her little cousin Jasper dashed over to her garden seat.

"Look!" he said. "Caterpillar." He held it in his hand for her to see. Green and white, wriggling across the back of his hand.

"Wow," she said. "What a cute little guy." The caterpillar reached the edge of Jasper's hand, making its way to his palm. Emilie held her breath as he slowly turned his hand palm up. She was studying his fingertips now. Each one of them was perfect, unblemished from the night of the Christmas party when he'd reached into the fire. Prick of tears, pressure in her throat.

"I found him in the dirt," he said. "I have to set him free soon."

She steadied her breath. "Incredible," she told him.

Goodbye to Margie and George and the twins. Goodbye to Mr. and Mrs. Santos. Goodbye to Rudy and Maurice and her distant cousins, whose names she was always unsure of.

She came back to the deck, nestled into a lounge chair across from Alice and Pablo, who'd been talking together on a sofa. She was so tired, but more relaxed now that most of the guests were gone.

"I want to tell you guys something." She hadn't been expecting to say it, hadn't known if she'd tell anyone. But the reception was over now, and she was tucked away in a corner with the people who knew her best. The people, she realized, she trusted most.

They were both nodding, waiting.

"I slept with someone a couple weeks ago."

"A stranger?" Alice asked.

"Sort of. We'd met once before, but a long time ago."

"And how'd you meet this time?" Pablo asked.

"She works at Yerba Buena. She's the bartender there."

"And exactly *when* were you at Yerba Buena?" Pablo asked.

"A few weeks ago. But it's not like that. I knew Jacob was out of town."

Alice sipped from her wineglass. "Fair," she said.

"I just . . . There's something about her. I knew it was right. It *felt* so right. And then . . . something happened. You know how I cut my foot?"

Alice leaned forward, set down her glass. "Yes," she said, face clouding over.

"I did it when I was at her house, in the middle of the night. I had been sleeping and then there were these sounds. I walked down the hallway in the dark and stepped on a shard of glass—it was the glass breaking that woke me up, I think. We'd had this *incredible* night. But something happened—I don't know what—and she didn't take me to the hospital. She didn't take my phone number. She just sent me away."

"Jesus," Pablo said. "I'm sorry, Em."

Emilie felt tears on her cheeks. She wiped them away, shook her head. "It's okay," she said. "Really. That's not even what I'm trying to talk about." She looked up, noticed that a few bulbs from the string lights above them had burned out.

"We're listening," Alice said.

Emilie nodded. "All this time, I've been so deeply lost. I don't even know why you're both still friends with me."

"What?" Pablo said. "Don't be—"

"*Pablo,*" Alice said. "Just let her talk."

"I just haven't known what I've wanted. But I finally knew that night. And I know something else now, too, but it feels impossible. It feels too big for me. I don't know how to do it."

"Tell us," Alice said. "I love big. I love impossible." So even though Emilie felt foolish, she told them.

"I want to restore my grandmother's house. I'll need help, I know, but I want to do as much as I can by myself. It probably sounds crazy."

Alice shook her head.

"No," Pablo said. "It doesn't sound crazy at all."

They sat longer in the warm night, tucked into their corner of the deck.

"Claire would be so happy," Alice said, and Emilie hoped so.

It was very late by the time Emilie got back to her grandmother's house, but instead of going straight to sleep in the garage apartment, she unlocked the back door instead.

She stepped into the house, made her way through it to Claire's room. She stood at the place where she'd promised she'd take care of Colette and wondered how it was possible that just weeks ago this room—this entire *house*—was full of furniture and papers and knickknacks, dust and rugs, TV trays, pictures of Jesus, antiquated electronics—and now held only her.

She couldn't do anything over again. The choices she'd made, or let be made for her, had all played themselves out, were over now. But here was her grandmother's house, ready to be restored. Here was the voice inside of her, telling her what she wanted.

Bas agreed to help.

He arrived at eight o'clock that Saturday morning. She handed him a mug of coffee she'd brewed in the garage apartment and they started a list of everything that would need to be done.

"How big is this room, do you think?" Bas backed up to get a better look. "Nine by twelve? Ten by twelve?"

"I left a measuring tape on the table in the apartment," Emilie said.

She noticed a chip in a windowpane. Made a note of it on her phone while Bas went out back.

"Those colors!" he said moments later, rushing in from the garage, measuring tape in hand. "I hadn't been since you moved in. It's like a circus tent in there!"

She laughed. "Oh yeah," she said. "I needed to cheer up."

"Oh," he said. "Was something going on that I didn't know about?"

She looked at his expression—concern, curiosity. How could she change her major so many times right before she was set to graduate, and have no qualms about moving out of her studio on a week's notice, and, to the best of their knowledge, have had no love life whatsoever for the last three years, and have none of this be the cause for any concern? Maybe to them she was someone content to give rides and show up for dinners. Maybe they didn't think it mattered to her whether she was arranging flowers or sorting pills, as long as she was keeping busy.

"Are you better now at least?" Bas asked.

She considered his question and imagined herself telling him all of it, every naïve hope and terrible mistake. She would tell him about the hikers in the canyon, that strange afternoon that haunted her still. She'd tell him about Sara, how she'd cast her out. Together they'd figure out what it meant.

Maybe she would, she thought, over these next few weeks or months. For now, though, she met his eyes and said, "Yes."

They worked on the house every day over the week that followed. One afternoon, after hours of ripping out carpet, dust billowing with each piece freed from the corners, they had escaped to the yard for air. Emilie massaged her hands, first the left, then the right. She knew the ache in so many small muscles—in her hands, her forearms and legs and back—meant she was getting stronger. She felt an unfamiliar pride, different from the satisfaction that once came with completing a floral arrangement, because this had nothing to do with arranging what was already beautiful and everything to do with how she felt when she collapsed walls and stripped floors and learned what tools to use and what to call them.

"Tell me about the other places you lived when you were growing up," Emilie said. "I looked through all the photographs and letters with Grandmother. I love how many were taken outside of their houses."

Bas took a swig of beer, leaned back onto his elbows. "Well, there was the one in Compton. That was their first, after leaving the projects. And then we moved to Inglewood, right next door to my cousins. Nice houses, but directly under the flight path. The sound rattled the windows. All the adults hated it, but as a kid it was fun sometimes. My cousins and I would lie down in the backyard and wait for the planes. They'd fly right over us. The *wind,* the *sound.* Such a thrill."

Emilie knew they were finished working for the day. Bas wasn't used to doing so much of the labor—it had been years, in fact, since he'd done any of it—and though his enjoyment of it was apparent, she could see that he was tired.

But this moment, this time with him—she didn't want it to be over. At points throughout the day, she found herself wondering if she could have had this, with him, all along. Had he always been willing to spend hours and days with her? Was he only waiting for the right project or reason? Could she have phoned him up, say, two years ago, when she was still arranging flowers for the restaurant and before Jacob had moved his workspace next to hers? Had she asked, would Bas have helped turn her apartment into a happier space? A place that filled her with confidence, so that when Jacob said, *I want to see where you live,* she would have been enough of a whole person to have known better, to have said, *Sure, bring your wife, I've been wanting to meet her.* Would Bas have shown up at her place with his tool belt and a box of tiles for a backsplash, butcher block for the counters, curtain rods and the right kind of hardware for plaster? But more than that, after that, when everything was finished and Emilie felt at home, would he have shown up empty-handed and climbed the stairs and sat with her, doing nothing but drinking coffee and listening to her talk, telling her about his day, asking nothing of her?

Maybe he would have. She would never know. But now she'd make it last as long as she could. He was finishing his beer, thinking of his past. His face had gone wistful. So she said, "The Inglewood house. Do you remember where it is?"

"I remember exactly."

"Let's go then."

He grabbed his keys from the counter but then paused. "Wait." He unlocked the side door of the garage. He dug through a drawer and then dangled an old keychain.

Emilie shook her head.

"No way it'll start."

"We can jump it," he said. "Come on."

The garage door opened for the first time in years—dust rising to the sky, must and heat—and there was the old Coupe de Ville, maroon with a white top and black leather seats, and Bas went theatrically weak-kneed at the sight of it.

"1974," he said. "A Saturday in March. Dad was working all weekend on a house. Mom wore a white suit and drove it off the lot."

"You were there?"

"She said she needed help negotiating, but then she didn't let me get a word in."

Emilie smiled.

It took more than a jump to get the car running—it took a few hours and the help of one of Bas's friends—but they finally did. Emilie slipped into the passenger seat and Bas drove them through the city of Long Beach and into Los Angeles, staying on surface streets because even though he kept saying the car ran as well as it did forty years ago, who knew how long that would last.

They took a detour past the Compton house Bas lived in as a child. She recognized it from the picture, thought of her grandparents, buying their first house in Los Angeles.

They turned onto Normandie and Bas slowed down.

"Now, I think it was . . . No, that one isn't right, maybe this block . . . Here!"

He pulled over. A modest house. Rosebushes. A green lawn.

Emilie recognized it from one of the photographs. Claire's short haircut and high-waisted pants. Her grandfather's wide smile and glasses.

"Are we getting out?" Emilie asked.

"Absolutely," Bas said. "I have big plans for us."

The evening breeze was picking up and she welcomed it. They shut their doors and Bas led them to the front door, where he rang the bell and then, a minute later, knocked. They heard a lock turn and then the door swung open and there was a Black man in a security guard's uniform, a few buttons at the collar undone. He held a glass of ice water and he leaned in the doorway, blocking the view inside the house when Bas, in his eagerness to see something from his past, craned his neck to look.

"Sorry," he said, and laughed at himself. "Bas Dubois."

"Michael," the man said, eyed Bas's outstretched hand and shook it.

"My family used to live in this house, back in the '60s. This is my daughter. I wanted to show her the place."

"Oh, yeah?" Michael took a slow sip of his ice water.

"Is the jasmine still out back? Growing over the wall?"

"Going strong. Smells real good back there."

"And the planes, do they still fly right over?"

"Sometimes all day."

"You ever lie out there and watch them?"

Michael narrowed his eyes. "You're losing me."

"I used to lie out there, wait for them to pass over. You never do that?"

"No," he said. "Never."

"Hey, so . . . How'd you feel about letting us into the back-yard? Just for a little bit? I want to show my daughter what it's like."

"I don't think so."

Bas nodded. "All right," he said. "I understand." He hesitated. "How about the front? Mind if we just lie out here for a while?"

"*In the front yard?*" Michael laughed.

"Yeah."

"Be my guest." He laughed again.

The door swung shut and Emilie looked at her father. Was he serious? He loped to the center of the lawn, tipped his head to the sky. "It's quiet now, but you just wait." He sat down, and then lay flat on his back, his arms straight by his sides, his palms up. A car passed and slowed; she saw the passenger squinting, and then the car sped up again. She sat next to him. She didn't think she'd lie down, but then a plane appeared in the distance and he said, "Believe me, you don't want to miss this. Right here, right here," patting the ground next to him, so she lay there, felt the dampness of the grass seeping through her T-shirt, the prickle of the blades on her neck, and she wondered when she'd last laid on grass, thought of the itchy rash she'd sometimes get as a kid after a day rolling down the hill at Griffith Park. The plane was getting closer, it was louder already than she had imagined.

"Okay," Bas said. "Okay. Get ready."

But there was no way for her to be ready; nothing could have prepared her for it. The earth below them shook. The belly of the plane was a meteor. Something must be wrong. An accident. An explosion. Bas was whooping, his mouth inches from her ear, and yet she could barely hear him over the plane's gigantic noise. She tried to keep her eyes open but she couldn't, she couldn't. And then it was over, and Bas's hands were on his head. "Oh my God," he was saying. His memories of it had been impressive, but the real thing was so much greater even, and didn't she think so? Didn't she? And now all was quiet, ears ringing, another car passing through the still-existing world.

She sat up, scratched her neck, wondered if it was pink and raw the way it was when she was a child, and she and Colette and Pablo and Randy stood at the top of the green hill, dropped onto their sides, and rolled and rolled, sometimes fast, sometimes crooked, always laughing, always dizzy.

"Let's wait," Bas said. "Who knows when we'll do this again? Let's wait for another; it won't be long."

So they waited, and it was what she wanted, to just sit there with him not saying anything important, and a little while later a speck appeared in the distance, and they watched it as it grew. It was eight o'clock already and the sky was bright gray and the lights of the airplane shone red and white. They lay back on the grass and soon it was here again—that wind, that noise— and this time Emilie kept her eyes open as the plane thundered overhead, and she didn't think about anything, and the belly of the plane was as huge as a planet, and after it began it was over in a moment.

They stood up, brushed the grass off their clothes, climbed into the Coupe de Ville, and drove back home.

By the end of their second week of work, they'd finished pulling up the carpet, exposing worn hardwood in some rooms, subfloor in others. The wallpaper was stripped and now the walls were discolored but smooth. The kitchen linoleum had been chipped away to reveal more linoleum. Chunks of the bathroom wall were missing from a grueling weekend of tile extraction. The toilet was torn out, as was the bathtub, as was the sad shower with its vinyl curtain.

The demolition looked like what it was—something hasty, something passionate—and now it was done and they still hadn't made plans for what would come next. "That's the fun part," Bas had been saying since the day they'd begun. "Better to do the hard work first, and then let the house talk to us." Emilie believed in that idea, that the house would tell them what was right, so though her mind often wandered to colors for the new tiles, and how they might play around with the floor plan, and what stain they'd choose for the hardwood floors, she tried to stop herself and instead focus on the task at hand, and how her body felt.

What new soreness. What new strength.

The house would talk to them when they finished. Each swing of the mallet and pick with the chisel, each nail pried out and tile clattered to the floor brought them closer to hearing it.

One afternoon when Emilie was working alone at the house, Lauren made a rare trip over, texting before she got there, and Emilie prepared herself for bad news about Colette.

But what she felt from Lauren when she appeared on the back patio was unusual. A nervousness, a tremor. Emilie went outside to greet her.

"Are you hungry?" Emilie asked. "I need to go to the grocery store, but I have almonds. Do you want tea?"

"Sit with me," Lauren said. Emilie followed her to the chairs and table under the bougainvillea.

"I'll put some water on."

"Just sit with me."

Emilie sat.

"I'm leaving your father." She took Emilie's hand. "I told him this morning. I go to New York for a week and I've asked him to find a place to live during that time."

The pink of the bougainvillea was an explosion, almost too bright to behold. Emilie found herself contemplating its weight, if it might be too heavy for the fence it had invaded, if it might pull the whole thing down. And then she returned to her mother, to the moment.

"So is this, like, a separation?" she asked.

"Yes. A permanent one."

"So a divorce?"

"Yes."

"Why?"

Lauren took a breath. "I've known for a long time. I've tried to make it work but it's never going to work." She went on, hands shaking, stumbling on practiced words. Emilie had never seen her like this, so unsure of herself. She was attempting to justify her decision.

Emilie was disarmed. She didn't want to be the source of her mother's discomfort. She squeezed Lauren's hand. "You don't have to feel guilty," she said.

"I don't feel guilty," Lauren scoffed, and Emilie regretted saying anything. "It's the best thing for all of us."

Emilie listened quietly for the rest of the visit.

When Lauren left, Emilie went back into the house. She noticed thorn pricks along her fingers, dirt she hadn't realized was under her short nails. She wanted Colette but she was somewhere on the coast without her phone. Pablo was busy with an upcoming show. She'd call him later that night. She tried Alice instead, but she was working and didn't answer. When did these calluses form on her hands? What were these scratches from? She would need to get herself gloves.

She forced herself up and made a pot of tea. Maybe she should have known it was coming, should have paid closer attention. As she fished the hot tea bag out of the pot and dropped it, steaming, into the sink, it hit her, what this might mean for them. How much it all mattered. The Christmas party, the brunches, even the dinners at Yerba Buena. The four of them—however strained it was among them. The four of them, the way it always had been.

———

Bas came over later, his eyes red and puffy, his usually clean-shaven face studded with scruff. She hugged him and even his smell was unfamiliar.

"I didn't know that she was telling you," he said, pacing. "I thought we were still seeing if we could work it out."

She had one bottle of red wine. She opened it without asking if she should. Filled two glasses and held one toward him.

"Oh," he said. "Thank you." He went to take a sip and then stopped himself. "Here's to . . ." Head shaking in confusion, glass extended.

"Dad," she said. "We don't need to toast."

"Fuck."

"I know."

"*Fuck*. What did she tell you?"

"That she was going to New York and you're moving out of the house."

"Like hell I'm moving out of the house. I built that fucking house."

"You're going to fight her for it?"

He gulped the last of his wine, got up to pour himself another glass. "I'll stay at the Davises."

"That's a good idea." She hated the thought of him staying alone somewhere. But the Davises were among his oldest friends, so this was good. They were Lauren's friends, too, though, weren't they? Her mind swarmed, trying to make sense of how this all would work.

"Listen," he said. "Emilie. I think I'm—I'm going to have to take a break with the job."

The job?

And then it dawned on her, heavy as an X-ray jacket. He

meant the house. The hours together. He meant the hammering and the measuring and the car rides. He meant the planes flying overhead. He didn't want to hear what had made her sad, or he'd forgotten entirely. All of it was over.

He pulled her in for a hug. "I just need some time to regroup. I hope you understand."

"Of course," she said.

"I'll check in with you soon," he said when he let her go. "I'll be back. Until then, you just stay right here, okay?" He opened the back gate, hesitated. "Hey, Em," he said. "Do me a favor and don't tell your sister if she calls you? It will be better coming from me."

"Sure," Emilie said.

The sky was darkening. Bas was gone. The overgrown yard seemed less full of promise.

And yet—something was stirring inside her.

Stay right here.

Her father saying not to look. Colette on a gurney. Her mother, telling her what kind of girl she was, telling her what she was going to do. She had waited so long. Had been waiting all this time, giving Colette the chance to catch up to her. It didn't make any sense—why she'd do this to herself. And yet here she was, alone again. The same words, in her father's voice this time.

Stay right here.

Colette was far away, taking care of herself. It was time for Emilie to do the same. Time to continue with Claire's house, with or without her father.

She went back inside. Stood under the exposed rafters where the ceiling used to be.

Maybe in the beginning she'd imagined an excavation rather than a demolition. Like if she got past the 1970s remodel she would find the 1920s glory: wood floors and antique details, some secret message etched in a doorway. But they had stripped everything away and it was barren. Not charming, not charmed. Wires from the walls they tore down were duct-taped to the beams. The walls that did remain were those of a haunted house: scraped and discolored. The floors were uneven, scattered with staples and nails, and the backyard was littered with debris, and two abandoned toilets, and a bathtub, and two pedestal sinks, one of which now had a broken neck.

What had they done?

Only another in a series of heartbreaks.

But no, she thought. It didn't need to be over. It was just the two of them now—herself and the house—as night fell and the breeze picked up, knocking the screen door around, rustling the magnolia leaves. There was an intimacy to the moment, not a loneliness.

"Talk to me," she said.

The weeks passed and her parents fought with each other and went to her, each of them with their grievances, with their needs and their anger. She listened, nodded, and when they left she took Claire's photographs, spread them carefully across the floor. Claire as a girl in New Orleans. Claire as a bride, the bouquet of gladioli in her hands. Claire hosting a Christmas party, pouring wine into a glass.

This house would pay homage to her.

She used the photographs, she used her memories.

Gold, she thought.

And flowers.

And light.

She had wallpaper patterns to select, buckets of crystal doorknobs to dig through at the flea market. She had a four-hundred-pound tub to be moved and restored, and paint colors to sample on the walls.

So *this* was how it felt—to be dealt a blow, to pause, to keep going in spite of it. Not to start over but to continue.

The Santoses recommended a contractor to advise Emilie along the way, a family friend of theirs, also from the Philippines. He was in his late sixties, close to retirement, a little sentimental. He caught sight of the Coupe de Ville the first time he visited and asked Emilie for a ride. It was early summer. She put the top down, drove him along the ocean.

"So you want to restore houses," he said.

"Hous*es?*" she said. "I don't know."

"You have a lot to learn," he said. "But I can see that you love it."

"I do," she said. "I do love it. Hey, Ulan, what made you leave your home? Back when you came to the U.S.?"

"Opportunity," he said. A single, definitive word. So much certainty in it.

"Did you have to give up a lot to come here?"

"Nearly everything. But that's the way it goes. I lost nearly everything, and then I built something better."

Ulan took to calling her to offer advice—not only for Claire's house, but for a career he could see for her. "I need a protégé," he said.

Each time she saw his name on her phone, she dropped what she was doing and grabbed her notebook to write down everything he told her, word for word. She hired his crew for the tasks beyond her abilities. She learned the rest on her own.

One night, when the tub was installed in the main bath, and a refurbished Wedgewood stove sat in the kitchen against the white tiled wall—her phone rang. It was Colette.

"Sister!" Colette said when Emilie answered. "Oh, it's so good to hear your voice. I miss you."

And even though, when Emilie thought of her sister, she felt the sting of rejection—the starkness of the choice Colette had made, to leave them all, to not offer a phone number to reach her, to disappear from everything on only her own terms—Emilie felt a rush of gladness, of *love,* upon hearing Colette's voice.

"I miss you, too. What's it like there?"

"It's been hard. It's been good. I've found new ways to cope."

"With what?"

"Everything. Addiction, shame, disappointment. All of it."

"What kind of ways?"

"A bunch of things. I've been getting into watercolor."

Emilie smiled. "Watercolor?" she asked.

"Yeah." Colette laughed. "I can lose myself in it. Not really care what anything looks like, just make these pools of water, add color, watch it change. It's this reminder."

Reminder of what? Emilie wanted to ask, but didn't, because another thought rose up.

"Have you talked to Mom or Dad?"

"Not recently."

"But you're doing okay? I can tell you something, even if it's hard?"

"Yeah," she said. "What is it?"

"They're getting a divorce," Emilie said. "Mom left him." She waited, but Colette didn't say anything. "Dad didn't want me to tell you. It's just . . . I didn't want you to come home and find out then. I thought maybe it would be better—"

"No," Colette said. "I mean *yes.* This is better. Wow."

"I know."

"I don't even know what to ask. Or say."

"You don't have to say anything," Emilie said. "I just wanted you to know." But the old feelings were creeping back. Colette, in her faraway place. Emilie, there in the mess of it.

"Who's living in the house?"

"Mom."

"Where's Dad?"

"The Davises."

"Oh. Well, that's good, at least."

"Yeah," Emilie said.

"I've been thinking about something," Colette said. "About when my months here are over. I can choose to stay, or I can go back home. And I was thinking—maybe, only if you'd want to—I was thinking maybe I could move in with you."

"Really?" Emilie said, and as quickly as it had rushed in, the resentment was swept away.

"Yeah. I could stay with Mom and Dad. Or *Mom* I guess, now, since she's keeping the house. But I just keep thinking about it. We do a lot of visioning here? Like of our right paths? And every time I do one of the meditations, it keeps leading to you. I don't want to pressure you at all. But I thought I'd ask."

Emilie slid open the door, stepped into the night. "I'm renovating Grandmother's house. Did you know that?"

"You are? No, I haven't talked to anyone."

The night was warm, the magnolia tree in full bloom. From hundreds of miles away, Emilie could hear her sister breathing. "Do you remember that time I had a headache and I thought I was taking Tylenol but it was your codeine?"

"When we were teenagers?"

"Yeah. You'd stashed them in the pill bottle we kept in our bathroom."

"I do," she said. "I do remember that."

"I was so scared—didn't know why I was so fucked up. So I went to you for help." The walk from her room to Colette's had been like walking through a fog. She was holding the pill bottle, ready for Colette to explain, to comfort her. "I knocked on your door. You screamed at me."

"I was in a really bad place, Em. How soon after that did I get sent away? Like just a few days, maybe, right?"

Colette, wild-eyed and furious, shaking the bottle. *This belongs to me! Don't touch anything that belongs to me!*

Emilie nodded even though Colette couldn't see her. "I know," she finally said.

"But I *am* sorry," Colette said. "We were so close before that. I want that again. Remember right before things got so bad, I was teaching you to play the guitar?"

"Of course I do," Emilie said. "I remember everything."

Quiet again.

"Hold on a second," Emilie said. She'd been staring at a low-hanging magnolia blossom, huge and white in the night. She set her phone on the step and crossed toward it. She buried her face in its petals, breathed in its scent. When she was finished, she picked up the phone again. "Hey," she said.

"Hey."

"I just put you on hold to smell a flower."

Colette laughed. "How did it smell?"

"It's one of the magnolias."

"God, I love that tree."

"Okay, so look. I don't know if I'll still be here. After the floors are done, all I have left is wallpaper and paint. And after I'm finished, I'm not going to stay. But I meant it, of course, when I promised Grandmother I'd help. So whatever you need, just tell me."

"It's not about money," Colette said. "I'll be working. We could split the rent. Or the mortgage, whatever. Just think about it. I understand if you don't want to. But think about it and let me know."

For a time, Emilie had assumed she'd keep the house.

But even though its dining room reminded her of Christmas brunches and its kitchen brought back memories of her grandparents stirring gumbo, shuffling decks of cards and teaching her to play, she found she didn't want to live there. Not for good. She carefully pinned a row of photographs to the wall of her bedroom. Gold pushpins against the bright pink of the wall, positioned around the edges of the pictures so that they wouldn't be damaged. In each of the photos, her grand-parents posed in front of a house they'd rented or bought. She arranged them in chronological order, from the family home in New Orleans, to the housing project in South Central, to the duplex in Compton, to the house in Inglewood where Michael now lived, to a bungalow in Watts, to the Long Beach craftsman where they'd stayed until they died.

Emilie wanted to choose a house of her own, now. Wanted to continue along the path they'd started.

Bas resurfaced in time to help Emilie with the final details. She hadn't told him everything she'd done—not even the half of it—and she watched as he took it all in. "Oh," he said. "Oh." He shook his head, speechless, walking through all the rooms. "This is not what I . . ."

She leaned against a wall, allowed him to search for the right words. She didn't need his approval. She already knew it was beautiful, had already heard it from Ulan and Alice and Pablo and Randy, who was listing the house for her to sell.

She was good at this. And she loved it.

"This is—" Bas began, but she got a call just then, lifted her hand.

"I need to take this," she said. "But I'm glad you like it."

She got fourteen offers on the house within two days of the listing. "Let's go celebrate," Randy said. "I'll call Pablo. Invite Alice if you want."

They met that night at a new tapas restaurant off Belmont, cooler than anything that had been in Long Beach when they'd been growing up. The four of them sat at a bright table, ordered sangria and paella and a dozen small plates to share.

"What's next for you, Emilie?" Alice asked.

Emilie sipped the wine. "I want to do it again," she said.

"Do you have a place in mind?" Pablo asked, and Randy made a show of cupping his hand over his ear and listening in. They all laughed.

"I guess I should be asking you, Randy. Got any diamonds in the rough for me?"

Randy's face changed. "Oh holy shit," he said. "I *do* know a place. I don't know if it's . . . I mean it's *rough*. But it could be spectacular."

"Expensive?" Emilie asked.

"Yeah, it's *on* Ocean Avenue. I mean, it's a mansion. Like for real. But with what you just made you could pull it off, no problem. We can go over and look together."

Emilie nodded. "Tomorrow," she said.

"Excuse me," Randy said, calling the waitress over, "can I get another pitcher for my best client?"

"Oh, no," Emilie said. "What have I done?"

"Watch out for this guy," Pablo said. "He's going to have you buying up all of Long Beach if you aren't careful."

But Alice didn't laugh along. Her eyes were fixed on Emilie, and Emilie cocked her head in question.

"Em," she said. "Look at you. And you're just getting started."

"You guys are too nice to me. It's only a house." But she knew it was more than that.

After dinner was over, Alice and Emilie drove back to Alice's bungalow.

Alice's guest room was a sanctuary—navy walls with white trim. A soft bed, a chest of drawers now full of Emilie's folded clothing. A coral-pink velvet lounge chair with an ottoman positioned under a window, perfect for reading. It was a gift to stay there while she sold Claire's house and searched for a new place of her own.

She and Alice said good night, and Emilie settled into the room.

She sat on the chair and looked at her phone. It was a little before ten. She took off her sandals and rubbed the scar on the underside of her left foot. Healed now, but still tender to the touch if pressed at a certain angle, with a certain pressure. At her last physical, her doctor told her it might remain sore this way for many more months. Perhaps forever.

"Bodies are mysterious," her doctor had said.

That night, months ago now, Emilie had found her way down the stairs and through the courtyard, past the fountain and under the ivy-covered arch to the sidewalk, with blood seeping through her wrapped foot, drenching her sandal.

There was the driver pulling up, bright headlights, speeding her to the hospital.

The triage nurse pursing her lips, ushering Emilie through a door.

The concern on the ER nurse's face when he untied the blood-soaked dish towel. The pierce of the syringe inside her cut. "This hurts," he said. "But the stitches would hurt much more without it."

She'd waited for the doctor for a very long time. By the time he pushed aside the curtain, the anesthetic had worn off. Alcohol burn, cotton press. She flinched and he said, "Oh, I'm sorry. This is going to hurt. Go ahead and squeeze my arm if you need to." Needle prick, thread through skin, twelve times.

She'd focused on a scar on his ear. Saw his jaw clench and re-
lease with each stitch. Tears down her cheeks. She squeezed
her own arm instead of his. Bruises would appear later, the
shapes of fingertips, bluish-purple.

"That'll do it," the doctor said. "You feeling okay?" He
looked at her. She wanted the pierce and pull back, the sting
of it, the knowledge she was being sewn up. Then he was gone
and there was a girl with a computer on wheels, asking about
her insurance and her address.

She rode back to West Hollywood, where the driver dropped
her in front of her car. But instead of heading home, she drove
slowly through the neighborhood, trying to remember exactly
where they turned, wishing she'd paid closer attention. Her
foot was throbbing, she was sore between her legs. Her head
was tingly with fatigue and, worse than that, she felt lost in a
way that was too familiar. She kept pulling into driveways to
turn around and start over. She was looking up at windows,
wondering if they were Sara's, even though she knew Sara's
windows overlooked the courtyard and other buildings, not a
street. She remembered standing outside under a streetlamp,
blood dripping from the towel as she waited for the car, but
which streetlamp? There were so many.

And what would she do if she found Sara's apartment?

She'd been wanted and then cast out. She didn't know why.

Maybe she'd understand if she remembered more clearly.
The bookshelves, the tile. Her dress, dropping to the floor.
Sara's breath on her throat. Sara's fingers, pulsing deep inside
her, and the taste of her in Emilie's mouth. Sleep, but too little
of it, under a worn blanket with the window open. And then

the shatter. Far away but not. And Sara gone. The hallway, and the light. The shard of glass after she pulled it out.

And Sara, the layer of stone over her face. No, not stone: resin. Just under the hard surface was a pain so deep it made Emilie's chest ache thinking of it. Unclear, if she was pulled over and staring into a courtyard (the wrong one, she realized, fountainless and quiet) out of lust or love or anger. Curiosity or desperation.

It didn't matter. She needed to go home.

She had never driven so tired, but somehow she made it to the driveway and into the garage apartment, where she collapsed on her bed, pulled the covers up, and slept under the heavy, yellowed ceiling.

She'd been able to lose herself in work, to think a little less about that night as she restored Claire's house. But now that she was finished, the memories were back.

That summer morning. Hearing Sara's voice. Looking up from her flowers and seeing her for the first time.

How their hands fit together as they introduced themselves and shook.

And then that night. Sara, appearing from behind the bar.

And how Sara had stared at Emilie's glass. *Spearmint's stronger, tougher. Yerba buena's a little more delicate.*

The night, wearing on.

I want to make you another one, but I don't want to get you drunk.

Sara taking her hips, drawing her closer.

It's just a cut.

Emilie moved from Alice's pink chair under the window

to the bed. Just after ten now. She pulled up Yerba Buena's number on her phone.

She'd spent enough time nursing her wounds. She would call and ask to speak to Sara. They'd make a plan to meet for coffee or just to talk on the phone. What happened that night must have been an accident, or a mistake, or a misunderstanding. One conversation would clear everything up, and then regardless of what happened next between them, at least Emilie would understand.

She dialed.

"Good evening, this is Richard at Yerba Buena. What can I do for you tonight?"

"Hey, Richard," Emilie said, relieved to hear a name she didn't know. "I'm calling for Sara. Is she working tonight?"

"Sara Foster?"

"Yes."

"She doesn't work here anymore."

"Oh," Emilie said. "Sorry about that. Thank you."

She hung up. Rubbed the scar on her foot.

It's okay, she told herself, even as the ache felt impossible to endure.

It's okay.

Emilie bought the mansion on Ocean Avenue. It had five bedrooms and three bathrooms and a living room; a sitting room, a parlor, a study, and a carriage house. It had a kitchen with an antique stove and a dining room with a bank of windows that overlooked sprawling blackberry vines, a squat palm, and a dying maple tree. It was in such disrepair that the listing called it a "contractor's special" and wouldn't show it to the general public.

She and Randy and Ulan spent three hours examining the foundation and the cracks in the plaster and the plumbing and the roof. It would need entirely new electrical and plumbing systems. It needed new shingles, and to be bolted to the foundation in case of earthquakes.

Thankfully, the foundation was sound save for a few slight cracks, expected for a building of its age. There were layers of peeling paint and damaged wallpaper, but that was a familiar problem. The wood floors were scuffed and stained. The bathrooms had been remodeled in the eighties. But it wasn't rotten. It wasn't going to topple over.

"Am I insane?" Emilie asked Ulan.

"You can do it," Ulan said.

She got a contractor's loan: short term, high interest, four hundred thousand dollars down. The rest of the money from Claire's house would go into the restoration, and then she would sell it.

The money mattered, of course, but the thrill coursing through Emilie came from the bones of the place, from the vision she had for it. From the carved wood columns and high ceilings. All of the natural light. The grand, curving staircase. So many rooms, some expansive, some small and tucked away.

She could see, already, what it would become.

She called Alice and Pablo over and they roamed the hallways saying *Oh my God, oh my God,* and Alice opened the door of the main bedroom, tested its balcony to make sure it was stable, and together the three friends stepped out to take in a view of the ocean.

"You're going to make so much money," Pablo said.

"It's going to be spectacular," Alice said.

"I know," Emilie said. "I know."

She had few belongings of her own, hadn't ever settled in at Claire's, so moving day was finished a couple hours after it began. She chose a small section of the mansion to live in—an upstairs bedroom next to a plain and functional bathroom. They tucked her round table in a corner of the grand dining room where it didn't look ridiculously small.

Every part of it was temporary. She'd enjoy her magnificent ruin of a house while it lasted. She'd make it gleam. She'd let it go.

She and Ulan made a plan. He was officially retired now, but his voice lilted when they sat at the table together, drinking tea, discussing everything that needed to be done. "In all my years," he said, "I never took on a house like this."

One month in—when the demo work had been done and the dust cleared away—Colette returned to Los Angeles. Her hair was lightened by the sun, her skin a deeper brown. She wore no makeup. Even her smile had changed. It was bigger now.

She was radiant.

"Hey, sister," she said, standing on the sidewalk.

"Hey, sister," Emilie said. "Welcome home."

Bas carried Colette's boxes, one by one, into the mansion and to the downstairs bedroom Colette had chosen. Emilie knew it was a risk, allowing herself to hope for closeness that would last. But Colette had chosen her over the others, even though it meant living in an unfinished, cavernous house, and Emilie, despite her fears, was glad.

They settled into a routine of sorts, a way of being together. Colette rose at five in the mornings to proofread for an online magazine. Her friend Rachel had gotten her the job, and Colette was careful to do everything right.

"The hours are horrible," Emilie had said.

"I don't really have a choice."

Emilie understood. Colette was smart and committed, but she had no formal education, no meaningful work experience. So after that conversation, Emilie was always supportive of her sister's early rising, her fastidiousness. She'd make Colette coffee first thing when she rose a couple hours later, and after Colette finished her first shift of the day, they'd walk the paved path alongside the beach together.

The more Colette explained the place where she'd been, the less Emilie understood it. Was it a cult? A retreat? A therapy center? A commune? No word for it, she finally decided. It simply was what it was.

Colette had fallen in love while she was there. His name was Thom, he lived in San Francisco now, but came to visit for weekends sometimes. He was a decade older, had a seven-year-old daughter named Josephine. Emilie was skeptical at first, but grew to like him as the months passed. And she liked Josephine even better. When the two of them visited together, Emilie made sure to lock the power tools away. On one visit, to give Colette and Thom an afternoon to themselves, Emilie took Josephine to the Long Beach aquarium. Emilie watched the girl gently pet a starfish with the tip of her index finger.

Soon I could be her aunt, she thought.

Emilie polished the original brass light fixtures, touched

up the paint on the medallions. Applied new plaster in the kitchen—none of the cabinets had been worth saving. She chose deep green tiles for the backsplash, so bold and dramatic that Ulan shook his head when they arrived in crates.

"You need to pick details that *everyone* will like," he said to her later on the phone. "If it's too bold, the buyer won't feel like it's theirs."

"I understand," Emilie said. "But the house told me it wanted green!"

"Do what you want to. Call me when it's over."

She felt bad about letting Ulan down, but she also knew she was right, and when he appeared again after the tiles were set, he paused, stepped back to take them in, and finally nodded his approval.

And then one night, out to dinner with Alice and Pablo and Randy at a restaurant Alice had chosen, Randy started a lecture on real estate trends, and Emilie leaned back in her chair, taking in the space as he spoke. Heavy velvet drapes covered stretches of the wall to give the place an intimate feeling. She liked the colors—deep reds and greens. Most of the other diners were young like they were. More relaxed than in most Los Angeles restaurants and more visibly queer, too. She saw a table of women in a corner, the two facing away from her were holding hands. And then she saw that one of the other women was looking at her. She averted her eyes—didn't want to be caught staring—until an understanding slowly took root, and she looked back, and Sara lifted her hand in greeting.

"I'll be right back," Emilie said to her friends. She rose from the table in search of the restroom. Let herself in. Her whole body trembled. She looked in the mirror, face flushed and hot. But her hazel eyes were clear, and her lipstick was even, and her hair looked pretty, falling over her shoulders in waves. She was as ready as she could be.

She opened the door.

Sara was there, waiting. "Hey," she said.

"Hi," Emilie said.

It was stronger than ever—the current between them.

Sara said, "My friends are leaving. But I'm wondering if I could wait for you, if you're free after this. If that's something you'd want. I'm assuming you're with the woman next to you at the table. I don't mean to overstep. I just would . . . I'd really like to give you an explanation. An apology. I'd like to talk to you, if that's something you'd want."

"Yeah," Emilie said. "That's something I'd want."

"Okay," Sara said. "Good." She ran her hand through her hair. A gesture of relief, Emilie thought. "I'll wait at the bar. There's no rush."

She began to turn away and Emilie said, "That's my best friend, Alice, at the table."

Sara smiled.

"That doesn't mean I'm going home with you," Emilie said.

"Oh, I know," Sara said. "I wouldn't go home with me either."

It was late by the time they'd finished dinner, but Emilie knew a bar just a couple blocks down where she and Sara would be able to get a drink before closing.

Their night together was months ago now, but walking out of the restaurant with Sara, down the couple of blocks, brought everything back. The yearning, the rush, the confusion. Emilie breathed deeply, tried to clear her head.

"Is this place okay?" she asked when they reached the bar.

"Yeah," Sara said. "This place is great."

They found a table in a corner and sat across from one another. Emilie kept her hands in her lap. She laced her own fingers together.

Sara ordered for them at the bar, came back with two old fashioneds. Emilie took sips right away, not even tasting. But Sara turned her glass round and round on the table for so long that Emilie wondered if she planned to drink it at all.

"I can't even tell you how many times I've thought about this," Sara said. "I've imagined apologizing to you in so many different ways."

"Did you ever try to find me?"

Sara looked up from her drink, surprised. "I didn't know *how* to find you. I asked Megan but she didn't know your number. I thought you'd come back. I watched for you every night."

"I don't go there anymore," Emilie said. "I just did that one night."

"I ended up quitting."

"I know. I called for you once, a few months ago."

"You did?"

Emilie nodded.

"It got to be too much. Every night. Hoping you'd come back in." Sara finally took a sip, set down her glass, and looked up. Emilie saw openness in Sara's face. She saw that she was telling the truth.

"I can explain," Sara said.

But Emilie didn't want an explanation—not right then. She was finished with the past, didn't want to stay there. She wanted to keep moving forward.

"Tell me something you want," Emilie said.

"Besides another chance with you?"

"Yes," Emilie said, heart pounding. "Besides that."

"Okay." Sara leaned back in her chair, swirled her drink, took a sip. "There's an empty storefront on Hollywood Boulevard, just a few blocks from Yerba Buena. I walk by it all the time. It's small, classic. Has that old Hollywood feeling. It has these amazing wood floors." She set down her glass. "Like this," she said, placing her fingertips together, so that her hands formed a point.

"Herringbone?"

"Yes! And a ridiculous chandelier—like something you'd see at the Chateau Marmont. It's been vacant for years. I want to turn it into a bar."

Emilie smiled, moved by the brightness in Sara's face, the energy of her movements as she described the space. "That sounds perfect," she said. "Have you called the owner?"

"There isn't a sign anywhere on it. It's just a fantasy. I haven't ever told anyone about it, actually. Until now. So what about you?"

Emilie wasn't ready to move on to herself yet, but Sara was leaning forward, eager to hear what she'd say, so Emilie said the first thing she thought of out loud.

"I'm renovating a house right now. A wildly huge and extravagant house. From the beginning the plan was to flip it, but I might want to keep it instead."

"Where is it?"

"It's here in Long Beach, right on Ocean Avenue."

Sara cocked her head. "Like . . . one of the mansions? Along the main strip?"

"Yes."

"And you bought it by yourself?"

"With a contractor loan. It was in really bad shape."

"You're a *contractor*?"

Emilie laughed. "I restored my grandmother's house after she died. I started the project right after that night with you, actually. And then I bought this new house with the money from that sale. I want to keep doing it. Bringing these old houses back to life. But saying goodbye after all of the decisions, all of the work . . ."

"How much of the work do you do yourself?"

"A lot. See?" Emilie showed Sara her hands, palms up, and Sara took them. She wondered if Sara remembered her hands as smooth and soft, the way they used to be. Her fingernails were still manicured and clean and short, but her palms were stronger, rougher.

"All this started after that night?" Sara asked.

Emilie nodded.

"That's so fast," she said.

"I know."

The bartender called out that it was closing time, but before they stood, Emilie reached out and touched Sara's arm. "I've been wanting to know about your tattoos," she said. "Ever since I first saw you."

So Sara showed her.

"Sara, Mom, Spencer," Emilie read, running her finger under the names. She felt their importance, knew better than to touch them. "Spencer's your brother?"

Sara nodded.

"He lives with you now, right?" She remembered the twin bed and the desk. But she saw Sara hesitate before speaking.

"He got arrested, that night we were together," she said.

"Oh," Emilie said, the mention of their night catching her by surprise. She thought they'd skip over it, let it be forgotten.

"I would have taken you to the hospital, and stayed with you, and brought you back when it was over," Sara said. "It was more than just a cut. Of course, it was."

Emilie felt a swell in her chest. She'd been right. The way they'd flirted at the bar, how they'd walked to Sara's apartment hand in hand, the way they'd made each other moan and gasp when they were in bed—all of that was real. What happened after was terrible, but it was a mistake.

"Did it turn out okay?" she asked. "With Spencer?"

"He's been serving some time." Emilie wished Sara would look at her, but she was still staring at the floor.

"I'm so sorry to hear that," Emilie said.

"His term's over in six weeks. So, at least there's that."

Emilie nodded. Sara stood. It was time to go.

Outside on the sidewalk in the dark, Sara said, "So what do you think? Do you want my number?"

And Emilie said, "Yes." She handed Sara her phone, watched

as she entered it in. But it wasn't enough, this promise of a phone call, of another night like this one. Who cared about decorum, about taking things slow? Not Emilie, not on this night. She took a step forward, placed her hand behind Sara's neck to pull her gently closer.

Sara's mouth was warm and soft against her own. She didn't want the kiss to end.

"Come home with me," Emilie said.

The sun rose the next morning, streamed through the windows of Emilie's room. Emilie had been awake for some time, the comforter kicked off, the breeze through the balcony doors on her skin when Sara stirred. Emilie watched as she flung her arm across her eyes to shield them.

"I'm having drapes made," Emilie said. "This incredible, deep ochre color. But I guess that doesn't help us right now."

Sara smiled and Emilie chanced a long look at her. Her smooth skin, her bare shoulders. The slight crookedness of her bottom teeth.

"Good morning," Emilie said.

Sara moved her arm, squinted. "Morning," she said. A stray eyelash curled on her cheekbone and Emilie resisted taking it between her fingers.

"I'll make coffee if you can stay?"

"Yeah," Sara said. "I can stay."

Downstairs, Emilie took three mugs from the cabinet. She ground the beans and heated the water. And then she found Colette at the table.

"You brought someone home," Colette said without glancing from her screen.

"Her name's Sara."

"From the sound of it, Sara is very good in bed."

Emilie looked to the ceiling. "*Hm,*" she mused. "So sound travels through the vents, I guess."

Colette laughed.

Emilie finished brewing the coffee, brought Colette her mug.

"I'm going back upstairs."

"Have fun," Colette said. "Get Sara to help us with the house later."

"I'll try."

Emilie climbed the curved staircase to her bedroom with a tray in her hands. Found that Sara was dressed now, at the balcony, looking out.

"*This place,*" Sara said.

"I know."

"Give me a tour?"

Emilie nodded. They poured cream into their mugs and Emilie led her through the house. The height of the ceilings, the ornate molding, the curved alcoves. The ceiling medallions and brass doorknobs. The inlaid patterns in the wood floors. Most people were impressed, but few wanted to be shown every detail. Sara wanted to be, kept asking for more. They finished their coffees, refilled their cups. Emilie made a quick introduction, was relieved at Colette's casual hello.

"Has Emilie told you what we're doing today?"

"No," Sara said.

"Scraping wallpaper in the foyer," Colette said. "Want to help?"

"Sure," Sara said. "I'd be happy to."

Soon they were eating eggs together in the kitchen, and Sara was looking through Emilie's closet for work clothes that fit.

Emilie collected paint rollers and scrapers and tarps. In the kitchen, she ran the water until it was hot and filled a bucket halfway in the sink. Stirred a pint of vinegar into it. The new Lorde album she and Colette had been listening to began to play in the front of the house. She heard Colette's and Sara's voices but couldn't make out their words. Blushed at the sight of Sara in her clothes.

It took hours. They made tiny cuts in the paper with a scoring tool, wetted the walls a section at a time, scraped, cheered when large sections fell away. Some areas were more stubborn, and they had to repeat the process. More water, more scraping. Emilie worried at first that Sara would feel trapped there, but she saw the concentration in her face as she focused on a section by the door. How Sara bit her lip and squinted, how carefully she worked the side of the stuck paper until it loosened.

They grabbed burritos from Super Mex for lunch and ate on the steps of the grand front porch. Got back to work, until, in the late afternoon, the walls of the foyer were bare.

"What comes next?" Sara asked.

"Tomorrow I'll prep the walls, make sure they're smooth. And then I'll put the new wallpaper up."

"What does it look like?"

"I'll show you."

Colette said goodbye—she was headed to meet a friend—and Emilie led Sara into the living room where boxes of light fixtures and rolls of upholstery fabric and trays of tools lined the perimeter.

"It's a little wild," Emilie warned, and then rolled the paper across the bare floor. Palms and flowers. Tropical birds in flight. Deep greens and blues, reds and yellows.

"It's beautiful," Sara said.

"I want people to walk in and know right away that they're somewhere extraordinary."

She felt Sara watching her as she rolled the wallpaper up and returned it to its box. Felt her gaze like a warm light, wanted it to last. The day was slipping away already, and then what would await them? She wanted Sara to stay and stay.

"Can I make you a drink?" Emilie asked.

Sara cocked her head in surprise. "Absolutely."

"Bold of me, I know."

The evening was warm, so after they'd cleaned up and gotten out of their work clothes Emilie told Sara she'd meet her out in the garden. "I'm way too self-conscious to make it in front of you."

Emilie'd had the dying maple tree taken out as soon as she'd closed on the home purchase, but the palm was still there at the garden's center. Blackberries grew in a thicket against the dining room windows and that's where Sara was when Emilie stepped outside. Sara held berries in her palm, offered them to Emilie.

"So good, right?" Emilie said. "The obvious choice would be to take these vines out before I sell the place, but I can't convince myself to do it." She handed Sara a glass. "Gin and tonic, extra lime. The only drink I know how to make."

They clinked glasses, sat side by side on a bench in the shade.

Sara sipped. "It's really good," she said.

"It's decent."

"It's the perfect drink for this moment."

"Okay, I'll accept that." She took her first sip. "So where do you work now?"

"I've been consulting. Designing the cocktail lists for a couple places. Leading some trainings."

"Waiting to buy your bar?"

"Maybe," she said, tapping her knee against Emilie's. "Tell me more about *this,* though. How you ended up here, taking on so much."

"I already gave you the short version."

"Give me the long one."

"It goes back generations."

"Even better."

"All the men on my dad's side of the family were builders. My grandfather and his two brothers. My grandmother's brothers, too. They all left New Orleans to come here to LA after the war. They followed each other in these old cars the whole way. Had to pull over when one of them broke down. Made the repairs themselves along the side of the road."

Sara leaned back, listening. And Emilie liked how it felt to be listened to. Liked the sound of her own voice telling the story. New to her, all of it. This confidence, this openness. She told Sara more. "They wanted to make new homes with each other, with their own hands," she said. "At least that's how I like to think of it. Actually, I have these amazing photos—want to see them?"

"Yes," Sara said.

So Emilie ran back in, returned with the box of letters and photographs and newspaper clippings she'd saved from Claire's things.

"Look," she said. "Here's a love letter my grandfather wrote. 'I kissed you. I was in love with you, but I was also a fool.'"

"*Oh,*" Sara said.

"I just love it so much. They were so incredibly young. Look at his handwriting! And here are the photos."

She handed them to Sara, each house in its order of possession. Modest houses, unassuming houses. A house they'd moved from during the Watts riots. The house she and Bas had laid in front of only months before, the photo taken decades ago.

"And now you're here," Sara said.

"Yeah, I am," Emilie said. She knew what Sara meant, felt it as the compliment it was, basked in it for a moment before the self-consciousness took over. "At least for now. But tell me about *you*," she said. "I've never been to the Russian River."

"Gorgeous to look at. More complicated underneath," Sara said. Emilie waited for more, but Sara shook her head. The sun was low in the sky now, their glasses were empty.

"Not much to tell," she said.

Emilie was going to press her, to ask a more specific question, but Sara stood, stretched her arms above her head. "I'm hungry," she said. "Let me take you to dinner?"

A week passed. It was Saturday, the three of them at work again. Emilie unscrewing the brass plates and knobs from all the doors, Colette and Sara spreading a drop cloth over the table out back. Emilie had mixed a baking soda paste, brought rags for them to rub with.

They each began to work, and after a little while Sara said, "So, Colette. I've noticed that you don't drink. Is that right?"

"Yeah," Colette said. "I'm sober."

"For how long?"

"A year and a half."

"That's a long time," Sara said. "Congratulations." Emilie saw her take in a breath to say more and then hesitate. Finally, Sara asked, "Does my job bother you?"

Colette shook her head. "Alcohol is the least of my problems."

"Ah," Sara said. "Okay."

"I did heroin. On and off for way too many years. Em, you didn't tell her?"

Emilie shook her head.

"She used to tell everybody."

"Not *everybody*."

"Oh no," Colette said. "You look shocked."

"No," Sara said. "No, I'm not shocked. It's not what you think."

But Emilie saw it, too. Sara set down her rag and the doorplate she'd been polishing. "My father dealt. My mother used."

The world quieted. Emilie felt the sun through the palm fronds, saw Sara's hands in her lap. Thought of how Sara evaded all the questions she asked about her childhood.

"That must have been hard," Colette said. "Did she get sober?"

"She did, yeah. But there was too much heart damage. She died from it anyway."

Sara, Mom, Spencer. Emilie thought she'd understood when Sara had shown her. But she hadn't understood, not at all.

She went to place a hand on Sara's back, but Sara stood suddenly.

"Fuck," Sara said, "I'm sorry. I'm feeling kind of . . . I just need a minute."

Emilie watched as she walked inside.

Later, Emilie and Sara in the bedroom. A candle burning, Emilie stepping out of her clothes and pulling on a nightshirt. Sara was sprawled on the mattress, turning the pages of her book. Emilie knew she could choose to let it go. But she didn't want that with Sara. She wanted to know her.

She knelt on the floor by the mattress. "Can I ask you something?"

Sara set her book down. "Sure."

"Why did you tell Colette about your family but not me?"

Sara sat up. "I told both of you."

"Yeah, but I mean the times I've asked before."

"It's not something I usually talk about. I mean, who really wants to hear about that?"

"I do," Emilie said. "I didn't even know you lost your mother. I assumed she was still back where you're from."

"I'm sorry."

"You don't need to be sorry. I'm not asking you to tell me everything. I just want to know you."

Sara nodded.

"How old were you when she died?"

"Twelve."

Emilie took Sara's hand and brought it to her mouth.

Pressed her lips against it. She saw the pain in Sara's eyes, could feel how deep it cut. She let Sara get back to her book. Didn't ask any more questions that night.

They were together as much as they could be. Emilie, perched on a stool in Sara's apartment, watching her slice the peels off oranges to soak them in sugar. Sara at Emilie's house, helping her spackle and paint and sand, holding the ladder steady as Emilie climbed it.

Emilie sampled Sara's new recipes and Sara weighed in on paint colors and wood stains. They read aloud to each other. Frequented their favorite restaurants. Took off their clothes, again and again.

One Wednesday night, Colette and Alice and Pablo joined them in the garden and they projected a Hitchcock film on the side of the house. For the rest of the week, they texted each other about the costumes and the sets, the long shots and the moody lighting. *Let's do this every week,* Alice wrote, and everyone agreed.

So each Wednesday afternoon Emilie set up the garden. She'd long known the pleasures of noticing her friends' favorite drinks and snacks, offering them when the moment was right. Now she also had a collection of etched glasses, a stack of white-glazed plates made out of a special clay from France, brass candlesticks—rare objects she'd found while combing the flea market for era-specific hardware and sconces for the house.

Pablo would appear at the garden gate, Alice behind him. Colette would emerge from the house or return from an errand, hair swept up, dressed for lounging.

And then, Sara in the foyer, amid the leaves and tropical birds of the wallpaper, shrugging off her jacket, greeting Emilie with a kiss.

The pizza was delivered. They sat in the dark, lights sparkling overhead as Grace Kelly snuck long looks out a window, as Tippi Hedren took a boat across Bodega Bay. "Oh no!" Pablo cried. "The birds came and Cathy didn't get her cake!" How lucky Emilie felt to be quietly at the center of them, to make sure they all had soft blankets on their chairs for when the breeze picked up.

After the movies were finished, they'd go inside, sit on the floor because there wasn't enough furniture to seat them. Colette and Emilie had inherited their parents' record collection and player, a casualty of the separation. One night Colette put on The Neville Brothers.

"The music of our parents' youth," Emilie explained to the others.

The morning Spencer was released, Emilie brewed coffee as usual in the grand, green-tiled kitchen. She dropped a mug off to Colette who was proofreading in the dining room.

"Mmm," she said, "thank you," her eyes fixed on her computer screen. Lately, the job had grown even more important to her, because she'd be able to do it whether she lived in Long Beach or in San Francisco with Thom.

Emilie stopped for the two other mugs and climbed the curved staircase to her bedroom, where Sara was waking up.

They sat on the mattress on the floor, facing the window to the ocean.

"How are you feeling?" Emilie asked. "Are you nervous?"

"A little. But happy, mostly."

Emilie saw that it was true—there was a lighter feeling to Sara. She drank her coffee faster, seemed more awake. Emilie wanted to be happy for her—was glad for her, of course—but there was something she couldn't shake. A memory of Colette, teaching her the guitar before shutting her bedroom door. Of Bas, tearing down walls with her and then leaving. Emilie knew that things could be good—beautiful, even—and then, without warning, they could be over.

Sara had been hers for these weeks. Yes, she still created recipes and trained bartenders. Yes, she saw her friends. But more than anything else she'd been with Emilie.

And now her brother was coming home. Emilie steeled herself for it, decided to get ahead of it.

"I know you might not be around as much," she said. "For a little while."

Sara leaned toward her, kissed her collarbone.

"I'll still be around."

And she was. A little less, yes, but not as little as Emilie had feared. And she brought Spencer over sometimes, too. Emilie almost laughed when she saw them together in her doorway for the first time. The same lanky bodies, the same short blond hair, their eyes a matching blue. Sara introduced them and Spencer said hello and smiled. The same single dimple on his left cheek.

He wandered the mansion, awestruck. "Your place is *hella* nice," he kept saying. And Emilie laughed.

"I know," she said. "I wish I could keep it."

Spencer was less reserved than Sara, not nearly as protective of their past. One afternoon Colette put on a Johnny Cash record and Spencer said, "Hey, Sara. Dad always played this, remember?"

Another night they decided to play poker. "Five-card draw?" he suggested. They agreed and he said, "Dave and Jimmy taught me after you left. Did I ever tell you we had poker nights? They started when I was like twelve."

Sara shook her head. "No, I don't think you told me."

Emilie watched her for more, wished she would say something, thought of the first time they met when Sara had asked to touch the fern. *These grew all over the place where I'm from,* she'd said. Wondered when she'd trust her with more.

Weeks passed, Sara's birthday approached. "I want to throw you a dinner party," Emilie said. "I know we barely have any furniture but we'll figure something out. Would that be all right?"

"Yes," Sara said. "That would be all right."

The day before the party, Colette and Emilie sat together in the dining room next to the neat stacks of family cookbooks.

Emilie knew which one she wanted. It was a small white paperback. Unfussy. No photographs, only recipes. It fell easily open to the right page.

"We can just follow the recipe, right?" Emilie asked Colette. "You don't think it's a problem that neither of us cooks?" Their knees touched as they flipped the pages. The one recipe took up five printed spreads of the small book.

"I think we can do it."

Emilie ran her finger over the long list of ingredients, the careful notes in their dad's handwriting filling the margins. "Well," she said, shrugging. "No matter what, Sara will know that we tried."

"And even if it's mediocre her friends will be obligated to respect it. It's the food of our people."

Emilie laughed, but she believed it. *I miss your gumbo on the stovetop, every moment with you,* their grandfather had written. And how many holidays had their parents spent in the kitchen, chopping and stirring until the house smelled like herbs and crab, until they ladled the dark stew over rice and carried the bowls to the table?

"What were they *thinking,* giving all of these to us?" Emilie asked, gesturing toward the books. "Like just because they're getting divorced they'll never make gumbo or scones or jambalaya again?"

"I know," Colette said. "It's crazy."

They made their way down the grocery store aisles, collecting everything they needed, double- and triple-checking the list. Bas came over later to help them make stock. They peeled the shrimp, removed the crabmeat from the shells. Next came raw chicken thighs and andouille sausage.

"Cut them into small pieces that will fit nicely into a tablespoon and into the mouths of your guests," he told them.

"That's exactly what you wrote in the margin," Colette said.

"What can I say? I'm consistent."

Emilie watched him move through the kitchen, aproned and thinner than he used to be. Her same father with his new life. She remembered how it felt when he left her at Claire's house, its walls torn down. How they'd embraced, how the sun had bored down on her after he'd driven away. It still stung, but she'd try to let it go. He was here now.

They put the proteins into a bowl together, covered it, and placed it in the refrigerator. They tossed the shells and bones into a big pot of water and left it to simmer on the stove with carrot peels and greens and onion.

The next morning, Emilie and Colette made coffee and toast and then got straight to work. It took them an hour just to prep the ingredients. To chop the celery and onions, bell peppers and garlic. To mix the spices in the right proportions. They burned the first batch of roux. "Should we use it anyway?" Emilie asked.

"I'll text Dad," Colette said. A moment later: "He says absolutely not."

So they poured the blackened, spiced flour from the pot into the trash and started over. A lower heat this time, Emilie stirring so often that it took ages to get brown enough. But once it did, the scent filled the room and they knew that it was right. Colette poured it into a bowl and set it aside.

"Time for the holy trinity," Emilie read. "That part's easy. We just mix the celery and onion and peppers together."

They cooked the proteins in batches. Browned the trinity in the same pan, making sure enough oil was left from the meat. They scraped the bottom from time to time as Bas had instructed in the margins. Mixed in the rest of the spices, lowered the heat. Emilie poured a can of crushed tomatoes and Colette brought over the bowl with the roux. They alternated, spooning tomatoes, spooning roux, mixing everything together until it formed a paste.

Emilie turned the burner with the pot on high, brought the stock to a boil. Colette added the paste they'd made little by little while Emilie whisked. When the paste was mixed in, they lowered the heat and put on the lid.

"We let it simmer for twenty minutes now," Colette said.

"Okay," Emilie said. "Let's set the table."

The dining room was her favorite space in the house. One side was covered in original windows—a little bit drafty but too beautiful to take out—looking onto the garden. It had French doors that swung open, and Emilie had found a massive chandelier at the Pasadena flea market that now hung regally from the center of the ceiling.

Below the chandelier were two long folding tables and a rack of wooden folding chairs from an event rental company Alice said owed her a favor.

Emilie ironed linen tablecloths. Colette laid out the placemats and napkins in alternating blues and pinks and greens. They lined up the tapered candles (deep green, Sara's favorite color) and set places for eleven.

They had matching dishes and flatware, also from the event rental, and wineglasses, too.

A place for Sara, a place for Spencer. Emilie, Alice, Pablo, Colette. And five of Sara's friends, only a couple of whom Emilie had met.

The timer rang and they went back to the kitchen. They added the chicken and sausage and shrimp to the pot and brought it to a boil. They lowered the heat, added the oysters and crab.

Emilie cleaned up their cooking scraps and discarded bowls,

turned to see Colette stirring, her right foot resting on her left calf just as she had at their parents' house that Christmas. How long ago that felt to her; how far each of them had come.

"Let's go take showers," Colette said. "Then we'll come back and taste it."

Emilie washed her hair under the stream of hot water in her newly tiled bathroom. She shaved her legs. She turned off the water, rubbed lotion into her skin. She put on jeans and a T-shirt and returned to the kitchen.

Colette was there, waiting, turning the pages of the cookbook. Emilie had the feeling that the book might hold answers for them, as though it were more than a collection of recipes. A manual for existing, perhaps. Step-by-step instructions for how to move through the world. Her sister turned another page.

"Do you ever think about being Creole?" Emilie asked. "Like is it ever on your mind?"

"Sometimes," Colette said.

"I wrote so many papers about it. All through college. I was trying to figure out what it meant. How I fit."

"I want to read them. Can I?"

Emilie shook her head. "I found a whole stack of them when I was moving out of the studio. They were so revealing. I was embarrassed for myself just skimming over them. I had to throw them away."

"Oh." Colette's brow furrowed. "But you were just learning."

Emilie shrugged, but her sister's compassion disarmed her. Maybe she needed to be gentler with herself.

She thought of Colette on the night she and Alice had her over, all those years ago. How different everything might have been had their conversation not taken a turn. Had Emilie not patronized, had Colette not fought back. Maybe Emilie would have shown Colette the papers as she'd written them. Maybe they'd have stayed up late lost in long conversations about identity.

"Remember when we were kids and we'd go to those big parties with cousins and dance the second line?" Emilie asked.

Colette leaned against the counter, wistful. "The aunties with their parasols."

"Grandmother told me that at the Creole dances in New Orleans bouncers stood at the door, checking boys' wrists. If they were too dark, they wouldn't be let in."

"That's fucked up," Colette said. "It barely makes sense. They moved here because *they* were discriminated against."

"I know."

Colette shook her head.

Emilie said, "No one's dancing the second line anymore. All the aunties are gone. I tried to learn all the stories but so much is lost anyway."

"We have this, though," Colette said, tilting her head toward the pot. "Ready?"

"*Nervous.* But yes, okay. Ready."

They each dipped spoons into the pot. Blew to cool them, placed them into their mouths.

"Oh my God," Colette said.

Emilie shook her head. "How did we *do* that?"

"It's gumbo!" Colette said.

They both looked at the pot. "I really thought it was magic,"

Emilie said. "Is it weird that it's making me sad? It tastes almost exactly the same."

"No," Colette said. "It isn't weird."

"No more Christmas parties," Emilie said.

"We could throw our own, though."

Emilie nodded. Maybe they could.

They made themselves sandwiches and went out to the garden to eat them. Sat quietly together in the shade of the ancient, squat palm.

An hour before the guests were due to arrive, Colette started the rice while Emilie lined up bottles of red wine and rows of glasses, placed bottles of Pellegrino in a bucket of ice. She assembled boards of olives and cheese and honey and fruit, one for the center of the borrowed table and another for her little round one in the corner. Emilie climbed the stairs to her room while Colette went into hers. A little while later, back downstairs, they stood in front of one another. Each of them in lipstick and dresses. Colette's hair swept in a bun, Emilie's falling over her shoulders.

"You look beautiful," Colette said.

"So do you."

Colette lit the candles throughout the house while Emilie picked which records to play. She placed *Where Did Our Love Go* by The Supremes on the player, wanting to start the party upbeat and happy. The Temptations for appetizers, Joni Mitchell for dinner. One of Sara's friends was bringing the cake. She'd select the dessert record later, depending on whether the party was boisterous or intimate by then.

"All right," Colette said, placing the matchbox on the kitchen counter.

"Okay," Emilie said, lowering the needle onto the spinning record. "I think we're ready."

And they crossed through the parlor and the living room and the foyer, out the wide, heavy door to the steps, to await their guests.

A couple hours later, Colette held out bowls of rice while Emilie ladled the gumbo over them and Pablo made runs to the dining room and back. Sara slipped into the kitchen. "I just want to do one quick thing," she said, and took some jars and glasses from a bag she'd brought. Just as the last gumbo servings were placed at the table, Sara set a rocks glass at Colette's place, one at her friend Erik's, and one at Spencer's.

"What's this?" Erik asked.

"You'll have to give me your opinion. Grapefruit shrub, tonic, rosemary syrup . . . I'm expanding my mocktail list."

"Your *what*?" Spencer asked.

Colette laughed. "Her nonalcoholic cocktails."

"*Ohhh*. But what's the point of a cocktail if it doesn't have booze? And you know I drink, right?"

"Yeah," Sara said. "But you're still underage. And I'll tell you what the point is—there's a whole story behind it—but I have to take a bite of this first."

Murmurs of enjoyment rose from around the table. "It's incredible, you two," Alice said. "It tastes just like Bas's."

Emilie took her first spoonful with rice, found it even more delicious than the bite she'd sampled earlier in the day. "Good job, sister," she said to Colette.

"Same," Colette said.

Emilie watched Sara from her spot across the table. Watched Sara's mouth as she tasted a spoonful of gumbo, her eyes as they closed to savor it. Her hand as she picked up the wineglass and took a sip.

The table was hushed, everyone waiting for Sara to begin.

"So, most of you know I left home when I was really young. I was sixteen, and I came to LA with this kid named Grant. I didn't know him when I left, but by the time we got here, we were friends."

Spencer had been eating ravenously, but now he set down his spoon.

"We didn't know anybody here. We didn't have any money. We found a shelter in Venice that took us in and hooked us up with jobs. Mine was at a restaurant. The woman who trained me asked if I'd take over the lease on her apartment. And when I agreed to, she got a bottle of Lillet out of her fridge and took down two etched crystal glasses. She sliced the lemon peel—the whole thing. We toasted. We sipped. It blew my mind."

"I don't think I've tried that," Spencer said. "What's it called again?"

"Lillet," Sara said. "But that's not what I'm getting at. It was good. I love Lillet, it's delicious. But more than that it was about the *moment*. Pausing to recognize something as meaningful. It was about all of that way more than the actual drink."

"So there's your answer, Spencer," Erik said, raising his glass and taking a sip. "It's almost as good as the real thing, Sara."

Sara smiled. "I'm glad."

"Okay, now keep telling us the story," Erik said, waving her on.

"So I was making good money waitressing. But what I

really wanted was to bartend. I was too young, but I still studied the names on the liquor bottle labels, asked the bartenders questions. I was relentless. I went in early—unpaid—to learn how they made simple syrups and tonics. One of the bartenders slipped me the bottles that had almost run out and gave me recipes to try out in my apartment. And then, on my eighteenth birthday, I could legally pour wine. Finally. Everyone toasted me at the restaurant's family dinner that night—the chef and the line cooks, the waitresses and the bussers, the hostess, the manager—everyone all sweaty from the long night, looking at me and lifting their glasses."

Emilie watched Sara from across the table, the candlelight on her face.

"It was one of the best moments of my life."

But Emilie could tell that there was more to the story. "What happened with Grant?" she asked.

Sara nodded. Brought her water glass to her mouth. Sipped, swallowed. Everyone else was still.

"I knew he'd want to share the apartment with me. It only had one bedroom, but we would have worked it out. We'd slept in a car for a while. It was luxury compared to that. I screwed up when I told him about getting the place, though. I just . . . I didn't read him right. I thought about him all the time, afterward. I kept a bottle of Lillet in my fridge, always, and I would pour some for myself and wonder where he was. That night, on my eighteenth birthday, after I got home, I wished he was there. I wanted to tell him everything."

"Did you find out what happened to him?" Colette asked.

"Nah," she said. "Not really."

"Tell us something about him," Emilie said.

"No," Spencer said. "Tell us a *few* things."

"All right. He had a chipped front tooth. Just a tiny one, in the bottom corner—super charming. He was from Idaho. His parents kicked him out when he told them he was gay." She leaned back, turned her face to the ceiling. "We had to do some fucked-up things to make it here," she said. "He had it worse than I did." She sat forward again, shook her head. "But anyway. I wanted to make something special for us tonight. I'm really happy to be here with all of you. Thank you, Emilie and Colette, for this incredible party. Thank you, everyone, for coming. And Spencer, I'm so grateful to have you back."

She lifted her glass, and around the table, everyone else lifted their own, and Emilie felt that she saw Sara more clearly as their glasses clinked, and she craved, as she always did, to know her better still.

The guests stayed until midnight.

"I think I'll hang back," Sara said to Spencer. "I want to help clean up. You can drive home—I'll call a car later."

"*Help clean up,*" Spencer said, and winked at her. "All right. Happy birthday." He held out his arms and Emilie watched them hug. Their tall, lanky bodies, their short blond hair and quick embrace.

"I'll see you in the morning, then," Spencer said. "Thanks again, Emilie. Good night, Colette."

He left and Colette said, "He seems really good."

Sara nodded. "He is."

"I'm so glad he's home with you."

"Yeah. Me, too."

"Okay," Colette said, yawning. "I know there are a million dishes, but I'm so tired. Please leave them. I have nothing to do tomorrow. I won't mind cleaning up."

They said their good nights and Colette left, and it was Sara and Emilie in the middle of the kitchen.

"Are we really cleaning up?" Emilie asked.

"Yes, we're cleaning up," Sara said. "I can't leave your kitchen like this."

"But it's your birthday."

"It'll be fun," Sara said.

"Okay, I'll wash. You dry."

They stood barefoot, side by side at the sink. Emilie's hands plunged into the soapy water, Sara drying with a white dish towel.

"Hey," Sara said after a few minutes. "Will you tell me if Spencer ever tries anything with Colette. To sell her something, or . . ."

Emilie turned off the water.

"Is he dealing?" she asked.

"He says he isn't. But I don't know."

Emilie wanted to understand what was going on. What Sara knew, and why she suspected. But Sara's expression was closed, her eyes cast downward.

"If Colette wanted drugs, she'd know where to get them," Emilie said. "But yes. I'll tell you."

Sara nodded. Turned her face to Emilie again and smiled—and Emilie felt her breath return, her heart steady.

It was all she needed. She had Sara back. She didn't have to understand everything.

She turned the water back on, gazed across the green-tiled kitchen and the dining room.

"This house is so pretty," she said. "I don't want to give it up."

"It's gorgeous," Sara said. "But what would you *do* with it? It's just . . . so *much*."

"I know," Emilie said. "I know."

They washed and dried and listened to records. And every so often they stopped to kiss, until the kissing didn't stop, and Sara let go of the towel, and Emilie turned off the water. Sara's hands found the hem of Emilie's dress, and Emilie's fingers undid the buttons of Sara's shirt, and they left the rest of the dishes for morning.

A THUNDERSTORM & THE RIVER

On an evening a few months after her birthday, Sara's phone rang. A woman, a hospital chaplain, frank but kind. Sara rose from the sofa, made her way to Spencer's bedroom. She stood in the doorway and put her phone on speaker as Spencer sat up in his bed to listen.

Their father was dead.

He'd spent a week in the hospital, had been lucid until the end, hadn't tried to reach them. He left a will and the directive to be cremated. He'd already paid to cover the expense.

"Let me know when you can come in," the chaplain said, and Sara said they would.

Sara needed to sit. Found the sofa and set down her phone. Spencer stood with his back to her at the window, looking at his reflection or the fountain or the night—she couldn't tell. She thought of the first time Spencer had come to stay with her, and she'd shown him the futon in the Venice apartment, and he'd waited for their father's call. How their father had appeared to her, a ghost in her living room. But now he was really gone.

"We have to go back," she said.

After Spencer fell asleep, Sara drove to Emilie's house. Emilie made tea and took Sara into the garden. Sara sipped, the tea warm in her throat, then cried so hard she gasped for breath. The heave of her chest, the tears down her face, unfamiliar. She hadn't cried in ten years. Now: a thunderstorm.

Later, in Emilie's room, Sara wanted to talk. The door to the balcony was open, curtains parted to the dark. Wood under her bare feet as she paced the room. The steady beat of her heart. She was elemental. She would open her mouth and something true would come out. She had to—couldn't hold so much in anymore.

"The last thing I heard him say was my name. My name as a question. Over the phone before I hung up."

Emilie sat up on her mattress, crossed her legs, and leaned back against the wall. Sara felt her waiting but she didn't know what to say next.

"Was he cruel to you?" Emilie asked. "Is that why you left?"

"Not usually. He was more absent than cruel. But before I left he did something . . . I still don't understand it."

But how would she tell Emilie about the drawing without telling her everything? She'd need to find a starting point.

Outside, a car sped by, engine revving.

Okay, she told herself. *Begin.*

"My mom was addicted to heroin most of my life but I didn't know it. They figured it out, somehow. My dad, just how much to give her. My mom, how to use and still take care of us. Then she went to rehab for a while. I got home from school—sixth grade—and she was back, and she explained it all. How addiction worked, how badly she wanted to stay clean. And my life started to make more sense. The marks on her arms made sense. Why she'd lock herself in the bathroom made sense. The whole thing of it, too—the way people would come to our door in the middle of the night, needing something from my father. Why the police were always driving by, why my dad had to go away sometimes. When she finished explaining it all, she held her arms out and it was like . . . like I was an organ she'd been missing, and now I was back inside her body. And it felt like we'd both be able to survive as long as we were together."

Sara closed her eyes, focused on the wood under her feet, needed to be anchored. Only then could she travel back into the living room of her childhood house. Home with her mother. The silver rings on all her fingers, pulling Sara close, petting her hair. *I'm here now,* she'd told Sara. Said it over and over.

"She stayed sober, but she got sick anyway. She was probably already sick then, just didn't know it. Or maybe she did know it and just didn't tell me. I'm not sure. But she was in the hospital for a long time and I stayed there with her until it was over. And then I was an organ without a body. Something that would die. But Spencer was only five, and our dad could barely look at us. I guess that's how he coped. He hung out with his friends, he started spending nights away. So

I did everything my mother had done. I cooked and I went to the grocery store and I put Spencer to bed. Made sure he had clean clothes. Brushed his teeth."

Incredible, how these facts she'd never spoken came out in sentences that made sense. All her life they'd felt too terrible. As though the speaking of them was what would make them true. As though they hadn't already been true all that time.

"He gave you purpose," Emilie said.

Sara nodded. "He did, yeah. And then I fell in love."

Emilie smiled. "Tell me."

"Her name was Annie. I'd grown up with her, we'd always been friends."

"How old were you?"

"Fourteen."

"Fourteen. So sweet."

They weren't the words Sara was expecting. Everything with Annie was cast in loss for her, but now she saw them in a different light. In a before time, still innocent. She and Annie in the forest, their young bodies, their hunger. So sweet—*yes*. But then.

"When we were sixteen, I noticed a mark on the inside of her arm. Recognized it from my mother. I thought if I ignored it, it wouldn't be real. We could just keep going." She swallowed. She'd never told anyone, had lied to the police officer, hadn't let herself remember. Her throat was thick with grief. But still—better to speak it aloud. "Then she went missing. They found her in the river."

"Oh no. Oh, Sara."

"After my mother, after Annie, all I cared about was surviving. I ran away the day they found her. I tried to get Spencer to come with me, and when he wouldn't, I left anyway. And then for a while all I cared about was keeping a job and getting an apartment. After a couple years I started dating other women but I never fell in love again. And then I saw you in the restaurant, that first morning. You had ferns in your hands. I had to talk to you. And then later, after so much time, you appeared at the bar. And I took you home, and in my bed something happened. I was with you—I was always with you—but I was also with Annie. Like I was living two parts of my life at once. I was with both of you, somehow, is what I'm trying to say. It sounds crazy, I know. It sounds fucked up."

"No," Emilie said. "It doesn't."

"I can't explain it."

"You don't have to."

"My father—the night before they found Annie—he drew me a picture of her. I still believed we could find her. I hadn't given up. But he drew me a picture of her dead in the river."

She watched Emilie's face—the dawning, the confusion. "Wait. I don't understand. He drew her dead body?"

Sara nodded. "I just never . . . I never understood it. Why he would do it."

"Did you ask him?"

The floorboards weren't enough—she felt them beneath her feet, but all she could see was his drawing, left for her on the table. She covered her eyes with her hands, pressed her palms against them until they hurt. Opened them when the pressure became too much.

Mattress on the floor. Chest of drawers. Stacks of green books. Chandelier. Glimpse of dark sky between the curtains.

Here she was, in Emilie's room, in Emilie's house.

"No," she said. "I never asked him."

Morning came. She had to go back.

But not yet. Here was Emilie next to her, the warm sun. Emilie stirring, waking up. Sara's heart pounded—a desperation that frightened her—the panic of needing something, of not knowing what it was.

And then Emilie opened her eyes, touched Sara's face, and Sara knew.

"I'll be back in a minute," Emilie said, and she slipped out of the room.

In her absence, Sara saw how it would happen.

Take me with you, Emilie would say, and Sara would wait while Emilie packed.

Spencer would be up and ready by the time they got to West Hollywood, and they'd stuff Sara's car with their suitcases and backpacks and be on their way. A long day on the road together, the three of them. She'd be able to do it this time— pull up to the front of the house, walk the path to the door, step inside—as long as Emilie was with her.

It would still be terrible, yes, but she would bear it.

Her heart was steady again. How right it was, to wake up in Emilie's room. To know that tomorrow morning, five hundred miles away in the place she was from, she'd wake with Emilie again.

And here Emilie was, now, appearing in the doorway with their two mugs of coffee. Emilie, who had offered her so much—her attention and her body, her gentleness, the daily joys of life with her, so many Sara could barely comprehend them.

Emilie handed Sara her mug, lowered herself onto the mattress next to her. She would go with her—Sara was certain.

"What time are you leaving?" Emilie asked.

"I don't know. Late morning?"

Take me with you. Sara waited for her to say it.

Emilie tucked her hair behind her ear and Sara noticed her hand shaking. Sara didn't understand—why would she be trembling?

She felt her chest tighten again. Told herself it would be all right. "I might be gone for a long time. We have to go through the whole house. Figure out what to do with everything. Get it ready to sell . . ."

She took a sip of the coffee. Swallowed. *Now,* she thought.

But there was only quiet.

"I'd love to help," Emilie said. "However I can."

Sara waited. There were so many ways Emilie could say it. But Emilie wasn't looking at her. She was clasping her hands together in her lap. "I could take care of your apartment for you? Water the plants?"

"No. I don't need that. My neighbor owes me."

Emilie nodded. "Okay," she said, and Sara heard a forced lightness in her voice. A crease formed between Emilie's brows. Sara wanted to smooth it away but kept her hands wrapped around her mug.

"You can come with me if you want to." They weren't the right words. She knew that as soon as she said them. But still—they were something. They were all she could manage.

"Oh," Emilie said. "Thank you. But I don't want to get in the way. You'll be there with Spencer . . ."

Sara's pounding heart gave way to blankness. Emilie was saying something about packing them a lunch. About calling when she got there.

"There's no cell service. I don't know if the landline works."

Okay, Emilie was saying, *then don't worry about calling,* and Sara was getting dressed, and ahead of her lay the long trip home, the threshold she'd be forced to cross again, her father's ashes, the river a body of water that still terrified her.

Soon they were outside on the front steps. Across Emilie's face was a distance Sara didn't understand. Sara kissed her, tasted salt.

It hurt too much. Sara turned away. She remembered what it was like, telling Colette and Emilie about her parents that day in the garden. She'd had to hurry away then, to the bathroom downstairs. Cold water on her face, a long look in the mirror to bring her back to herself. This was so much worse.

There, in front of her, was the wide street. The ocean beyond it, blue and glinting. She only needed to take a step, to make it down the first stair, the second, one at a time.

On the sidewalk now, keys in her hand now, car door open, engine started.

She caught sight of Emilie in the rearview. Still there. Still watching. Still time, maybe, for Sara to turn back. Somewhere in the last hour lay a misunderstanding, but what exactly it was she didn't know. How to recover from it, impossible to tell. Emilie's face, impossible to read. Behind her, the house rose grandly from the street. What a gift it had been, each time she'd arrived there, all those wild birds greeting her as she stepped into the house. What utter joy it had been—to kiss Emilie, to hold her close, to stand barefoot on the floorboards, to share meals, to wash dishes. And how lonely it was now—how horrible it was—to drive away.

They left Los Angeles, drove through the mountains, past fields and hand-painted signs about Jesus and drought, the cattle ranch with its awful smell. Marshland. Orchards. They drove alongside truckers and families and people making the journey through the vast expanse of central California on their own.

After seven hours, Spencer held up his phone.

"No signal," he said. "Must be home."

They drove across the green bridge and turned onto River Road. Here was the sign for Armstrong Woods. She felt a sharp and sudden urge to turn toward them. *Now.* Before going to the house. Instead, she made the immediate right and then left down a narrow road to where they had lived.

There was the red mailbox. She drove up to it this time. She parked in front of the house. Their father's pickup was in the driveway.

"I can't believe he still had that truck," she said.

"He loved that thing."

They carried their bags to the front porch. Spencer took out a key he'd kept and unlocked the door. He stepped in first.

Sara waited.

Took a breath.

Followed.

It was just as she remembered it. The scent, first—of dampness, of wood, of cigarettes.

She took a step deeper in. The gray sofa in the living room, the table in the breakfast nook, the dark hallway. Spencer dropped his stuff in the living room and picked up the cordless phone. He disappeared into his room, and she walked toward her old one, hesitated outside of its closed door, standing where her father had stood the last time she'd seen him. What had he been thinking as he cast his gaze down the hallway? When he'd drawn her that picture, what had he meant? He'd never tried to find her. Never called her even though he could have gotten her number from Spencer. Once she'd turned eighteen, she'd come out of hiding. She thought of his voice on the phone. *Sara?* He could have reverse dialed her. He could have tried. But she'd made the choice to run away, and he'd let her disappear.

Just as Spencer had as he straddled his bicycle, and Grant had when she moved into the apartment, and now Emilie had, too, saying goodbye to her on the steps. It gutted her—how easy she was to let go.

She heard Spencer's voice in the bedroom, talking to someone on the phone.

She pushed the door open. Two bicycles. Some stacked boxes. She looked closer, found the boxes were labeled in her father's handwriting: *Sara's things.*

She shut the door again. He hadn't erased her. *All right,* she thought. All right.

Spencer came out of his room. "My friend's working at Tino's now. He can deliver us a pizza."

The pizza came. They ate in the living room, watching TV. When they got tired, Sara went to the hall closet for a blanket and a bed pillow.

"You can have Dad's room, you know," Spencer said as she carried the bedding to the sofa.

"I'd rather sleep out here," she said.

"Okay," Spencer said. "Good night."

The house's smell kept her awake. The dampness, the staleness. And she felt the murmur of something—some meaning pressing against her as she tried to sleep. She missed Emilie, still didn't know what had happened between them. Thought about calling but didn't. Back in Los Angeles, in her own apartment, in the life she'd made for herself, she would find out what went wrong. She'd fix it if she could. Now, in this place, she would try to sleep. To get through each day until the days here were over.

She thought of Spencer down the hall. So much about him she didn't know. He'd taken her to breakfast on the morning of her birthday. He'd chosen one of her favorite restaurants. It wasn't cheap. She'd found him a job washing dishes at a restaurant, but it only paid minimum wage, and she'd been adding up how many hours he'd have to work to pay the check when she caught sight of the bills in his wallet—a stack of them.

She wanted to look away, pretend she hadn't seen. But not this time. He couldn't go back to prison, she couldn't keep losing him over and over.

"What's a gram going for these days?" she asked.

Spencer grew still. "A gram of what?"

"Heroin? Coke? You tell me."

He looked at her. "Now why the fuck would I know that?"

It was her father, across the table. "Spencer," she whispered. "Come on."

He sighed, more himself again. "It's nothing," he said. "You don't have to worry about me."

"That's a lot of money."

"I said don't worry."

She'd taken him to Emilie's place that night for the party and he charmed everybody there. She saw him the way the others did—so much younger than they were, handsome in his button-down shirt and jeans, sweet with his slight swagger, his eagerness to rise from his chair to help. When she saw him talking to Colette in a corner between courses, she told herself not to think anything of it. Her brother could talk to Emilie's sister—*should* talk to her. But those new sneakers he was wearing. The thick stack of bills.

She thought it would mean something—driving back to the river together—but as she lay awake on the couch she was aware of the distance between them.

Around midnight, she gave up on sleep. She took the keys to her car, shut the door quietly behind her.

She drove a couple miles down a forested, windy street, out of Guerneville, into Monte Rio, where she pulled into the Pink Elephant's gravel lot. The bar's sign was off, its lot empty. She got out and tried the door to confirm what she suspected. It had closed down.

How foolish, anyway, to think her old friends would find her there.

She'd vanished. A decade had passed, and she'd never called them. Had rarely thought of them at all, if she was being honest. She'd had to sever her ties with this place as cleanly as she could. It had been a matter of survival.

And now here she was, imagining that they might still come to meet her if she showed up in a parking lot without warning in the dead of night.

She drove back home. Tossed and turned as the hours wore on.

The chaplain called the landline twice over the first two weeks they were home. Sara ignored the calls both times, had to force herself to listen to the messages. "This is Alison Tarr from General again, checking back to see when you'll be able to come in."

"We should go through everything," Sara told Spencer. "Box up what you want to save."

"Okay, yeah."

"And we need to go to the hospital, too."

"Soon, yeah. I've got some people to see."

He slept until noon most days, then went out to meet friends. One day, he emptied the crowded hallway closet, its contents spilling through the hall. She thought he was starting to pack, but no—he was searching for something. His bicycle helmet, he told Sara when she asked. She wanted to believe him, but he'd been keeping secrets from her. He never even told her the whole story of why he got arrested. She'd tried asking over and over, in as many ways as she could.

Who was there?

Just Spencer and his girlfriend and a few people they knew.

And this man he hurt, was he a friend?

No, none of them had ever seen him before.

And how hurt was he?

Rushed away in an ambulance, bleeding from a gash to the head.

"He disrespected me," Spencer said.

"Okay," Sara said. "But *how*?"

He never gave her an answer, and Spencer's girlfriend broke up with him, didn't see him again after that night, and all of it felt off, wrong.

She stood at the window now, saw him take off riding from the house, helmetless and unconcerned. Her little brother, a stranger.

She kept herself stuck indoors, in the house, waiting to discover where to start. She forgot why she was there at all. Why she'd come back, when her home was four hundred miles away. What exactly was it that she'd intended to do?

On the third Monday, when Alison Tarr called again, Sara finally picked up. Yes, Sara said. She'd go in the next day.

She waited for Spencer to come home that night. Heard his keys on the other side of the door, the undoing of the lock. He stepped in and she said, "We have an appointment for eleven tomorrow to go to the hospital."

"What for?"

"To talk to the chaplain."

"Right," Spencer said. "Okay."

But in the morning, he emerged from his room. Poured himself a cup of the coffee she'd brewed. "Would you mind if I stayed home?" he asked.

And Sara thought maybe that was why they were here together. She would handle everything for them, and maybe it would make up for the way she'd once left him. Maybe, if she did as well as she could now, she'd stop seeing him watching her, ever smaller in the rearview.

"Yeah," Sara said. "Sure. That's okay."

She pulled into the parking lot, the same lot they'd parked in when her mother was dying. She entered the hospital and was led to a small office with a Bible and a Torah and a Quran. Soon Alison Tarr took the seat across from her. She was in her sixties, with a kind face and a shirt buttoned up to the collar. Sara could tell she was a practiced listener, trusted her intentions. And still.

"Your father's ashes are being held at the funeral home. It's just a couple blocks from here. I'll walk you over when we're finished," Alison said. "He asked me to tell you and your brother, Spencer, that he wants them scattered in the river near the house. Now, I'm not sure that that's legal, so I advise you to check. But know that those were his wishes."

Sara nodded.

"And this," she said, taking a piece of paper from a folder, "is his will. He wrote it here while in the hospital. He took a reverse mortgage on the house, but you'll still make a small profit if you sell it. He left it to you and Spencer equally. He also owns a 1993 Ford truck, as I understand. He left that to you."

"Both of us?"

"No. To you alone."

Sara dug her fingers into her palm.

"Now," said the chaplain. "May I ask, do you have anyone with you through this to support you?"

Sara nodded. "My brother's at home." But she had a flash of Emilie taking her out to the garden, draping a blanket over her lap, giving her tea.

"I want you to have my card," Alison said. "If any questions come up for you, if there's anything you want to know about your father's last days, please call me anytime. We had quite a few conversations before he passed."

"We weren't in contact with each other."

"Yes," she said. "Sometimes that makes the loss all the more difficult."

Sara turned to the office's only window, which looked onto a staff parking lot. "Why did he leave me the truck?" she asked.

"He didn't tell me. I'm sorry. I don't know."

Back in the parking lot, Sara placed her father's ashes on the floor of the passenger seat. She turned on her phone for the first time since she'd been back. She'd kept it off in Guerneville; all it did there was search for service. She waited for it to come alive, and soon they showed up on the screen—texts from her Los Angeles friends, emails from restaurants, and a voice mail with Emilie's name.

She wanted to listen. Ached to. Her heart raced with it— imagining Emilie's voice saying that she missed her, that she wanted her back, that everything between them was fine. But the ache was too familiar. Her desperation, like a warning. *No,* she thought. Not in this place. She would do what she needed to do. She would get back home. She would listen then.

She drove to the house and found Spencer in the living room watching TV.

"I have Dad's ashes in the car. He wanted us to scatter them in the river. Can we go do that?"

"*Now?*" Spencer asked.

"That's what I want," Sara said. "If it isn't what you want, we can wait."

Spencer turned off the TV. Sat still. "I'll be ready in a minute."

She sat on the front stoop while he got ready, and then drove them to River Road, past the Safeway, to a small street where she parked. They walked through an unmarked alley between a row of houses, down narrow steps to the shore. Sara carried the ashes because her brother didn't want to touch them.

This had been their favorite spot on the river, before everything had gone wrong. She found herself briefly out of time, on her father's shoulders, her mother smiling up at her. And then on Dave's deck, watching Annie's body rise from the water. And then she was back.

"We should find a deep place," Sara said.

Spencer pointed. "Let's go to that dock."

They crossed the rocks, gained their footing on the dock's unsteady surface. Sara set down the box.

"I don't know how to do this," she said. "Is there anything you want to say?"

But Spencer was crying, shaking his head no.

"We can wait, if you want to."

"No," he said. "Let's just do it."

Sara took off the lid. Inside was gray ash and small frag-ments of bone. She reached in her hand, cupped as much as she could, and flung it into the river. Some of it fell, some of it was carried away by the breeze. She took another handful, and another. Spencer reached in, too, let it go. When the box was empty, they headed back to the car.

"I'm gonna meet up with a friend," Spencer said as Sara un-locked the door.

"Okay," Sara said. "Can I drive you anywhere?"

"Nah, she's close. I'll walk."

Sara was in the kitchen, cleaning out the refrigerator, when he came back just an hour later. She was glad to hear him—thought he wanted to be with her, after all—but then she saw that he had a girl with him. Red hair, freckles, around his age.

"Tina, this is my sister, Sara," he said. His voice was quiet and low, like it was hard to get the words out.

"Hey," Sara said. "Nice to meet you."

"Nice to meet you, too. I'm sorry about your dad."

"Thanks." She watched Spencer stand still in the hall, saw the darkness under his eyes, his numbness, recognized it all. He continued down the hall to his door and Tina followed. Sara would finish what she was doing and then leave him to be comforted the way she'd been before they left. She thought of blackberries, the movies projected on the wall. She thought

of Emilie, taking her to bed. It came back to her in a wave—
the ache in her pelvis, the wetness between her legs. Emilie's
hands and her mouth and the warmth of her, sleeping soundly,
when it was over.

She went to her bag for her phone. No signal.

She rinsed out the last Tupperware. Scrubbed the sink. She
looked out the window, through the parted gingham curtains,
at the thick trunk of a redwood tree and the ferns below.

She picked up her phone again and framed a picture. The
kitchen sink, the window, the walls around them. She found
Emilie's number and pressed send. She watched the blue line
begin and then get stuck in the middle.

She heard a moan from Spencer's room, remembered the
girl. She'd let them have the house to themselves.

A decade had passed since she'd walked into town. New businesses with city signage and upscale facades were squeezed between the old familiar places. The Juicy Pig was still there,
taking up an entire block, and next to it, the Appaloosa Bar,
where her dad and his friends would go to drink. The bank
that had been closed for years now advertised ice cream, pies,
and home goods. There was a general store with expensive
cheese and kombucha. It was November, but tourists were
there anyway. They used to only come in the summer.

But despite its attempts at transformation, the town was still
the town. Still not quite paradise. Sara weaved off Main Street
toward the small white church where Lily's dad preached.
The windows of the chapel were boarded up. She rounded

the corner to see if the adjoining apartment where they'd lived was occupied. Thick curtains hung in its windows. Impossible to tell. She walked a few blocks farther to where Annie and Dave had grown up with their parents, but there were children playing in the front yard, a man who was not Dave playing with them. The window boxes their mother tended were gone, and the old door had been replaced by a modern one with a panel of frosted glass through its center. It was someone's vacation house now. They didn't live there anymore.

La Tapatia had a sign in the window saying CLOSED FOR THE WINTER. Wishes & Secrets Hair Salon still stood next to it, but the bar down the block was new. She looked at the menu posted in its window. Tequila and mezcal, citrus and ginger. Nothing like this had been here before. She entered the bar, part local, part tourist, not sure how to feel. But a drink sounded good, and so did a quiet table in a dim room where no one would recognize her.

She ordered the house cocktail from the young bartender and chose a seat where she could watch out the window. At another table, a group of dressed-up tourists sat huddled together in hats and ponchos, cell phones out to take photos. One of the girls' voices was raspy, loud in a way that showed how much she liked to hear herself talk.

Sara studied the wallpaper—colorful flowers and metallic stars—and wondered if Emilie would like it. Sipped the drink without tasting. Turned back to the window to see a woman her age passing slowly outside, looking in at her. The woman lifted her hand in greeting, and Sara squinted, scanning her memory, took too long to place her. *Crystal,* she thought, but Crystal was gone by the time the name came to her.

She checked her phone. The blue line, still stuck in place. She made the photograph bigger. The stained enamel sink. The dingy curtains. Wondered what she was doing, sending it at all.

She left the bar and walked back home. It was right to come here. Right to get the ashes and throw them to the river. But she didn't want to stay.

Cars were parked in front of the house. Inside, Spencer's friends filled the living room. Had he been waiting for her to leave all this time? Someone made a joke and they all laughed. Weed smoke, windows shut.

"Hey, everyone, hey. This is my sister. Sara."

"Hey," Sara said to the boys on the sofa and the girl on the chair. Tina was pouring a giant plastic bottle of Coca-Cola into red plastic cups, topping them off with whiskey.

"She's a bartender in LA," Spencer added.

"Want one of these?" Tina asked.

"No," Sara said. "No thanks."

She watched Tina as she poured, felt herself exposed.

Not a symbol of celebration. Nothing beautiful about it. Maybe she'd been tricking herself all this time, thinking what she made was special. Maybe she was a glorified version of this kid she was watching. Maybe she was just like her father, selling drugs. Only she dressed them up and made them sweeter.

Sara went down the hall, toward the backyard, but stopped in front of her bedroom door. All of it confused her. The sounds from the living room. The fact of her, back here. Her feet on the brown shag carpet, her hand on the doorknob, and the way she was turning it. Why was she going in?

But here she was. The stacked-up boxes labeled with her name in her father's handwriting. The bicycle Spencer hadn't been using, leaning against the window. Bare carpet where her bed used to be. She crossed to the closet, slid open its door. Her old chest of drawers was there. She opened a top drawer. Nothing. She pulled the handle of the drawer next to it.

Just as light, but inside was a drawing.

What was he doing, leaving her his truck, leaving *this* for her to find? She stared at the paper in the darkened closet for a few moments before picking it up. It had frightened her on the night she'd first found it. She hadn't wanted to look for long. But now she stood in the center of the room under the overhead light to see it as clearly as she could.

He'd drawn rocks on the shore and ripples on the water. He'd drawn Annie's curly hair. Her jeans with a hint of a tear at the corner of one knee. The backs of her high tops, disappearing into the water. He'd drawn her in a T-shirt, had sketched in the stripes. One of her arms was submerged, but the other was floating, turned in at a strange angle. There was the crease of her inner elbow, and just above it, where a needle would go in, a single small mark.

Sara's vision doubled, a sharp pain in her chest.

She shoved the paper back in the drawer, slammed it closed.

It rushed back: The quiet of the living room the evening she got home. The tension through it. Eugene telling her to sit with him. The two brothers playing cards. Her father, at the door. *Now why the fuck would I know anything about that?*

He'd known everything.

She heard the sound of the front door opening down the hall, more voices joining the rest. And then Tina's voice from outside her door. "Sara," she said. "Your friends are here."

"My friends?" Her head pounded, a sudden ache.

Tina nodded. "Come on."

Sara followed her back into the hall and through the crowded living room until she reached the open front door.

Her friends, just outside.

She stepped out and shut the door behind her.

"Holy fuck," Dave said.

Lily, her hair in a braid falling over one shoulder, took a step forward. "Is it really you?" she asked.

"Yeah," Sara said. She rubbed her temple, tried to ease the pain. "It's me."

"Let me see you." Lily stepped closer still, touched Sara's earlobe, smiled. "Look at your short hair."

"I heard you finally got a tattoo," Dave said. "You know I took over The Stick and Poke, right?"

"No," Sara said. "I didn't. But how'd you hear that?"

"Are you going to show us or what?" Dave asked.

Sara pushed up her sweater sleeve.

"Sara, Mom, Spencer," Lily read. She looked into Sara's face. "It's about your mother, at the center."

"No," Dave said. "It's about Spencer. Always, always about Spencer."

"But anything about Spencer is really about her mother. Remember the hospital bed."

"Oh, yeah. I remember now."

"What do you mean?" Sara asked. "What *about* the hospital bed?"

"What your mother said," Dave reminded her.

"What did she say?" Sara had tried for years to remember their hospital conversations, but all she was able to call back was the flamingo pink, the tiny diamond printed sheets, the paleness of her mother's hair against the pillow. The rose-colored eyelids, the yellowed eyes, the cracked white lips.

Lily stared.

Dave stared.

Lily said, "She told you to take care of him."

"What else?" Sara asked.

"Seriously?" Dave asked.

Lily said, "She told you to get him away from your father. She said you should steal him away if that's what it takes."

"It was the most boss thing any of our parents ever said. You remember, right?"

Sara didn't remember. She pictured herself in the hospital room, but nothing came back. Could her mother have really said that? What else had she forgotten, or chosen not to see?

"That's what happens when people leave." Lily drew a heart with her finger on the dust-coated window, pierced a crack through it. "They forget."

Dave said, "I knew you would turn up again. And here you are."

"I expected you to be in love," Lily said. She stepped even closer to Sara, put her hands on either side of her face. Waited until Sara met her eyes. She nodded. She'd found it. "Poor thing," she said. "Let's get out of this place. Spencer and his parties. We tried to keep him on the straight and narrow, Sara, I promise."

"We could only do so much," Dave said.

"Come on. I'll make us hot chocolate."

A black pickup rolled up. The engine kept running but windows inched down. Crystal and Jimmy.

"You found her," Crystal said, looking at Dave and Lily instead of at her.

"Sorry about earlier," Sara said. "It took me a minute, and then you were gone."

"It's been a long time," Crystal said, shrugging, but Sara could tell she wasn't forgiven.

"Still," Sara said. "You look exactly the same. I should have known. And Jimmy. Hey."

"What's up, Sara?"

"We're headed to my place," Lily told them.

"All right," Jimmy said. And they rolled up their windows and turned the truck around.

"They're married now," Lily said. "They have a daughter. Her mom lives with them, watches the baby."

Sara shook her head, didn't know what to say. They'd all grown up without her. She'd vanished, and here they were.

Lily and Dave climbed into an old white Cadillac, a mini disco ball and a rabbit's foot dangling from the rearview.

"I'll just go in and get my keys."

She turned—and then remembered. She got into Dave's car instead.

"Phew," Lily said. "For a second there I thought you'd forgotten everything."

"Ride together, die together," Dave said.

"What is that even from?" Sara asked. Some dirt caked on

the floor of the backseat, but a soft blanket was tucked in to cover the old upholstery and Sara allowed herself to lean back and close her eyes as she listened to her old friend make up some bullshit story. His voice sounded so good. Deep and always loud, on the verge of nasal. She wanted him to talk and talk, and she wondered if she could feel where they were going even with her eyes shut.

"You okay?" Lily asked.

"I have a headache."

A rustling. Pills in a bottle, being poured out. "Here," Lily said, and Sara opened her eyes to aspirin and a tin water bottle with a pink lid. She took the medicine and handed the water back. Closed her eyes again. Wished it was only a headache.

"Look at her back there," Lily whispered. "Just look at her."

"Do people still die here?" Sara asked.

"Ummmm," Dave said. "Isn't that why you're in town?"

"You know what I mean."

"Two kids last year."

"Together?"

"No."

"In the river?"

"Yeah, one of them."

Sara opened her eyes. Light from the disco ball danced over the car's roof. "I think about Annie all the time."

"We all think about Annie all the time," Lily said.

She felt the quiet between them, the silence heavy. Whatever happened to Annie, her father had been there. He'd known.

The car stopped on the street in front of the white church with its shuttered windows and its small steeple that reached into the sky but didn't get far, the moon and the clouds high above.

"I walked past here earlier. Wondering if you were still here. I drove to The Pink Elephant one night, too. You don't hang out there anymore?"

"In the parking lot of a closed-down bar?" Dave laughed, incredulous. "We aren't *children*."

All three of them had sharper faces, adult voices; there were strands of early silver at Dave's temples. But, to Sara, being in the car with them was like being sixteen again—the sweetness and the ache of it. She could feel the whisper of the friendship bracelet Lily had braided for her, see its pink and red and white. Just one of the things she'd left behind.

Crystal and Jimmy sat on the steps of the church, waiting, as they pulled up and parked. The five of them entered through the apartment door, climbed the stairs. Sara remembered the space from before, and while the structure remained the same, she could see that only Lily lived there now. It used to be all needlepoint and Jesus. Now a bubblegum-pink sofa took up most of the living room and framed posters of faraway places hung on the walls. Jimmy and Crystal took the sofa and Dave sat on the floor, leaned against the wall with his legs out straight. Sara followed Lily a few steps, into the adjoining kitchen. A photograph of Lily and a man hung on the refrigerator.

"Who's this?"

"Billy McIntire? He was three years ahead of us in school. He's stationed in Alaska right now."

"You must miss him."

"Every moment," Lily said.

"What happened to your dad's congregation?"

"New church in Forestville," Lily said. "They drew everyone away. My dad moved to Arizona with his new wife."

"Do you ever hang out in the chapel?"

"Sometimes," Lily said.

"I always liked it there," Sara said. "Even though we weren't religious."

"Take her down there, you guys," Lily said. "I'll be right behind you."

Dave and Crystal and Jimmy led Sara through the hallway and down another flight of steep stairs to a door. Then they were in the little church with its high ceilings and its pulpit, its rows of pews. Jimmy and Crystal sat in the first pew, Dave and Sara on the steps that led to the stage, and soon Lily was there, too, five mugs of hot chocolates on a tray. Sara took her mug, felt its heat between her hands.

She sipped. Warm and sweet.

"Thank you for finding me," Sara said. "I didn't think you lived here anymore. It's been so long."

"Not everyone goes away," Crystal said.

Her friends—they were still the same people. She thought of them, huddled together on the deck that terrible morning.

Sara said, "Tell me about Annie."

Annie. Her messy ponytail, bobbing with every step. Her light, raspy voice and her silly jokes that would break them all down eventually, once they were tired or drunk enough.

"Please," Sara said. "I need to know what happened. I just found something . . . I know my dad was part of it."

Jimmy held Crystal's hand, twisted her wedding ring in circles around her finger while Crystal watched. Lily and Dave looked at each other. Lily nodded.

"Your dad and his friends," Dave said. "All of them. That's what people say."

"Okay," Sara said. "All of them." The aspirin wasn't working. She rubbed her temple. "I still don't understand."

"I guess it was an accident," Dave said. "She went to them for drugs and they did some in your house. She took too much." She felt dizzy. She leaned forward, head against her knees. "People say they tried, but they couldn't save her. They didn't call anybody."

"They knew they'd be fucked if they did," Jimmy said.

"So they waited until it was dark," Dave said. "And they hid her body in the river."

"How do you know?" Sara asked.

"When your dad got arrested a while back a lot of things came out," Crystal said. "The group of them fell apart, people started talking. But there was never enough evidence. So much time had passed."

"And no one did anything?"

Lily said, "We talked about it, but what was there to do? She was dead. Everyone's life was ruined already. John and Mark were so addicted by then that not even their parents would take them in. They were trying to con tourists into giving them money, sleeping under the bridge. Everyone just felt sorry for them."

"What about Eugene?" Sara asked. "Why didn't anyone go after him?"

"Eugene," Dave said. "That fucker. We heard you went to his house with some guy on the day you left."

"I needed money. He said he'd help me."

Jimmy snorted.

"I was desperate," Sara said. "I believed him."

"Did he give it to you?" Crystal asked.

She didn't need to tell them anything. Found that she wanted to. "He made me earn it."

"Fucker," Dave said again.

When Sara sat up, Lily was looking at her, waiting.

"People like Eugene . . ." Lily began, locking eyes with Sara. "*Men* like Eugene. They rarely suffer for the things they do."

She nodded. She lowered herself onto her back. The hot chocolate had filled her. Her head still pounded. Above her rose the arched ceiling of Lily's father's empty church. "This fucking town," she said.

Dave rested his hand on her knee. "We missed you," he said.

The house was quiet when Dave dropped her off. She let herself in and found it was only Tina and Spencer now. Tina was sleeping on the sofa, her head in Spencer's lap.

"Hey," Sara said quietly.

"Hey," he said. "You stayed out late. I'll let you have the couch."

Tina looked so peaceful. Almost a shame, to make her move. She watched as Spencer smoothed a red curl away from her face. He leaned forward to speak in Tina's ear. "We gotta walk to the bed now," he said, and she stirred and said okay.

Tina woke easily, stood without wobbling. She stretched and turned around.

"Oh," she said. "Hi, Sara. Good night."

"Good night," Sara said.

"I'll be in, in a minute," Spencer told Tina, and Tina nodded.

Strewn across the living room was evidence of their night. Pizza boxes, beer bottles, stacks of plastic cups. "Sorry about this," Spencer said.

"It's okay."

"Here, just give me a minute."

He circled the room, cleaning up, and Sara joined him. She poured warm beer down the drain, rinsed the cups. As she dropped them into the recycling, she realized she'd been worried over nothing. She wasn't like her father. She wasn't a nineteen-year-old girl, mixing whiskey and Cokes.

She thought of Lily's five mugs, balanced on a tray. The mug she'd chosen, clasped in her hands.

How special it was, that first sip, and each sip that came after.

How it had settled and warmed her, made her feel that she was welcome.

That's what Sara did.

The house was decent again. "I'll do the rest tomorrow," Spencer said, and Sara said okay. They were in the kitchen together, and he wasn't turning or leaving. And so she asked:

"Do you remember Annie?"

"Yeah," he said. "Only a little, but I do."

There was something in the way he was standing here that let her know he'd been expecting this. He was still, solemn almost.

"You know what happened?" she asked.

He leaned against the counter. "I do."

"Why didn't you tell me?"

She felt his eyes searching hers, telling her something. Finally, he smiled sadly and said, "I tried to talk to you about life here, but you never wanted to hear it."

She thought of the framed picture when he was still so young. His comments about Johnny Cash and poker nights. He'd been inviting her in, but she hadn't wanted to see it.

"I don't know what your friends told you," Spencer said. "But Dad and those guys—they didn't kill her. You know that, right?"

She shook her head.

"She *asked* for the drugs," Spencer said. "She paid for them."

Sara saw herself in Eugene's house, taking off her clothes. Three hundred dollars in cash in her hands, exactly the amount they'd agreed to.

"He could have told her to go home. He could have thought, 'This is my daughter's best friend. Might be better if I don't.'"

"Yeah," Spencer said. "He could have done that. That would have been the better thing to do."

It wasn't what she'd expected him to say. She realized how much she'd steeled herself for disappointment, never knowing when he might act too much like their father. But here he was, still himself.

He reached out and took her arm, turned it so that her tattoo faced upward. "It was never that," he said. "It was never just you and Mom and me."

She nodded, eyes flooding. "I know." The omission had been a lie she was telling herself, a lie that never made her feel any better.

"He made a lot of mistakes. He was fucked up in so many ways. You know I know that—we weren't even speaking at the end. But he wasn't a monster."

"I don't know if that's true." It was becoming hard to breathe. "I asked him for help. He drew me a picture. It was of—"

"I know about the picture. You don't have to describe it."

"Like it wasn't horrible enough, what he'd already done." She gasped, couldn't fill her lungs. "It wasn't brutal and terrible enough that he let another person I loved die. He needed to *taunt* me."

"No," Spencer said. "No, no, listen. You have it wrong."

He put his hands on her shoulders, left them there until she could breathe again.

"Listen," he said. "He knew you'd find out one day. He knew you'd never forgive him. He was letting you go. It wasn't a taunt, Sara. Sara, look at me."

She did. Her brother's face, certain and kind.

"It was never a taunt," he said. "It was a confession."

Two days passed. On the third morning, she rose and went to the kitchen.

She opened the refrigerator, took out a carton of eggs. Cracked them into a bowl.

Spencer came into the kitchen when she'd put the eggs on her mother's old plates and poured them each a cup of coffee. They sat together and ate.

"We need to talk about what'll happen next," she said.

He set down his fork. "Okay."

"I don't want to do this. I don't want to go through all of the stuff and pack it up. I'd rather pay someone to come and take everything."

He picked up his fork again. Didn't answer her.

"We'll get some money for selling the house. It could pay for community college, if you want to try that. Or a trade school. Or an apartment of your own."

He took a bite. She waited. The quiet stretched on. Her throat ached, knowing what was coming. She wasn't ready to hear it yet.

"What do you remember about the day I left?" she asked.

He took a sip of coffee, set it down, looked at her.

"I remember I was riding to Henry's house, like I always did after school. And you pulled over in a car I'd never seen before. With a guy I'd never seen before. And you told me you had to go."

"What else?"

"I remember that you looked like shit. Like scary-bad. I'd never seen you look like that before."

She was waiting for one thing. She needed to know. Her throat was so tight she didn't think she'd be able to get the words out, but, somehow, she did. "Do you remember that I asked you to go with me?"

Spencer nodded. He looked to the window. The redwood tree, still there, after everything. "Yeah, I remember. You asked me a few times."

"Why didn't you come?"

Tears were streaming down her face now, and Spencer put a hand over his own, wiped his eyes. He shrugged, took in a ragged breath. "We were just kids," he said. "How were either of us supposed to know what to do?"

She never thought she'd be forgiven. Didn't know if she deserved it.

"It wasn't terrible for me after," Spencer said. "I mean you took better care of me, but Dad came through. Microwave dinners in the freezer, whatever, you know. No one cut the stems off my strawberries anymore, but it was fine."

She smiled. He remembered.

"You want to stay," she said.

"I only left because Dad and I couldn't get along. But my friends are here. Tina's here. LA is cool, but this is my home."

It wasn't what she wanted, but she knew. He was her brother, and she loved him, and his life was his own.

That evening, just after six, Sara rummaged through the junk drawer for the keys to her father's truck. Found them.

Its door groaned when it opened. She smelled rust and cigarette butts and her father's cologne, the only smell of his she'd ever liked. She climbed into the seat, remembered how he'd taught her to drive. Winding down the roads in the shade of the trees. His arm hanging out the window, perfectly at ease.

The smell was stale, it made her sick now. She rolled down the window for air.

Dave's Cadillac was parked out front of The Stick and Poke when she got there. She let herself out of the truck and crossed the lot to the door.

She saw his eyes brighten at the sight of her, light brown and wide. Had Annie grown up, her face would have looked something like his did now. Sara had been right to keep her distance. Being here split her open.

"Come for a ride with me," she said.

"Anywhere," Dave said. "I'm just closing up."

But when they walked out, he squinted at the truck parked across the lot.

"I'll drive," he said.

"No," she said. "We need the truck."

"*Sara*. There's no fucking way I'm getting in that truck."

She wanted to convince him. But she took another look at him—his jaw set, his eyes angry—and understood that he meant it.

"Okay," she said. "Okay."

She'd run away, had stayed gone for ten years. Didn't sit through a funeral or live in a house of mourning.

"I'm sorry," she said. "I wasn't thinking."

"No," he said. "You weren't."

"I'm sorry."

He nodded.

"Will you follow me?"

He followed her out of the lot and down Main Street. They turned right and neared the river. She pulled over at the corner of Eugene's block, left Dave room to park behind her.

"What is this?" he asked at her window. "A tour of horrible men?"

"Something like that."

He sighed, walked around to the passenger door. "Fuck it," he said, and climbed in. He shut the door and took a breath. Opened the glove compartment and riffled through it, ran his hand along the dashboard. "Okay," he said, now still. "Jack Foster's truck."

She nodded. She couldn't stop her body from trembling.

"Hey," Dave said. He took her hand in his own, and his hands were nothing like Annie's. They were broad-palmed and warm, and she allowed herself to be comforted.

"I loved your sister," Sara said. "You know that. I'm *still* in love with her."

"Yeah, I know. That day when we all split up to find her? I still think about the look on your face. The way you stood there as we were talking. How you said you'd go into the woods. I knew that if she was still alive you'd be the one of us to bring her back."

"I was sure I would, too," Sara said. "I couldn't believe it when she wasn't there."

"Life is a fucking heartbreaker," he said. He sniffed, wiped his eyes on his sleeve. Cleared his throat. "Okay, so tell me. What are we doing?"

"Eugene's the only one left, right?"

"Yeah," Dave said. "The rest of them are dead or gone or in jail."

"What do you do when you see him?"

"Head in the other direction."

"I keep thinking about that afternoon at his house, before I ran away. He let Annie die and he still needed more. And we don't even know what else happened to her that day. I'm sorry to even say that, but—"

"Oh, believe me," Dave said. "My fucked-up brain has thought of everything."

"He can't just get away with it."

"You want to confront him?"

"No," Sara said. "I don't want to confront him. I want to sink this truck into his dock."

Dave's eyebrows shot up. "He'll know it was you."

"Well, yeah."

"You're not worried?"

"He can't go to the police. After everything he's done? I'm going to push this truck down the hill, and he can clean it up if he wants to. Or he can look at his friend's wrecked truck every time he goes outside and be reminded about everything."

Dave was staring at her. "You're serious," he said.

"Of course I'm serious."

"All right then. Let's do this."

She drove the truck the rest of the way up the block. Plenty of cars were parked in the gravel driveways and on the street. Night was falling, but it wasn't dark yet, and Sara and Dave would be easy to identify if anyone cared. But why *would* they care? Anyone who knew Eugene would know that he deserved it. Anyone who knew Sara—the girl who'd lost her mother, the girl whose father dealt their drugs, the girl who'd vanished and finally come home—would turn the other way.

The house next to Eugene's was a vacation rental. Lockbox on the door. Empty drive. Perfect for what they needed: an easy path to push a truck over, enough space to angle it right. Eugene's door was open, only the screen shut. He'd hear all of it, probably. He'd come out and see them after the crash.

"Ready?" she asked.

"Yep," Dave said.

She released the emergency break and they got behind the truck and pushed. Slowly, slowly it moved, and then the pushing became a little easier, and then its tires were turning without them. The screen door banged open, Eugene rushed outside to witness it. The truck rolling over the edge of the drive, strangely quiet, before careening over the stumps and the shrubs, smashing into the middle of his dock. It sank. Rested. Sank further, until most of it was submerged, but its bed jutted out.

Eugene's mouth hung open. His face reddened. Sara thought of his living room on that afternoon. The slant of the light through his shutters. How the floor had seemed to tilt under her feet.

Now, beneath her, the ground held still.

They were yards from each other, but Eugene turned to them in recognition. Across the distance Sara could see how he'd aged—his stomach hung lower, his hair was gone. His eyes were venomous but she and Dave were grown. They were living their lives in spite of the things he'd done. Shoulder-to-shoulder they stood, each of them twenty-eight years old. They could have torn him apart with their hands, slashed him with their teeth.

But this would have to be enough.

Some of the neighbors, summoned by the noise, stood on their porches, staring.

Finally, Eugene said, "That's a waste of a perfectly good truck."

Sara shrugged. "I don't want it," she said.

Above them towered redwoods. Below them ran the river. The dock Sara used to lie on with her mother on warm summer days was now a mess of splintered wood. The truck her father drove through town, a sunken wreck of metal.

Nothing left for them to do.

Together, Sara and Dave walked back down the forested block, past the onlookers who'd turned away from so much in their lives already. Who would turn away again, she knew, from this small thing.

"I'll drive you home," Dave said.

"It's okay. I feel like walking."

"It'll be dark soon."

"I know."

"Okay." He opened his door and slid in. "Hey, Sara," he said. "I needed this. Don't know why I didn't do something years ago."

She nodded. Lifted her hand to wave goodbye.

He started the engine of the Cadillac, waved back, and was gone.

Once he was out of sight, she followed after, along the curved blocks of the neighborhood and up to River Road. There was the sign, pointing her to Armstrong Woods.

She could walk there, she realized. And then walking there felt like the only thing she could do.

Two miles up the gentle slope of the street, she walked. Past the old café and the bookstore until she was officially out of town. Her feet grew tired but it didn't matter. She was heading home.

She reached the ranger's station, didn't need a map. And here it was—the moment when the air changed. She inhaled as deeply as she could. She wanted to swallow it, to fit the forest inside of her. She hiked the steeper trail. She hiked up and up, feeling her way through the dark, resting sometimes to catch her breath as hours passed.

Above, the moon shone through branches, and she could

see better. As far as she was off the trail, she wanted deeper in, wanted the moss that spread over fallen trees. Wanted the slick wet of banana slug in her palm. Wanted ferns on her face and dirt on her skin. She walked and walked. And there before her was a cluster of young redwoods, rising around a hollowed, ancient stump. *Home,* she thought, and climbed into the hollow.

Every part of her ached from exhaustion. She lay down on a bed of pine needles, found a flat, smooth section of the hollowed tree. Rested her head atop it. She hugged her arms close for warmth. Closed her eyes, felt Emilie's cheek against her chest, felt the banana slug sliding over her stomach and Annie's, saw the glittering trail it left on their bare skin. She imagined them both, showing up here. Annie alive, still sixteen, saying, *Of course I'm fine. Why were you worried?* Emilie's dark hair falling softly down her back, bringing her close for a kiss. She was lifted onto her father's shoulders, heard the rush of the river, felt powerful and unafraid. *Come here,* Emilie said, and held out her arms. *We're with you,* Annie said. *We're here.* And Dave drove her around in his car, the disco ball lights dancing across the ceiling, and her mother took her hand and said, *I'm sorry. You're perfect. I should have loved you better.* Tiny Spencer's body tucked against hers. Grant saw her through the window, clutched his heart. And Sara's breath grew steady, her body gave in. She fell asleep in the deep of the forest.

YERBA BUENA

The night after Sara left, Emilie dreamed she was in Guerneville. She was walking down a long street in the dark, looking for Sara. She saw a light on in a house, saw Sara's car parked out front. She followed a moss-covered path to the door. Stood still. Planned to knock, but changed her mind.

In her dream, she drove to a motel instead. Took off her clothes and swam to the middle of its swimming pool. She floated, eyes open to the black sky.

But something startled her, and she pulled her head from underwater. Cutting through the night was the rumble of a truck—far away, and then closer. Headlights, bright, and getting brighter. She was alone and floating in the water. She needed to move but couldn't, needed to scream, but no sound came out. And then the truck was upon her, and her mouth was wide open, and the water began seeping in.

———

She woke up startled and shaking, sprang from her mattress as though it might drown her.

It was the middle of the night. Flashes of the dream pressed against her. Sara's house. Black pool and black sky. Headlights. Water pouring into her mouth.

She took a sweater from her drawer, pulled on jeans, tucked her phone into her pocket. She rushed down the curved staircase. Grabbed her keys and wallet, pulled on her shoes in the foyer. Then she was out in the quiet night, sliding into her car and starting its engine.

She pulled onto Ocean Avenue, her body shaking. It hadn't stopped trembling since the morning before, no matter how she'd tried to talk herself down.

She knew how this worked, had been through it before. Someone she loved would leave her. Her job was to stay quiet and still and out of the way. To wait, to not need anything, to trust they'd come back.

All those nights Jacob had disappeared as she slept, and then reappeared in the mornings at the restaurant, or in the evenings with his knock at her door.

All the years she'd thought Colette was lost forever, until the morning she arrived on Emilie's front stoop with all her possessions.

The afternoon she waved goodbye to her father from her grandmother's house, certain it was over, but then found him with her again, months later, stirring gumbo on her stove.

Even Sara, after the first time, had caught Emilie's eye from across the restaurant, had found a moment to talk to her alone, had told her she wanted her back.

Emilie followed her headlights through the streets of Long Beach and onto the 405, heading north.

Sara's father was dead. She had business to attend to. *It has nothing to do with me,* Emilie thought. But every time she told herself that, the shaking got worse.

Sara had paced the floor, had told Emilie about her life, had eventually curled on the mattress, fallen deeply asleep. Emilie had watched Sara's breath steady, her chest rise and fall, had felt a love so vast it terrified her. She needed Sara to stay.

But her job was to hide what she needed so that Sara could be free to go. That way Sara wouldn't have to think of her or worry about her, could do what she had to without Emilie in the way.

Where was she going? Not the Russian River. She didn't even know where Sara lived. The roads from her dream were not real roads. The house was not Sara's house. She wasn't really drowning.

She pulled off the freeway, drove a few blocks, and parked. Took her phone from her pocket. Her hands were still trembling. It was two in the morning. She wanted to wake Sara up.

But the call went straight to voice mail, and she remembered that Sara had said there would be no reception. She'd leave a message, then, but what would she say? The tone sounded, no time to think.

"I feel selfish calling you like this, with all that you're going through. I hope you'll understand." Her heart was racing, her throat tight. "I didn't know what to say when you were leaving because all I wanted was for you to stay. I thought I needed to act like it was fine that you were leaving, and fine that you didn't need me, but I *want* you to need me. I shouldn't be saying any of this right now—I know. Your father died, you're back in a place that you hate, you have so many terrible things to do and here I am being a mess, but I can't keep not saying it. I had this horrible nightmare. I got up and got in the car like I could just drive to you, like I knew where you were or if you'd even want me. Did you mean it, when you said I could come? I thought you were just saying it for my sake, like you could tell I was afraid of being left behind. I *am* afraid of it. I hate it. I hate that you drove away yesterday. I want you to need me but you're fine on your own."

She barely recognized her own voice—loud and plaintive—but speaking each word was a relief. As embarrassing as it was, as pathetic as she must sound, she felt the unveiling of herself. Like taking off her clothes on the night they first went home together.

Here she was, all of her.

"I try so hard to be good. To be easy. To not be a mess. But maybe it'll be okay with you if I'm messy. If I fuck up and do the wrong things. If I care about myself even when you're going through too much already. Or maybe you'll hear this and think I'm ugly and needy and selfish. I don't know. I wish I could drive to you but I don't know where you are or even when you'll get this. You probably won't get it until you're finished. But when you're finished—*please*—come back to me."

She was done talking but she didn't want to hang up yet. She held the phone, sat back against the seat, looked around her.

Found that she was on Sunset, in Silver Lake. Her old place was just a block away, the Mexican grocery below it.

She laughed. "I drove to my old studio apartment," she said.

"I didn't mean to, I just pulled off the freeway, but I ended up here." She checked the rearview, drove up the block to see it better. "*Oh,*" she said, breath catching. "There's this motel across the street from it. The whole time I lived here its vacancy sign was always flashing. But now there's no vacancy. I've never seen it this way before. It's incredible. I . . ." She didn't know what else to say. She needed to hang up or she'd get cut off. "I wish you were here with me," she said. And then she ended the call.

She sat at the stoplight. In her old window, a shade was drawn. The NO VACANCY sign shone steadily, no flashing.

When she looked at her hands, they were still.

Back home, once it was light out, she called Randy. "The house is ready," she told him. "I need to make enough from this sale to buy my own to keep, and another one to flip. And I need enough to invest for Colette, too."

Sunlight filled her room, cast across the mattress on the floor and her simple chest of drawers, warming the house that was never meant to be hers—at least not for good. She couldn't afford it—wouldn't have anything to put into a next project, wouldn't have anything for Colette, would have to get an investor to carry on restoring houses. And even if she did that, it wouldn't make any sense to have so much space of her own.

Still, she felt that she deserved that kind of beauty if she craved it, especially if she made it for herself. She didn't feel out of place in it. Her grandparents had known their worth and kept reaching. They'd dressed in tuxes and ball gowns despite being turned away from restaurants and jobs. They'd written love letters in the midst of a war. They'd danced through displacement and heartache. They'd made rich lives for themselves from the little they were given, posed in front of their houses as the camera shutters clicked.

She'd continue what they started. She'd do it in her own way.

"I know a financial advisor," Randy said. "I'll give you his number. For the houses, do you want to buy outright or get loans?"

"Loans," she said. "I'm not delusional."

He laughed. "Okay, good to know. I'll talk to the broker; we'll figure it out. Shouldn't be a problem."

"Great," she said. "Then let's list it."

She went downstairs and brewed coffee as she usually did. She carried the mugs into the dining room, set Colette's next to her computer.

"I have something to talk to you about," she said.

Colette looked up. "What is it?"

"The house."

Colette scanned the room and Emilie followed her gaze. Each fixture was in place, each doorknob and windowpane. The paint was bright and clean around the intricate molding. Everything gleamed.

Colette smiled. "Ah," she said. "It's finished."

"What will you do?" Emilie asked on their walk along the beach later in the morning. "You're welcome to stay with me again once I find a new place."

"Actually . . ." Colette stepped to the side of the path to tie up her hair. "It might be time for San Francisco. Thom's been asking me."

"Why have you waited?"

Colette shrugged. "I've wanted to ride this out," she said. "With you. It's been an adventure, right? I've loved it."

"Yes," Emilie said. "It has." She thought of how it felt to stumble upon Colette when they lived in side-by-side neighborhoods. The painful small talk, the forced pleasantries of surprise. She never wanted that again. "I'll really miss you," she said. "But I'm so happy for you, too."

"I'll miss you, too, sister."

Later in the afternoon, Emilie was working in the garden when she felt a tap on her shoulder. "Take off your headphones," Colette was saying from above. Emilie removed a muddy glove, pressed Pause on the music.

"I have the perfect plan," Colette said. "I'm taking you out to Yerba Buena. I got us a nine o'clock reservation."

Emilie wanted to laugh. Yerba Buena. Of course.

She wondered what hold the place might have on her if she walked through its doors tonight. Cut stems and blossoms. Breakfast at Jacob's table. The first sight of Sara, her first hello, the moment their eyes met and the tremor coursed through her. And *before* that, with her parents and her sister, when she still believed in their family, as flawed as they were, as tenuous. And Claire. *Claire.*

"You don't feel like it?" Colette asked.

"No, I do," Emilie said. "It's just . . . Jacob Lowell. We were involved. For a while."

"I knew it!"

"Then why didn't you ever ask?"

"I thought you didn't want me to know. But we don't have to go there tonight. We can pick up Super Mex, watch a movie out here."

But it made sense to her to go. It felt right. Enough time had passed, hadn't it? They'd all moved on. Nothing there for her to be afraid of. "No," she said. "Let's do it."

Colette drove them out to West Hollywood, down Sunset, past the Chateau Marmont. There was Yerba Buena, grand and glowing on the corner. It felt right to park a few blocks away and walk toward it. Right, to enter through its heavy curtains, wait between the potted palms under the high ceilings. "Colette Dubois," the host repeated, scanning the list. "Yes! Wonderful. Right this way." But as they walked through the front dining room, Emilie caught sight of Jacob, seated with his family. She didn't turn to look at him as the host led them past their table and—thankfully—into the smaller dining room near the back.

"Did you see?" Emilie said when the host was gone.

"Yes. Are you sure this is okay?"

"Yeah," Emilie said. "I think it's fine. Let's just enjoy our dinner."

It felt good to be back. She ordered a Yerba Buena and Colette ordered tonic with lime. When the drinks came Emilie took a sip, tasted more of what she didn't know.

She hoped Sara would come back. Still wanted to know her, as fully as she could.

They ordered the olives and the bread, a salad, two servings of ragout.

"I'm going to use the restroom," Emilie said, and Colette nodded. Emilie crossed through the dining room to the restrooms, but when she got out, Jacob was waiting.

"Follow me?" he said, and led her through the doors to the kitchen and into the walk-in refrigerator.

"What are you doing here?" he asked.

"I didn't expect you'd be here."

"God," he said. "You look gorgeous. But I'm going to have to ask you not to come in again."

"Okay," Emilie said. "It's just . . . I really miss the food."

He flung his head back and laughed.

"You remember Zack? He opened a place on La Cienega. Stole half my dishes."

"Does he make the ragout?"

"Yes, that bastard."

"Thanks for the tip."

"You got it."

He took a step back to look at her before leaving. She wanted to tell him that she'd found a passion, that she'd fallen in love, that she often cooked for herself now.

She wondered if any of it showed.

"Are you still doing flowers?"

"No," she said. "But I'm growing them in my garden."

"So you moved."

The tiny studio rushed back to her, its dingy walls and bare windows. "You thought I still lived there?"

"I had no idea. The only thing I know about you from the last couple years is that you once went home with my bartender."

"Someone told on me."

"Well, it *is* my restaurant."

She nodded. "Fair."

"I can't blame you. Everyone wanted to go home with her."

"I fell in love with her," she said. "I'm still in love with her." She stifled a sob, her hand flew to her mouth. "Look at me," she laughed. "Years later and I'm still crying."

He wiped a tear from her cheek. Had he always been so kind?

"I have to go," he said. "My family . . ."

"I saw them."

"It's good to see you," he said. "I mean, it's terrifying to see you—my stomach's all fucked up right now—but it's good, too. Can you stay in here for a few minutes? I don't want anyone to see us together."

They were surrounded by cheese and milk and cream, thick slabs of meat, long sheets of pasta. She shivered, she could see her breath. What was she doing, standing there in the cold?

"No." She laughed. "I'm not waiting in a *refrigerator*. You can, if you want to."

She unlatched the heavy door, stepped into the warmth of the kitchen.

She made her way past the dishwashers and the cooks and the runners, through the bar and the curved hallway and then the doorway into the dining rooms. Another family was in her family's favorite booth, number 48. She thought of Claire in her suit with her sparkling jewelry, asking Emilie the names of the flowers. She saw the sky, dark through the windows. Saw the moon and the gray clouds, the sidewalk she and Sara had stepped onto together, on the night she learned what it felt like to be sure. She saw the golden flicker of the candles at the tables, the bright blossoms of the bouquets. And finally, across the restaurant, Colette. Catching sight of her, and beckoning.

The Ocean Avenue house listed on a Wednesday morning. It entered escrow on Friday afternoon with a preemptive, all-cash offer so high that Randy showed up in person to give Emilie the news.

"The buyer's agent wants to know if you have other properties in the works," he told her. "She said she's never seen a flip that good."

"Good," Emilie said. "That's really good to hear."

But first, she wanted to find a house of her own to keep.

Randy drove her around Long Beach and Los Angeles in his BMW. They'd both scoured the listings, had an agenda long enough to fill an entire day, arranged by neighborhood.

The Long Beach houses came first, but though Emilie loved her home city, she found herself thinking of her grandparents. Of how far they'd traveled, how they'd moved from place to place to find the home that felt most right. Long Beach was too familiar, she realized, standing in the foyer of a house with high ceilings and original floors—a truly lovely house that she didn't want to own. She wanted to be somewhere else.

They got back in the car, followed the coastline north. Rolling Hills offered white ranch houses and canyon views. Horse properties and pools. Exquisite, but so quiet, so far away from everything.

In Hermosa and Manhattan Beach, they looked at small,

modern houses with tiny front yards, just a couple short blocks from the ocean. In Venice, a six-hundred-square-foot stucco off Abbot Kinney charmed her, but she knew before long she'd want more—more windows, more rooms, more floor space to pile with rugs and wall space to hang artwork. She'd need a place to console her each time she finished a new house and put it on the market. A place that felt like a dream to return to, night after night.

They moved on.

Saw a few places in Santa Monica.

Drove by one of them without going in.

Headed east, away from the ocean.

Traffic slowed on Pico and Emilie glanced at the list of addresses that remained. One in Beverly Hills, one right off the Sunset Strip. A few in Hollywood and several in Silver Lake and Echo Park.

They'd exhausted conversations about Randy's and Pablo's parents and their cousin Marisol, about how the Santoses' family business was doing and whether they'd ever retire. They'd talked about Lauren and Bas's divorce, and how Colette and Thom were vacationing in Tahoe right now, where Emilie was sure Thom would propose, out on the glistening lake somewhere, a diamond ring zipped up in a pocket. And now they were quiet, the radio on, making their way through West Hollywood. They looked at a couple more houses, one of which was almost right. And then they got back in the car and turned right onto Sunset Boulevard. Traffic creeped along. Emilie watched out the window.

There was Yerba Buena on the corner.

They moved past it. Emilie rested her forehead against the glass. Noticed, ahead of them, an empty storefront on the corner of Hollywood Boulevard. A memory stirred. Traffic came to a dead stop in front of it. Up ahead, a light turned red.

"Hold on," she said, and opened her door.

She ran out of the car, just for a moment, to look inside the window. Herringbone wood floors. An ornate chandelier—crystal and brass—huge for the intimate space.

Sara's bar.

She ran back to the car as the light turned green.

"What was that about?" Randy asked as they pulled into the left lane.

"It just called to me," Emilie said.

"It's a cool location for something. Interested in going commercial?"

"Maybe someday," she said.

And then they were turning off Sunset, onto Laurel Canyon Drive, heading up into the hills, higher and higher, until they reached Mulholland.

"I didn't know we were seeing a house up here," she said.

"It's not on the market yet. An agent I know told me about it. It'll be listed next week, but there's a lockbox already and she said we could check it out."

They turned onto a narrow street. Verdant and quiet with views of the city far below.

"There's no way I could afford this."

"Well, it's a bungalow, not a mansion. And it needs a lot of work."

He turned into a driveway and she caught sight of the house, tucked beyond a moss-covered brick patio. Kelly green shingles, diamond-paned windows, palms all around.

She stepped out of the car.

That night, Emilie's phone lit up while she was sleeping. In the morning, the first thing she saw was the photograph of Sara's kitchen, delivered just after midnight, no words to accompany it.

Emilie sat in her bed, holding the phone close to her, zooming in to study each part of it as clearly as she could.

She saw a stained sink, imagined Sara standing over it.

Saw the worn curtains, the loneliness, the grief.

Saw the ferns and the redwoods through the window.

She waited for a message to come, but nothing else followed.

And still.

She recognized a love letter when she saw one.

In the Los Angeles summer heat, her legs against the leather of her truck, Emilie pulled over in front of the familiar storefront. Still unabashedly beautiful with its sidewalk plants—fuller and taller now—startlingly green against the blue-black facade.

But the flower shop had changed, Emilie noticed, as she pushed open the door and the bell chimed. Just then two men were leaving, so she held open the door to let them by. The first man carried a large ficus, his arms wrapped around the pot, gold wedding band catching the light. And then his husband behind him with a baby in a front pack, sleeping against his chest.

"Thank you," the second man said to Emilie. He smiled and she noticed a small chip in his front tooth. Felt a swell in her chest.

"You're welcome," Emilie said, and then he was gone.

A young woman worked on an arrangement at the counter. She greeted Emilie, and Emilie said hello. "Let me know if I can help you with anything," the girl said, before returning to her work.

The back of the shop had been pushed out to make a much larger space. And it had increased its inventory, too; it wasn't only a florist anymore. Emilie browsed a rack of letterpress cards. Read the labels on a row of candles, picked one up to smell it.

"Emilie?" she heard, and turned to see Meredith, setting a houseplant on the counter.

They embraced.

"The store looks incredible."

"Thank you," Meredith said. "I've been busy."

"I can see that."

"And what about you?

"I've been busy, too. Actually, I just closed on a house."

"Congratulations! Where is it?"

"It's in the Hollywood Hills," she said. "Tucked away off Mulholland Drive."

"Wow," Meredith said. "Good for you."

Emilie laughed. "It needs a lot," she said. "But yeah—I'm happy."

Meredith cocked her head and nodded. Emilie could see her mind at work. "What is it?"

"It's just—you *do* look happy. You look . . . satisfied."

"I guess I didn't used to look that way."

"Not quite," Meredith said. "I'm glad to see it now. I have to get this order ready, but is there anything you need? Or just here to browse?"

"Here to browse," Emilie said.

"I'll leave you to it."

Meredith disappeared to the back and Emilie turned again to the candles. One smelled like the beach—salt and coconut. Another like the forest. She moved on to an assortment of hand-carved wood spoons. In a flurry of movement and noise, the girl behind the counter dropped her scissors, bent over to retrieve them, rose again.

Emilie walked past the cut flowers to the shelves of vases. So many more now than the shop used to carry. Glass along the upper shelves, ceramic in the middle. On the ground clustered stone and concrete and terra-cotta. All of them waiting to be filled.

I was a vase.

The thought struck her as she gazed at the wall of them. She had been a vessel; it was true. She'd stepped into this shop, introduced herself, asked for a job, hoped it would fill her.

And then, for a time, sitting with Jacob at the community table, she'd been a flower. Snipped from the root, quick to wilt, temporary. She'd existed to be lovely and to be chosen. No one had expected her to last.

But she hadn't been a flower when she'd gone to live with Claire, had she?

Emilie traveled deeper into the shop. She was in the addition now, its ceiling higher, its rows of tables laden with houseplants. *Water,* she decided. That's what she'd been with Claire. Shapeless, colorless, but necessary. She'd done what she had to. She had been there for her grandmother. She'd kept her family afloat.

But what was she now?

At the back of the shop were modern glass doors, flung open to an enclosed patio. She crossed the threshold. Vines grew along wires strung across the space, forming a roof of leaves and bright pink flowers. Shoppers wove their way through the displays of plants and clusters of modern patio furniture.

"You know," Meredith said, passing Emilie with plants under each arm. "You're welcome to make yourself your own arrangement if you'd like to. For old time's sake. Just tell Mabel at the counter that I said it was okay."

Emilie had come for a bouquet, it was true. But now there was so much, and she didn't want that anymore.

"Actually, I'm going to choose a plant," she said. "I want something that'll grow."

"That's *exactly* why I expanded," Meredith said. "You always understood." And she brushed past her, into the shop again.

Emilie browsed the trees and vines and flowers, found herself in a corner where the edibles were displayed in tiers atop upturned metal troughs and wood risers. Tomatoes and squashes and eggplant. Arugula and little gems. Blackberry bushes. Several varietals of blueberries. Below them were the herbs—rosemary, lemon balm, thyme, verbena.

And then she spotted a small plant with delicate green

leaves. A swell in her chest, a longing. She read the description to be sure.

Yerba buena. "The good herb." Native to California, especially abundant on the coast. Fragrant leaves, white flowers from spring to summer.

Carefully, she tore off a single leaf and placed it in her mouth. It was subtle and sweet and just the faintest bit bitter.

She read that it grew best as a groundcover, that its companion plants were the wood strawberry and flowering currant. Meredith had those in her shop, too. Emilie bought them, nestled the plants on the floor of the passenger seat of her truck, and drove home.

She found a spot for them in her garden right away, in the shade of an old oak tree with branches that hung strong and low. She dug small holes with her trowel. Coaxed the plants from their containers. Pressed them in.

The yerba buena took root.

And by the time the doorbell rang at Emilie's new house a month later—Emilie's perfect house, nestled under the Hollywood sign, ivy growing up the sides—the plant had formed a soft, green groundcover in a small patch of her garden.

Emilie heard the bell from her bedroom, where she was reading. Set down her book and went to the door.

Here she was. The curve of her cheekbones. Blond tips of her eyelashes. Freckles across the bridge of her nose like specks of pollen. Hair just the slightest bit longer, falling into her eyes. Standing in a sweater and jeans on her doorstep.

Here was Sara.

"You sold the house," Sara said.

"I did. How did you find me here?"

"I showed up at the other place first. And then I asked Colette for your address."

"You called Colette instead of me?"

"I wanted to see you in person."

"You did?" Emilie asked.

"I got your message," Sara said.

Emilie nodded, tears rushing her eyes. "I got yours, too."

"I want to tell you everything."

"Okay." But she knew it already. Saw how Sara stood straighter. Saw their future, unfurling, across the clear blue sky.

Let me in? Sara would ask, and Emilie would open the door and lead her into her house. She'd show her both bedrooms, the guest studio, the dining room that overlooked the city. They would talk. They would take off their clothes. They'd rise together in the morning, the two lost months behind them.

Tell me what you meant by this, Emilie would say, and she'd open the image on her phone, the one of the kitchen sink and the gingham curtains and the trees. She'd tell Sara what she understood and ask if she was right.

Yes, Sara would say.

And Emilie would ask, *Did you notice the place on the corner, before turning up the hill? It's still vacant.*

And, of course, yes, Sara would have noticed.

The bar would be intimate, lovely. No kitchen. Brass and

marble, wood and mirrors. Sara would shake and stir, taste small-batch whiskeys, make her own bitters and shrubs. Emilie saw her already: mixing drinks and laughing, leaning against the counter under the grand chandelier.

They would understand each other, make room for each other. Each of them driven, each of them in love.

But then, something would go wrong. The pain inside of Sara would rise up again. Emilie would fall silent instead of fighting. They'd lose one another for a time, and what would they do, then? Sara off, searching for her brother, tending to her wounds. Emilie, craving something of her own. A new house to flip, maybe, and months sunk into it. Lunches with Alice and Pablo, a trip to San Francisco to see Colette and Thom and Josephine. Hands in plaster, head in plans. Time of her own, no one to tend to, until Sara returned, and Emilie took her back, and they continued the dance.

So right while it lasted. So sweet, and bitter, too.

Emilie had suffered enough heartache already. Surely, there were wiser choices. Surely, she knew enough to know better.

But here was Sara, now, on her doorstep, just as Emilie had hoped.

Here was Sara's hand, reaching for hers. How warm, how right.

"Let me in?" Sara asked.

And Emilie opened the door.

ACKNOWLEDGMENTS

Thank you to my friend and agent, Sara Crowe, who, book after book and year after year, makes my dreams come true. And thank you to all of Pippin Properties, especially Holly, Elena, Cameron, Rakeem, and Ashley, for being such a joy and a force. I am immensely grateful as well to my film and TV agent, Dana Spector, and my attorneys, Diane Golden and Sarah Lerner.

Caroline Bleeke, here is a story: One night, early in the submission process for this book, a feeling washed over me. I felt an overwhelming, otherworldly sense that someone out there was reading my novel—*right then*—and falling in love with it. The next morning, I woke up to the email you wrote to Sara, saying so many beautiful things about the story. What an absolute pleasure and gift it's been to work with you every step of the way. Thank you for all of it.

Thank you, also, to the entire Flatiron team for your passion, professionalism, creativity, and tremendous care. If I've learned anything about publishing over the years, it's that so many people work tirelessly behind the scenes in order for books to be placed into readers' hands. I am so grateful to all of you, and especially Sydney Jeon, Megan Lynch, Malati Chavali, Bob Miller, Nancy Trypuc, Jordan Forney, Amelia Possanza, Keith Hayes, Kelly Gatesman, Erin Gordon, Donna Noetzel, Frances Sayers, Vincent Stanley, Callum Plews, and Talia Sherer.

Thank you also to Joanne O'Neill for capturing the essence of my novel so perfectly for the cover design, to Julie Gutin for your impeccable copyediting, and to Deni Conejo for your wonderful editorial eye for FORESHADOW.

I would like to thank all of the booksellers, librarians, bloggers, and readers who have supported my work over the years. You're the reason I have this career that I love.

I used a great deal of real family history in the Emilie sections of the story, from the houses my grandparents lived in to the love letters my grandfather wrote to my grandmother during the war. To my cousins, my aunt and uncle, and my father: I hope that the love I put into the story shines through. I'd also like to acknowledge that my aunt Joe is the person who cared for my grandparents in their final years, allowing them to stay in their house on Cherry Avenue in Long Beach until the end. Words can't express what a gift that was.

Thank you to my friends Brandy Colbert, Eliot Schrefer, Nicole Kronzer, Mandy Harris, and Jessica Jacobs, who read this novel in its early stages and gave me invaluable feedback. I appreciate you all so much! Thank you to Jandy Nelson for inviting us to live in the Magic Circle; I loved knowing you were writing on top of my head all year. Thank you to my writing group—Carly Anne West, Teresa Miller, and Laura

Davis—who read pieces of this book for over a decade and a half and have cheered me on and guided me all that time. Your friendship and support mean so much.

And thank you, Elana K. Arnold, for motivating me to write the first complete draft over the pandemic summer, for spending dozens of hours on the phone with me talking through plot points and thematic threads, for reading more drafts than I can count, and for your steadfast and exuberant belief in this novel—it got me through many spells of self-doubt. You make my writing bolder and braver. I'm so grateful for your devotion, generosity, and brilliance.

Thank you to my mother for taking me to the Russian River as a kid, where we walked in Armstrong Woods and stayed in the motel I reimagined for Sara's job. Those are memories I cherish. Thank you to Sherry, Robyn, Jeremy, Riley, Katie, Sophie, and Charlie for being my family. Thank you to Dad and Raewyn for always being here for me, for your excitement and nourishment and unconditional love. Thank you, Jules, for being the very best brother. I hope we cook gumbo together until we're old. Amanda, everyone should be so fortunate to have a best friend like you. Thank you for telling me I'm perfect and meaning it. Juliet, simply having wonderful you as my kid is enough. You inspire and delight me every single day. Kristyn, I could not have written this book without you. Thank you for sharing your life with me, for knowing what I need and being so good at giving it to me, for the coffee and the cocktails and the innumerable, exquisite moments of joy.

Nina LaCour is the award-winning and bestselling author of six novels for young adults, including *We Are Okay,* a Printz Award winner and national bestseller. She lives in San Francisco with her wife and daughter. *Yerba Buena* is her first novel for adults.